FROM TIME TO TIME

B.B. Jones

Best wishes

B.B. Jones

FROM TIME TO TIME

B.B. Jones

© Copyright B.B. Jones 2024

FROM TIME TO TIME

All rights reserved.

The right of B.B. Jones to be identified as the author of this work has been asserted in accordance with the Copyright, Designs and Patents Act 1988.

No part of this publication may be reproduced, stored in a retrieval system, or transmitted, in any form or by any means, electronic, mechanical, photocopying, recording or otherwise, nor translated into a machine language, without the written permission of the publisher.

This is a work of fiction. Names and characters are a product of the author's imagination and any resemblance to actual persons, living or dead, events and organisations is purely coincidental.

Condition of sale

This book is sold subject to the condition that it shall not, by way of trade or otherwise, be lent, re-sold, hired out or otherwise circulated in any form of binding or cover other than that in which it is published and without a similar condition including this condition being imposed on the subsequent purchaser.

ISBN 978-1-3999-9181-0

More from this Author

The Chatelaine Series

The Chatelaine series chronicles the lives of Annie and two of her daughters, spanning a period of over fifty years. The story follows the three women as they navigate the challenges of life and love in the 20th century, staying true to their duties and aspirations.

The Chatelaine: Annie

The Chatelaine: Kate

The Chatelaine: Isabelle

The Sundered Path

From Time to Time

This book is dedicated to my family and friends, whose love and support are invaluable to me, both in my writing and in my life. Thank you.

P.S. Rest assured, I've changed your name in my books.

Prologue

Overwhelmed with frustration and gripping the pen firmly in her fingers, Mary Mattleton abruptly stopped writing in her journal and slammed the book shut.

'How *can* I concentrate with that incessant ticking going on?' she complained, a hint of frustration in her tone as she listened to the grandfather clock ticking away in the great hall below.

Mary was not prone to being easily spooked despite her unfamiliar surroundings. She'd accepted North Hall Manor's imposing grey stone building, standing alone on a desolate hill, even during the daylight hours; it was intimidating. However, as she went to the window to peer out, she soon discovered that, at nighttime, the Manor had taken on a new persona.

'I can't see anything beyond these windows,' Mary remarked on finding nothing but an endless expanse of darkness and the sound of the wind's mournful wail outside. 'I wonder what on earth made me up sticks and come here,' she mused, moving her head from side to side. 'It's not just the isolation, the atmosphere of this place is suffocating,' she observed.

The silence was suddenly broken by the grandfather clock striking the hour, startling her. Its loud sound reverberating through the house. One, two, three … Each chime of the clock sent a shudder through her being.

Mary glanced at her watch. 'It's nearly midnight. The witching hour!' she murmured aloud.

Sensing a sudden chill in the room, she clasped her arms around herself and turned back from the window to retrieve her dressing gown from the end of her bed.

As Mary walked past her dressing table, she noticed a flicker of movement in the mirror's reflection. It was a fleeting glimpse of something lurking just beyond her perception. Mary stood rooted to the spot. An icy shiver ran through her as she looked into the mirror.

She inhaled deeply. 'I need to calm down,' Mary reminded herself. 'It's just my mind messing with me,' she whispered.

She held her breath, waiting and counting each chime.

Four, five, six, seven …

While simultaneously listening to the steady tick-tock of the clock, its constant reminder that time was slipping away as it counted down the hour to midnight …

Chapter 1

The silence in Mary's study was shattered by a forceful knock on the door. She looked through the window to see who had been crazy enough to venture out on such a stormy Australian mid-winter morning. Torrential rain was pelting down with such a relentless force that it sounded like a thousand tiny fists pounding on the tin roof and the glass of the ill-fitting windows. She could see gum trees swaying wildly and hear the branches of the Oleander bush thrashing up against the wooden boards of the remote green weatherboard house that belonged to her Aunt Molly. Her aunt had passed away five years ago, and the peeling green paint of the weatherboard home stood as a haunting testament to the passage of time and apathetic neglect.

Mary hurried to the door to open it.

'G'day Doc! It sure is a bucketin' down out here today, huh?' the postman remarked in a thick Australian accent, his words laced with friendly familiarity, as he handed over a large brown envelope.

Mary took the envelope. 'Thank you, it certainly is, so you be careful, you hear? We don't want any accidents and you ending up in my surgery, do we?' she replied, tilting her head and smiling.

'Nah, don't you worry about me, Doc? I'm as tough as old nails!' the postman replied, laughing loudly, his hand waving dismissively. 'Better watch out for those gum trees, though. They sure are thrashin' about in this wind. Don't want them flattenin' your place, do ya?'

'I'll keep an eye out, don't worry …'

He mounted his bicycle. 'Hooroo, catch ya later…' he called out cheerfully over his shoulder before cycling off down the track.

Clad only in her thin cotton frock, she watched him briefly, wrapping her arms tightly around herself as protection against the chilly wind and the icy touch of raindrops as they bounced off of the wooden verandah onto her face. The scene brought back the stark realisation of the harshness of the unpredictable Australian weather as she watched the postman, head bent, battling against the wind as he disappeared down the track.

When the postman was out of sight, Mary turned and hurried inside, shutting the door behind her. The bare wooden floorboards, once shining and polished, now bore the scars of neglect, hinting at a history of apathy and indifference since her Aunt Molly's death. They creaked like a mournful groan as she walked along the hallway to her study. She sat at her desk and studied the mysterious brown envelope the postman had handed to her. The postmark on the envelope was from Yorkshire.

'I'm curious to know who this can be from. I don't know anyone in Yorkshire?' she said aloud, studying the handwriting of her address written neatly on the front of the envelope. Mary's heart raced with anticipation as she tentatively opened the envelope, her curiosity intensifying as she pulled out a letter inside.

J. B. Nicholson & Co.
31 Castle Street
Ellerby
Yorkshire

19th July 1981

Dear Doctor Mattleton,

We act as executors for the estate of your great-uncle, the late Leonard Mattleton dec'd, owner of the estate of North Hall Manor, High Brow, North Yorkshire. We have been instructed to dispose of Mr Mattleton's assets. As a named descendant in Mr Mattleton's last wishes, we would be obliged if you would attend this office at your earliest convenience to discuss this matter further.

I look forward to hearing from you.
Yours faithfully,
Robert J. Hart LLB
Partner - J. B. Nicholson & Co.

'Travel all the way over to Yorkshire? That's quite a long way to go to see if, on the off chance, I've inherited a few dollars!' Mary said light-heartedly. She glanced at the letter again. 'Still, on the other hand ...' Mary pondered. 'It's been some time since I took a vacation. I wouldn't mind taking a trip overseas, and who knows, I might discover some long-lost relos over there,' she mused.

Mary reached for the envelope and retrieved a large bundle of paper headed '*Last Will and Testament of Leonard Mattleton*' As she held it in her hands, a knot formed in her stomach. A mix of excitement and apprehension intertwined like a tangled web, making it hard to distinguish between anticipation and dread as she carefully spread out the document on her desk, eager to uncover its contents.

As Mary scanned the first page, the words on the document appeared to dance before her eyes, creating an almost hypnotic effect. She noticed a faded wax seal in the corner, leaving her further intrigued and curious about the enigmatic nature of her inheritance. Feeling a brisk breeze blowing through a small crack in the window, she adjusted the scarf around her neck and continued to read the words in the document. Mary quickly scanned the words from one paragraph to another, finding she couldn't read fast enough to absorb its contents.

'This can't possibly be true, can it?' Mary muttered under her breath in disbelief when she'd finished reading the Will, her voice barely a whisper despite the oppressive silence of her study. 'Out of nowhere, I learn that I have become a beneficiary in the Will of a distant and previously unknown relative.' She wondered aloud, her voice trembling with uncertainty.

Mary glanced over the solicitor's letter once again. It was clear, there was no doubt, that the letter was definitely addressed to her. Yet she found her mind racing with countless unanswered questions and the fear of the unknown growing stronger, adding more pressure to her already burdened shoulders. Her eyes wandered to the view outside. Menacing storm clouds loomed low in the sky, throwing a shadow of doubt over her and intensifying her feelings of concern about what was written in the letter and the Will.

She turned back and looked around her study. The faded family photographs on the walls, their presence filling the room, transported her back to happier times. The photo of her father lifting her high above his head. Next to it was a photo of her aunt in the garden, dressed in her khaki dungarees, her then greying curls tied back loosely at the nape of her neck, harvesting the crops from the seedlings she had lovingly grown. Mary sighed as she looked at the photograph below. It was of her mother smiling down at her as she blew out the five candles on the cake. This was to be the last photograph taken with her mother and the last cake her mother would bake for her before her untimely death. As Mary looked around the remaining pictures, she could almost hear the whispers of her father's gentle words and the melodic sound of her mother's laughter, amplifying her emptiness at her loss.

In life, her father, Thomas, had shared very few details with her about his family other than he had been born somewhere in the north of England and, when he was around eight years old, he'd made the journey over to Australia just after the First World War. With hopes of a fresh start, he embarked on the trip in a large boat, accompanied by his sister, Aunt Molly, and his parents, James and Sybil, who were her grandparents.

Mary's gaze lingered on her parents' wedding photograph. Her parents were both in their early twenties when her father met her mother, Catherine. They married quickly and settled down as a family when Mary was born some nine months later. From a place of love and affection, her world was shattered when fate intervened and tragically snatched away her parents when she was a child of five, leaving her an orphan and searching for her family in a vast and unfamiliar world.

Once again, fate played a role in the events that unfolded. The authorities stumbled upon the discovery of Mary's long-lost Aunt Molly. An enigmatic individual who lived a reclusive life. Her green weatherboard house stood alone, nestled deep within the Australian bush, surrounded by towering gum trees which acted as a guard, keeping Aunt Molly away from prying eyes. Mary soon found the locals instinctively veered away from her aunt. Rumours had circulated that Aunt Molly was a witch and that misfortune would befall anyone who crossed her path or ventured too close to her cottage. This cast a shadow of fear and uncertainty among the townsfolk.

Although her aunt was initially reluctant to take Mary in, she treated her well over the years. She provided both education and practical skills, such as baking, sewing, and gardening. They lived a self-sufficient life, albeit in a closed-off environment. Mary had everything she needed except for the one thing she yearned for — her parents.

As Mary gazed at a photo of herself and her aunt on the back verandah, she reflected on how much time had passed since the death of her Aunt Molly, leaving her all alone once more. Mary retrieved the solicitor's letter and looked at it. However, perhaps she should contemplate a trip to Yorkshire, she thought. She might find the key to unlock her mysterious past and locate her long-lost relatives who were living in England.

'Yeah, I'll do it.' Mary said aloud. 'It might be worth the trip, and I'd like to see where my parents were born.'

A glimmer of hope flickered within her, just thinking about the possibility of visiting her parents' country of birth and the possibility of discovering long-lost relatives.

Chapter 2

Mary leaned against the back of her seat and exhaled with relief as the taxi pulled away. She had finally arrived in London and was heading to the hotel to check in. Mary attempted to absorb the sights surrounding her while the taxi swiftly manoeuvred through the busy traffic. Her eyes were tired and gritty after little or no sleep on the long and exhausting flight from Australia. All she longed to do was to close them and sleep.

On arriving at her hotel, the concierge opened her taxi door. 'Good morning, miss. Welcome to The Ambassador Hotel.'

Mary acknowledged him with a smile and a nod.

The concierge picked up her suitcases from the pavement where the taxi driver had dropped them. Mary followed him up the stairs and into the foyer. She glanced around the lobby. A crystal chandelier hung suspended from the middle of the ceiling, each of the crystals sparkling and giving the room an air of grandness. Sumptuous, crimson-buttoned velvet couches were scattered around the foyer on a deep-piled cream carpet. It was a far cry from her Aunt Molly's modest furnishings. Mary was in awe and started questioning herself if she would fit into this life.

After checking in at reception and clutching her key, Mary entered the lift to take her to her room. She glimpsed herself in the lift mirror as it transported her to the third floor. A tired and drawn face stared back at her, with thick black circles under her eyes and unkept-looking hair.

She unlocked her bedroom door, dropped her luggage just inside, then raced straight to the king-size bed and, flopping down on it, stretched out her arms wide.

'Ah! Horizontal at last!' she exclaimed. 'All I need now is a long hot shower, a good night's sleep, then Yorkshire, here I come!' she said out loud to herself.

The following morning, Mary was refreshed and excited for her train journey to Yorkshire. After breakfast, she ordered a taxi to Victoria Station, where she would catch her train to Harrogate.

Mary was drawn to the sight of the sleek silver train, its polished exterior gleaming like a silver bullet in the morning sunlight as it neared the platform. On boarding the train, she discovered the carriage was nearly empty as she placed her cases in the luggage rack just inside the carriage. Mary settled into a nearby window seat, which gave her a panoramic view of the countryside as they travelled along. As the train sped up, the rhythmic clatter of wheels on the track and the gentle swaying of the carriage lulled Mary into a state of tranquillity. Jet lag started to take its toll. Her eyelids closed, and she fell into a deep sleep.

A loud voice boomed over the Tannoy, 'Harrogate station!' it said, jolting Mary awake from her peaceful slumber. 'Harrogate station!' it repeated. The sound reverberated through the train.

In a slightly unsteady fashion, Mary stumbled down the aisle of the carriage, hastily gathering her cases from the luggage rack before stepping off the train. After passing through the ticket barrier, she exited the railway station, crossing the road to the car rental offices opposite. She had rented a car to drive herself to her overnight accommodation at The Wheatsheaf Inn in Ellerby.

'Ah! Yes! Doctor Mattleton, your car is the red one over there.' Sarah, the friendly receptionist at the hired car office, greeted Mary warmly, instantly putting her at ease. 'I'll get you to sign the paperwork, then I'll grab the keys for you.'

'Thank you,' Mary responded with a smile, then enquired about the location of her overnight stay in Ellerby, where she was due to meet the solicitor, Robert Hart, the following day.

Sarah proved to be a wealth of local knowledge. 'Your best way is across the Buttertubs Pass,' she said, showing the route on the map she'd spread out on the desk.

'The Buttertubs Pass?' Mary frowned.

Sarah nodded. 'Yes! The pass is this road here that crosses the moors. See?' Sarah said, pointing to the map and tracing her finger along the twisting road that cut through the rugged hillsides towards Ellerby.

Mary examined the map and frowned. On the map, the only thing visible to her was the endless emptiness of the moors, with a narrow winding road cutting through it.

'But…But where are all the houses, the towns?' Mary asked.

'There are none. These are the Yorkshire Moors.' Sarah laughed lightly.

'Oh! Are the moors a safe place to drive over?'

'Yes! You don't need to worry. You'll be quite safe if you follow this map. This route will get you to Ellerby the quickest, and the moors are absolutely breathtaking at the moment.'

'They are? I was led to believe the moors were just scrubland – what's breathtaking about that?'

Sarah smiled. 'Get ready for a delightful shock then. In August and September, the heather on the moors is in full bloom, turning them into a blazing carpet of vibrant shades of pinks and purples as far as the eye can see.'

'Really? I had no idea. How wonderful… Judging by the size of the moors on the map, I could be in for a pleasant surprise then.' Mary replied as she headed out of the office, clutching the map.

Mary hoped the girl was right, lovely as the moors might look. She hoped the journey across the moors was safe and that she would get there before nightfall.

As she gripped the car keys, their coolness against her palm mirrored that of the uncertain yet exciting journey ahead. Mary climbed into the car, put the key into the ignition, and started it. Despite doubts about her journey ahead, she was determined to conquer her fears and embrace her adventure.

With the map conveniently placed on the passenger's seat next to her, Mary set off on her journey to Ellerby. She was eagerly looking forward to her forthcoming meeting with Robert Hart, whom she had been corresponding with via email, to discover more about a potential inheritance and a chance to reconnect with long-lost family members.

After a while and in search of some relief from navigating the narrow, steep and meandering roads across the moorlands, Mary pulled over and stopped at a lookout point high on the moors.

Mary got out of the car, grateful for the break. She stretched and faced the wind. Mary thought she heard the distant cry of a lone bird – maybe it was the wind, she told herself. As she stood admiring the scenery, the wind's relentless force caused her long blonde hair to whip around her face, prompting her to wrap her silk scarf around her head.

The heather-covered moors, as Mary discovered, were a breathtaking landscape, just as Sarah had described them. The scent of the heather and crisp, earthy air filled her nostrils. She could see sheep dotted around in the distance, their gentle bleating echoing through the grandeur of the dramatic cliffs and deep valleys, filling her with awe. In the far-off distance, she spotted the outline of a grand house positioned on a hill. Its golden lights flickered like beacons amidst the rugged landscape, providing warmth and comfort in stark contrast to the bleakness of the surrounding moorland.

Unbeknownst to Mary, the mysterious silhouette of the building in the distance held within it the key that would unlock unanswered questions and grant her the fulfilment of her deepest, long-held aspirations.

As the biting chill stung her face and penetrated her bones, Mary hunched her shoulders and hugged herself to protect her from the wind and to stop her teeth from chattering uncontrollably. However, she couldn't resist admiring the vast open space despite the cold. The Yorkshire Moors' vibrant hues and captivating plant life were a stark comparison to the scarce vegetation of the Australian outback that Mary knew well. The landscape's beauty filled her with awe and appreciation.

She was reminded of a book from her childhood Aunt Molly had given her, a copy of *Wuthering Heights*, set in the Yorkshire Moors. She'd found the book, its pages now worn from countless rereads, simultaneously romantic and haunting. As a romantic at heart, Mary envisioned herself as the heroine, Catherine Earnshaw. Her imagination had been captivated by the tumultuous and ultimately doomed love affair between her and Heathcliff. Their brutal yet passionate liaison had held her spellbound.

Mary shivered uncontrollably. She dug her hands deeper into her pockets, prompting her to realise her unpreparedness for an English winter and the need to purchase warmer clothing. A smile crept across Mary's face as she recalled that only a few days ago, she was running around in shorts and a T-shirt back home and having to find relief from the sweltering heat by standing beneath a fan. But there she was, all bundled up in a scarf and coat, albeit the chill of the winds still managed to seep through into her bones. Her mind wandered, trying to picture the winter months in this place. The moors blanketed in a fresh cover of snow, transforming the place into a winter wonderland. It would be a dramatic change from the mild winter she was used to back home.

Prompted by the fading light, Mary realised it was time to get back on the road and continue her journey to Ellerby.

She returned to the warmth of the car, turned the key and the engine roared to life.

She soon caught sight of Ellerby, a short distance away. Upon arriving in the village, she immediately spotted The Wheatsheaf Inn. Mary pulled up and parked outside the ivy-clad pub, its weathered façade telling tales of centuries past. She could hear the sound of a lively folk band playing, their harmonious melodies blending with the laughter and animated conversations of the local patrons inside the pub, creating a vibrant symphony of sounds. The cheerful atmosphere brought a touch of warmth and liveliness to the scene, unlike the cold and solitude outside.

As soon as she stepped inside, she was immediately aware of the powerful smell of ale and stale tobacco in the air. Mary spotted the sign *Reception*. With her suitcase in tow, she proceeded along the corridor, following the sign. As she passed the bar, she saw a mysterious older man sitting alone in the bar, his head wrapped in a cloud of smoke from his pipe. He gave her a toothless grin and raised his hat. At the very end of the corridor was a stunning stained-glass window, casting vibrant patterns of light onto the worn wooden floors. A gallery of vintage photographs and faded paintings adorned the walls on both sides of the corridor, showcasing the rich history of The Wheatsheaf Inn. Standing as a centrepiece was an intricately carved polished oak desk with ornate brass accents and a gleaming glass countertop.

Mary lingered for a second, listening to the distant murmur of conversations and the gentle clinking of glasses before ringing the vintage bell perched delicately on the reception desk to announce her arrival with a soft, melodic chime.

Almost instantly, a jovial character emerged from a door behind the reception desk, the buttons on his waistcoat straining against his robust figure. His larger-than-life personality immediately putting Mary at ease.

'Nah then, 'ow do,' he boomed in his broad Yorkshire accent and with a twinkle in his eye.

Chapter 3

The piercing sound of the telephone abruptly awakened Mary from a deep sleep, leaving her disorientated momentarily.

Partially opening her eyes, she surveyed the room. 'Where am I?' she mumbled.

The telephone rang again. Mary's hand fumbled from under the warm covers to retrieve the telephone from her bedside table. Hesitantly, she picked it up and pressed it to her ear.

'Hello,' she mumbled in a sleepy voice.

'Morning, miss,' a chipper voice replied.

'Morning? What time is it then?'

'It's nigh on eight, miss …'

Mary desperately tried to gather her thoughts. 'In the morning?' she asked incredulously.

The voice gave a loud chuckle. 'Aye, Miss,' the man said, still chuckling. 'Thou asked for a wake-up call at eight of the clock.'

Mary sat bolt upright in bed and checked her watch. 'Oh! … Yes! … Yes, I did, didn't I? Thank you.'

'Thas reet,' the voice responded in a cheerful tone.

Mary heard a click, and the line went silent.

She sank back into the soft mattress, enjoying the warmth of the covers enveloping and cocooning her, lulling her into a sense of peace after her initial confusion caused by the abrupt awakening. Mary stared up at the ceiling, pondering over what the day's events might bring. She found herself immersed in the picture hanging on the opposite side of her room. It showed a remote cottage set among the rolling purple heather-clad moorland, just like the moors she'd crossed the day before.

Mary could smell the aroma of freshly brewed coffee wafting up from somewhere downstairs. She checked the clock on her bedside table; it was almost eight thirty. If she was to make her nine-thirty meeting with Robert Hart, her solicitor, on time, she'd better get up now, she told herself, swinging her legs out of the bed.

After breakfast, Mary set off to Robert Hart's office, carrying her black leather briefcase filled with paperwork and letters he had sent her. She could sense the feeling of nervous anticipation. *Or was it hunger, perhaps?* All she'd had for breakfast was a piece of toast and a cup of coffee. She was undecided about what to eat at this hour. Was it breakfast time? Or dinner? *Who knows!* She mused wryly. She guessed it would take some time for her and her stomach to get used to the time difference.

On following the directions from the Wheatsheaf Inn's receptionist, Mary reached Castle Street. She spotted the large brass number *thirty-one* displayed on a black panelled door with a semi-circle fanlight above it nestled amidst a row of Georgian stone-built four-storey terraced houses. The windows were framed by ivy-covered walls and colourful flowering window boxes, creating an inviting entrance.

Mary followed the instructions on the door. She knocked on the brass fox door knocker, then pushed open the door to reveal a polished black and white tiled corridor. The click-clack of her heels on the tiles echoed off the walls as she approached the efficient-looking receptionist wearing a grey-tailored suit and a white blouse, sitting at her immaculately organised desk with neatly stacked files positioned on each side of her typewriter.

'Good morning,' Mary addressed the bespectacled

fifty-something female who was peering at her over her glasses. 'I'm Doctor Mary Mattleton. I have an appointment with Mr Hart.'

'Good morning, Doctor Mattleton. Please, have a seat, and I'll let Mr Hart know you've arrived,' she replied, gesturing to the upholstered wooden chair placed outside a white-painted door with a sign in black lettering: Robert J. Hart LLB.

The receptionist picked up the telephone. 'Doctor Mattleton, to see you, Mr Hart,' she announced.

A few moments later, the door opened. A tall, dark-haired man stepped out into the corridor wearing a grey three-piece pin-striped suit, a crisp white shirt and a red-and-black striped tie.

'Doctor Mattleton! Come this way.' He smiled warmly, gesturing with his hand into his office.

Mary entered the office. Sunlight streamed through the two windows on the opposite end of the room while bookcases loaded with leather-bound books graced lined both sides of the room. An oak pedestal desk stood majestically in the centre, its polished top covered in files and an overflowing in-tray piled high with paperwork.

'Please, do take a seat,' he said, gesturing to a green leather button-backed club chair facing the desk. A stack of well-worn magazines sat on a table by the chair.

'Would you like coffee or maybe tea?' he asked.

Mary nodded. 'Coffee please, black, no sugar. Thank you!' she answered, placing her briefcase alongside her on the floor.

He picked up the telephone. 'Would you please bring in a tray of coffee, Miss Ives?'

Robert Hart replaced the receiver, took a thick file from the top of the overflowing in-tray, and proceeded to thumb through it.

There was a gentle tap on the door. 'Come...' Robert answered.

'Your coffee, Mr Hart,' Miss Ives announced as she advanced into the room.

Miss Ives balanced the tray on top of the desk corner with one hand and, with the other, proceeded to clear a space for the tray, revealing a small, framed photograph of Robert Hart with another young man who seemed to be around the same age smiling at each other.

'Help yourself to milk and sugar if you wish,' she instructed as she pushed the tray of coffee and biscuits squarely on to the desk.

'Thank you, Miss Ives,' Robert replied. 'That will be all for now. See that I'm not disturbed, please,' he added.

'As you wish, Mr Hart.' Miss Ives inclined her head as she closed the door.

'Now then, Doctor Mattleton,' the solicitor began.

'Please ….' Mary raised her hand. 'Call me Mary!'

'Mary — then you must call Robert,' he smiled, his eyes crinkling up at the side. 'Have you got the paperwork I sent you?'

Mary bent down and retrieved her briefcase from the floor. She placed it on her lap and pulled out a large brown envelope containing all the paperwork she'd received from Robert in the post.

'Yes, I have it here,' she replied, holding it up before her and replacing the briefcase back on the floor. 'I've been guarding it with my life, afraid it might sprout legs and run away.' Mary chuckled.

'Good! Now, let's discuss Leonard Mattleton's last wishes.'

Mary lifted her hand. 'Just before you do?'

'Yes? What is it?' Robert asked.

'In one of your letters, you said Leonard Mattleton was my great-uncle?'

'That's right.' Robert replied.

'I didn't know I had a great-uncle Leonard, or indeed that I had any living relatives at all — are there more relatives I don't know about?'

Robert reclined in his chair. 'Leonard Mattleton is, or was, your grandfather James' older brother …'

'My grandfather had a brother?'

'He did. Were you not aware of his existence?'

'No! I don't recall my grandfather nor my father ever mentioning it. But then I was only quite young when they both died. In fact, I know very little of my relatives, really,' Mary replied softly. 'When Aunt Molly died, I believed I had no family left …'

'But Mary, you have lots of family living here in Yorkshire and other parts of the United Kingdom. So much so, I had quite a job untangling your family tree to find you!'

Mary's eyes welled up with tears, overcome with emotion. *She had lots of family!* Robert's words echoed in her ears. Yet, she'd spent these past years since her aunt's death believing she had no-one, only now to discover she *did,* in fact, have a family after all. Mary dug into her pocket for her handkerchief and blew her nose.

'I have a family?' Mary's voice cracked as she whispered. 'I never knew …' she uttered with a shake of her head.

'Are you okay, Mary?' Robert asked with concern. 'I didn't intend to distress you…'

Mary dabbed her eyes with the handkerchief and gulped back the tears before replying. 'Yes! I'm okay. It's just that your news that I have family came as a surprise because I thought I had none left.'

Robert leaned in towards Mary. 'What led you to believe you had no family?' he asked softly.

Mary sat up straight in her chair. 'My grandparents died soon after I was born. My parents died in a fatal car crash when I was five years old, and my Aunt Molly, my father's sister, who took me in, died a few years ago, too. I assumed I had no living relatives left.

'I'm sorry to hear about your parents' accident, Mary. That would have been a tough time for you and being so young.'

Robert was right. The accident often came back to haunt her. The picture of herself in the back seat of the car remained as fresh in her mind as if it had occurred only yesterday. Her mother sat next to her father while he was driving. Without warning, her father emitted a loud groan, released the steering wheel, clutched his chest and the car swerved into an oncoming vehicle. Mary shuddered as she relived it once again.

'Indeed, it was a difficult period.' Mary's voice faltered. 'They were killed outright!' she added, blinking back her tears.

Robert promptly stood up from his chair and knelt beside her. He gently touched her arm. 'Are you alright?' he asked.

Mary blotted her tears with the handkerchief before she replied, 'Yes! I'm okay. It's just that it's the first time I've spoken or even given thought to that day in a long time.'

'You say your parents were killed instantly, yet you miraculously survived.'

'Yes! I was in shock when they found me still strapped into my seat, surrounded by broken glass. But miraculously, I walked away without a scratch. I must have been lucky.'

'Yes! Very lucky. I can only imagine what a tragedy it must have been for you to lose your parents when you were so young.'

'Yes, it was.' Mary's voice quivered. 'There was a time when I felt abandoned with no one to look after me. Well, that's what I believed back then.'

'That's what you believed back then? What changed your way of thinking?' Robert asked.

'The Welfare took care of me while they tried to find any remaining family members. Australia is a vast country, and the distance between cities and towns can be immense. So, locating any remaining family of mine proved challenging for them. Finally, it was uncovered that my grandparents, along with my father and Aunt Molly, had relocated to

Australia many years ago. Despite the deaths of my parents and grandparents, they discovered that I still had a living relative… my Aunt Molly.'

'Ah! So, did they find your family then? That must have eased your sense of isolation?'

'No, not really….

Robert raised an eyebrow, clearly intrigued. 'Despite finding your family, did it not make you less isolated?'

'No! Not to begin with, anyway. Aunt Molly, a confirmed spinster, was in her forties and living alone in the outback. She'd been estranged from the remaining family for several years and didn't even know of my existence, I believe. She initially resisted the idea of taking in a strange five-year-old, conjuring up all sorts of excuses. Welfare stood their ground, unwavering in their determination to secure me a home with my aunt. They informed my aunt that, as my only living relative, she had an obligation to give me a home. Otherwise, I would be sent to an orphanage. Aunt Molly begrudgingly agreed to take me in, on trial, for the summer holidays.'

'But I assumed you were living in her house when I contacted you?'

'Yes! I was.' Mary giggled.

Robert looked puzzled. 'Did you not say she only agreed to take you in for the holidays?'

'Yes, she did say that …' Mary grinned. 'But summer after summer went by, and as each summer ended, she would say I could stay until the following summer. So, I stayed.' Mary laughed.

Robert relaxed in his chair and smiled. 'So, your childhood turned out okay, then? I am delighted for you after all the hardships you endured.'

Mary nodded. 'Yes, it was fine, albeit somewhat unconventional. Aunt Molly homeschooled me and taught me to bake, sew, tend the garden and, grow vegetables. We lived a self-sufficient life. I even became used to seeing her converse with invisible figures as though they were present in the room.'

Robert frowned. 'I'm curious. Are you saying she saw and talked to people who weren't visible? Was she … How can I put it?' Robert coughed. 'Er… Mentally unbalanced?'

Mary burst into laughter. 'No! Not at all. Aunt Molly was what I believe you'd call a clairvoyant, a spiritualist? She could see things and people that others couldn't. She called it The Gift.'

'You mean black magic, the occult? Those people are dangerous, Mary. They're playing with fire, and you need to keep away from individuals like that!'

Mary chuckled and gave a little shake of her head. 'Not at all, nothing like that. Aunt Molly was quite harmless and quite sane; she said she helped people. The townsfolk, however, believed she was a witch. Whenever we stepped foot in town, whispers and glances of disapproval followed us,' Mary added. 'Still, I guess her presence added some excitement to our quiet little town,' Mary said, grinning.

'Did her interactions with unseen spirits never trouble you?'

'No! On the contrary, I loved living with Aunt Molly and grew to love her too. Now she has gone; she has left a huge void in my life.'

'She sounded a remarkable woman, just like you, Mary.' Robert remarked.

'I'm not so sure about myself.' Mary blushed. 'But, yes! Aunt Molly was remarkable, and I credit my successes to her unwavering belief in me. Her dedication to my education propelled me from a humble home-schooled student to a thriving scholar. I gained a scholarship to a prestigious grammar school. I earned a place in a prestigious university, making my dream of a future in medicine possible. Regrettably, because of the distance, I had to board at university. Oh! How I missed Aunt Molly. However, my determination drove me to work hard and make her proud of me. I was so happy that my aunt lived long enough to see me graduate from medical school …'

'And judging by what I've heard, I'm sure she was proud of you,' Robert remarked.

'I hope so ….'

Mary paused. She reminisced about the joyful moments shared with her aunt and the void left by her passing, leaving her with an overwhelming sense of emptiness. A yearning for the warmth and connection that only a family can provide. Mary blew her nose and drew in a deep breath before continuing.

'Since Aunt Molly's passing, I've wished I had family …'

'What about friends? Do you have friends you can turn to?'

'Yes! Of course, I have friends … good friends. But, even with their support, no one can replace the special understanding and unwavering love of a family. When Aunt Molly died, I felt like I had lost my entire family and faced the prospect of being completely alone once more.' Looking down at her uncle's Will in her hand, Mary added. 'Now it appears that might not be the case….'

Chapter 4

'It's as if time stands still in this place,' Mary mused as she sat on the wooden park bench overlooking the lake, inhaling the earthy smell of the newly mown grass. Shielded from the wind by the surrounding tall oak trees, Mary turned her face to catch the midday sun's warmth on her bare skin. She was still reeling from the bombshell Robert had dropped a short while ago during their meeting.

She took the copy of her great-grandfather's Last Will and Testament from her leather briefcase and scanned through the pages.

'I never dreamed I'd be facing such a tremendous undertaking,' Mary admitted with a heavy sigh, her mind overwhelmed with doubts and misgivings and questioning her ability to fulfil her great-grandfather's wishes as she replayed her meeting with Robert in her mind.

***

'I must warn you,' Robert's voice carried a tone of caution as he spoke. 'Prepare yourself, because what I'm about to tell you will change everything we've previously discussed. Are you ready?'

'Go on, I'm listening,' Mary replied, sitting slightly forward in her chair.

'It seems Leonard Mattleton was a sad and bitter man

when he made this Will,' Robert said to her, holding up the bound bundle in his right hand.

Mary's brow furrowed in surprise. 'Oh? Why do you say that?' she asked curiously.

Robert sighed and ran a hand through his hair. 'Where do I start…?'

'From the beginning.' Mary chuckled.

'Leonard Mattleton never married….'

'But, if I remember correctly, you mentioned in one of your letters that he had a son named Jack, and he's mentioned in the Will?'

'Yes, he's survived by his son, Jack, who was the son of one of the maids here at the Manor. However, they never married; therefore, his son, Jack, is illegitimate.'

'That doesn't matter too much these days, though, does it?' Mary asked.

'As a rule, it doesn't really matter. But it does matter when it comes to inheriting the Mattleton estate.'

Mary leaned forward, her brows furrowing. 'You've lost me. How does being illegitimate affect the inheritance? Please explain.'

'It's slightly complicated….'

'I can't see the complication. As the eldest son, my great-uncle Leonard would have inherited the Mattleton estate after his father, my grandfather James, died? Since his father, my great-uncle, is no longer alive, shouldn't Jack be the one entitled to the estate?'

'Ah, this is where it gets a little complicated.' Robert responded while reclining in his chair. 'Let me order more coffee, and I will try to explain.'

While they waited for Miss Ives to bring in a pot of fresh coffee, Robert shuffled the papers in the folder before him. Mary looked out through the window. It overlooked a picturesque garden at the back of the building. The vibrant colours of the delicate blooms added a touch of serenity to the scene, Mary noticed as she absentmindedly played with a lock of her hair. A habit she'd cultivated when she was anxious or lost in contemplation.

'There's some coffee left in the pot,' Miss Ives announced, interrupting Mary's reverie after replenishing the empty cups with the fresh coffee. 'Help yourself and to the milk and sugar,' she added before turning and leaving the room.

'Thank you, Miss Ives,' Robert said.

Robert leaned back in his chair after having a sip of his coffee. 'Now then … I suppose it all started with the fire back in; let me see … ' Robert shuffled through the file. 'Ah, yes, back in the early nineteen hundreds. April 1920, to be exact.'

'There was a fire at North Hall?' Mary asked.

'Yes. In the west wing. It was believed it originated in the servants' hall, which is now used as the great hall, just off the kitchen,' Robert replied. 'It was nighttime, and Molly, the young daughter of James Mattleton, sounded the alarm by waking up one of the servants and her young daughter, who was sleeping in a room off the hall. The butler was alerted, but when he reached the servants' hall, the room was already filled with smoke, making it difficult for him to breathe and forcing him to retreat. He summoned the fire brigade.'

'Was there anyone else in that wing?' Mary asked.

'Yes. It was the start of the season, and all the servant's rooms were occupied.'

'Did the servants get out?' Mary asked anxiously.

Robert nodded. 'I believe so. The butler and the maid went round to each room, raising the alarm.'

'Was anyone hurt?' Mary asked earnestly.

'No, thankfully, they were fortunate to escape unharmed. There was panic, as you can imagine. One of the kitchen maids jumped to the ground from her bedroom, which was quite a considerable drop. She hurt her hip and her ankle, but other than that, she survived the fall. Another climbed out of her window onto a ledge, then climbed down a drainpipe.'

'They were lucky by the sounds of it!' Mary said, trying to imagine the terror those girls must have experienced to risk their lives like that to escape. 'But what of those elsewhere in the house?'

'The butler sent the servants to the east wing to raise the alarm and, with instructions from their master, to retrieve as many valuables as they could. The brigade arrived just in time to contain the fire to the west wing, preventing it from spreading. However, by that time, it was far too gone to save anything inside it. It had destroyed everything in its path. The only interior features that remained intact, although blackened by the flames, were the large stone inglenook fireplaces in the servants' hall and library and the stone spiral staircase leading off the hall.'

'Oh, my goodness, it would have been a terrifying sight!' She exclaimed, her hands instinctively flying up to her face. 'Did they find out how the fire started?'

'No, not for certain. Some believed it started in the chimney of the servants' hall. Some believed it began in the library. There were even rumours of a servant leaving a burning cigarette. Suffice it to say that the incident left an indelible mark on the building and its occupants.'

'They never found the cause of the fire then?'

'No!' Robert shook his head. 'Not only that, unbeknownst to anyone, the fire that night was just the beginning of a series of events that would uncover the hidden truths within the walls of the house, ultimately altering the lives of those involved.'

Mary sat on the edge of her seat, eager to delve deeper into the mysteries that Robert had spoken of. 'I don't understand?'

'Well … on the night of the fire, your great-grandfather, along with his sons Leonard, your uncle and, James, your grandfather, salvaged as much as they could carry. It must have been then …' Robert paused. 'Your Great-uncle Leonard discovered the secret.'

'A secret? Is that the hidden truth and secret you spoke of?' Mary asked.

Robert placed his cup down on the saucer. 'Yes! And it's something that has only recently come to light, which, as it turns out, is something that has redefined everything we believed to be true.'

'That sounds intriguing! Please go on, what did you discover?' Mary said, her curiosity growing.

'An old servant, who was just a child back then and who still works on the estate, reported that on the night of the fire, she'd seen Master Leonard hurrying off with a metal box under his arm. On hearing this, I suspected at the time that there could have been important papers in this box. But this box has remained lost until now …' Robert said, pointing towards a tarnished old metal box that sat innocuously on the edge of his desk, concealing the answers to decades-old questions.

'Is that the box he was seen carrying?'

Robert nodded. 'Yes. That's our opinion so …'

Mary leaned forward and touched it lightly. 'Oh, my goodness! Who found it? The old servant you just spoke of?'

'No! The box was discovered quite by chance recently, and that's why I've not had the opportunity to tell you. The restorers were repointing the stones in the great hall fireplace when they found a loose stone. On removing the stone, they discovered this box in the cavity!' Robert said, picking up the box.

'What was in the box?' Mary asked, anxiously wanting Robert to get on with the story.

'As it is part of the estate, we opened the box and found Leonard Mattleton's secret among these legal documents.' Robert held up a bundle of paperwork. 'This is also part of it,' he added after pulling a yellowed sheet from the bundle and passing the document to Mary.

With her arm extended, Mary examined the faded

writing on the document, dated 11th January 1895, at the bottom of the page, with a large X alongside it. 'It's no good. Apart from the date, I can't make out what it says!' she said with a frown.

Robert laughed aloud. 'Don't worry, even with my glasses on, I couldn't either! But we've had an expert on this who has deciphered it for us.'

'And?'

'Essentially, it appears you are not related to Leonard Mattleton after all …'

Not related to your great-uncle. Robert's words resounded in her ears.

'Of course I am! He's my great-uncle, my grandfather's brother! You told me he was!' Mary retorted indignantly.

Robert lowered his voice. 'Mary…. I'm sorry to tell you Leonard Mattleton isn't legally your great uncle. This document tells us he was a foundling.' Robert replied, holding up the yellowed document.

'A foundling? What does that mean?'

'We've learned that Leonard's mother was a young woman from the community who died while giving birth to him. Her sister took the baby in and looked after him until he was around a year old. On finding she was pregnant again and as she already had several children, she couldn't afford to keep Leonard, so she had to find someone else to take care of him. This document is the agreement between her and your great-grandfather that he would take over Leonard's welfare and treat him as one of his own.'

'So, that means Leonard is not my blood relative, given that he was adopted?'

Robert nodded. 'Yes! Although there was no formal adoption process in those days, just informal arrangements like this,' Robert replied.

'So, what does all this mean regarding me, then?'

'What this means, Mary, is that, although Leonard

Mattleton holds the family surname, he has no legal entitlement to the Mattleton property.'

'But in the copy of his Will you sent me, it states he leaves the estate to his son Jack and a small bequest to me?'

'The discovery of the agreement between your great-grandfather and Leonard's mother showing Leonard Mattleton as a foundling invalidates Leonard Mattleton's Will. Leonard Mattleton isn't the rightful heir to the estate. Your grandfather James was.'

Mary's voice wavered as she tried to contain her emotions. 'But he's dead! What now?' Mary sunk into her chair and sighed.

Robert pulled out another bound bundle of papers.

'This is your great-grandfather's last wishes. It clearly states that the entire estate on his death is to be passed down to his son, James Mattleton, who is your grandfather, and then to his offspring, which would be your father, Thomas.'

'But he's dead too,' Mary interjected.

'That is correct,' Robert held up his hand. 'The document continues. Subject to any specific bequests. The estate goes to those who bear the name of Mattleton through its bloodline. So, Mary Mattleton, as the only remaining family member, you are the rightful heir to the Mattleton estate.'

Chapter 5

28th August 1981

I didn't get much sleep last night. I tossed and turned, my head replaying yesterday's meeting with Robert. He's taking me to see the Manor this morning. The idea of it makes me feel both nervous and excited. My mind is occupied by all the changes in my life I will need to face. What if I cannot fit it in? What if I dislike being the Mistress of North Hall? After all, it's a far cry from my life back home! Although I can't wait to see the astonishment and envy on the faces of my friends back home when I tell them. Bet I'll get called Mistress Mattleton!

Lingering over her breakfast in the Wheatsheaf's dining room, Mary soaked up the warm morning sun streaming through the large, arched window. A rush of nostalgia washed over her as she gazed around at the old-world surroundings of the dining room, with its polished oak furnishings, vintage chandelier, richly patterned wallpaper and, a grand fireplace with intricately carved marble surrounds. Despite the opulence, Mary couldn't escape the restlessness that gnawed at her, the conflict between the grandeur of her newfound status and the longing for simpler, familiar times.

Mary's face took on a pensive expression from being unexpectedly reminded of her heritage. She longed to hear the familiar sound of Aunt Molly's laughter. To be able once more to sit around the table eating breakfast in her aunt's cosy kitchen on a lazy Sunday morning. To taste her aunt's homemade jam spread onto the hot, buttered pikelets made fresh that morning. Preoccupied by her own musings, Mary absentmindedly toyed with the mushrooms on her plate. Her stomach churned as she gazed upon them, imagining their slimy texture in her mouth. She silently made a note to herself to ask the waitress not to serve them to her in the future.

Her gaze shifted to the clock on the wall. It was almost ten o'clock. Soon, it would be time for Robert to collect her and transport her to the Manor. She was beginning to feel a combination of excitement and trepidation. *What secrets await me at the Manor?* She wondered while she gathered up her cardigan and bag and left the dining room to wait for Robert's arrival at the front of the inn.

Upon stepping outside, Mary's attention was drawn to a dilapidated wooden bench nestled beneath an ivy-covered archway, its vines intertwining to create a leafy canopy. The morning sun filtered through the gaps in the ivy leaves, casting dappled shadows on her face, providing a sense of seclusion and intimacy. She sat down on the seat. The rough, textured wood was uncomfortable against her bare legs. Still, the bench offered a perfect vantage point to admire the row of quaint stone cottages and their colourful flower gardens on the other side of the road against a backdrop of lush green fields stretching out into the distance, along with undulating hills in the distance dotted with grazing sheep and cows. It reminded her of the postcards she'd seen in a local shop. A wave of tranquillity overcame her. This was indeed god's own country, as she had once heard it called.

An unexpected chill swept over Mary, causing her to wrap her cardigan around her shoulders, offering a comforting layer of warmth. It had looked sunny and warm when she'd looked out of the window of her bedroom earlier, so she had dressed appropriately, she decided, in sandals, a blue cotton dress and a matching cardigan. Now, with a cool breeze having picked up, the weather looked unpredictable. As she sat wondering whether she would have time to go back to her room to get changed, Mary suddenly heard a piercing blast of a car horn, jolting her back to reality. A bright red sports car with its top-down and Robert in the driver's seat was frantically waving and beaming at her as he pulled alongside her.

'Good morning!' Robert shouted cheerfully. 'A lovely morning, isn't it?'

'Er. Yes …. yes, it is, isn't it?' Mary said, getting up from the bench and going over to the car. 'It is warm enough to have the roof down?' Mary hesitated, glancing at the clear blue sky overhead.

'I can't imagine a better way to start the day than experiencing the wind in your hair and the sun on your face!' Robert's voice brimmed with infectious excitement, his eyes sparkling with anticipation.

Mary's hesitation was evident in her voice when she replied, 'I must admit, the idea of driving with the top down does sound exhilarating, but I have my reservations.'

'Reservations? Have you tried it?'

Mary moved her head from side to side. 'Well … no, but …'

Robert chuckled. 'Trust me, it's a wholly unique experience. On a day like this, it's exhilarating and gives you a sense of freedom!'

'It won't be such a unique experience for me, I fear. Midges and mozzies make a beeline for me, and I end up with big red welts all over!' Mary frowned.

'Midges and mozzies?'

'Mosquitoes,' Mary explained.

'Ah! I see – Aussie slang, no doubt. No worries, mate,' Robert replied in his best Australian accent.

'Also, I'm not exactly dressed for an open-top car ride this morning?' Mary frowned, pulling her cardigan tighter around herself.

'Don't worry, you look perfectly dressed against flying creatures to me,' Robert teased, giving her the once over.

With her mind filled with amusement. 'Oh, so you're an expert on bug-repellent fashion?' she replied, laughing. 'I meant I'm not dressed warmly enough.'

Robert leaned over to the back seat. 'Here, take this coat and put it on. That will keep you warm and safe from the mozzies.'

Mary donned the oversized sheepskin coat which reached down below her knees. She pulled a quizzical face.

'A tad on the big size methinks?' Mary expressed her doubt with a raised eyebrow.

'Don't worry, it's mosquito-proof fashion at its finest!' He laughed as he opened the car door, revealing plush leather seats and inviting Mary to sink into their comfortable embrace. 'Buckle up, hang on tight, and off we go!' Robert exclaimed, revving up the engine. The car shot forward like a rocket, taking off from the launch pad. Mary was thrown back in her seat.

'Hey! Whoa!' Mary burst into laughter, her hands gripping the dashboard as if she were on a rollercoaster ride.

'Sorry, I got carried away. I promise to drive sedately for the rest of the trip,' Robert said with a mischievous grin.

Mary turned to Robert and smiled. 'You're forgiven. How far is North Hall?' she asked, excitement bubbling within her.

'Depends on the traffic.'

'The traffic? My impression was that the Manor was in the middle of nowhere. I wasn't expecting to see many cars?'

Robert chuckled. 'Indeed, you're correct. It is in a remote spot. I wasn't referring to cars, but rather to the sheep as the ones taking over the roads!'

Mary gave him a wry smile, wondering what she should believe of what Robert told her. 'Sheep traffic? You jest?'

'No! I'm serious. Sheep have lived and grazed on the moors for hundreds of years and roam freely. You'll get to see them up close, I promise you. In fact, they often lie across the road and refuse to budge!'

As they drove deeper into the countryside, Mary could see up close the rolling hills she'd seen earlier while waiting for Robert. They passed cows and sheep grazing lazily in the nearby meadows, basking in the warm rays of the sun. The lush green fields separated by ancient dry-stone walls stretching across the landscape, weathered and moss-covered, standing strong against the backdrop of a clear blue sky. Along with the occasional farmhouse dotted about the landscape. Their modest charm adding to the picturesque countryside setting.

Mary experienced deep calm as the quiet beauty of the countryside embraced her during their silent drive.

'Look, you can see North Hall from here!' Robert exclaimed, breaking the silence and pointing to the weathered façade of a stone building sitting ominously on top of a hill in the distance.

'I see it!' Mary replied, staring through the car window in the direction Robert had pointed.

As Robert veered onto a side road, Mary experienced a sudden, strange sensation come over her. It was a mixture of excitement and trepidation as she was about to embark on an adventure into uncharted territory.

Mary held onto the sides of her seats as Robert drove along the uneven, unmade track to the Manor, leaving a trail of dust behind them. He came to an abrupt halt at the front of the imposing stone building and turned off the engine.

'I'm a little nervous about coming here, Robert. After all you have told me, I have no idea what to expect,' Mary confided before she got out of the car.

'It's been ages since I've been here, so this is a bit of an adventure for me as well. Still, I love a good mystery. Come on, let us explore!' Robert exclaimed.

Chapter 6

A flood of emotions surged through Mary as she walked up the gravel path. 'I can't believe I'm actually here and about to see my new home!' Mary muttered, her voice trembling. Her footsteps echoed ominously on the gravel, sending waves of unease through her and an urge to turn around and run.

On reaching the entrance, Robert positioned himself facing the solid oak door and, holding up a large iron key in his hand, exclaimed. 'Here we go!' as he turned the ornate vintage key in the large lock.

The large oak door groaned in protest as it swung open on its rusted metal hinges, simultaneously releasing a piercing screech. With Robert leading the way, Mary entered the dimly lit great hall. She was met by the musty scent of old books mingled with dust that hung in the oppressively dense and lifeless air. It was as if the place concealed centuries of secrets.

Mary stood transfixed with her senses overwhelmed by the splendour of her surroundings. The room was crowded with big, heavy pieces of antique furniture along with a display cabinet containing a collection of antique treasures, she supposed. A dark, stained wooden settle rested up against the far wall, its once plush cushions now threadbare and faded. At the heart of the room was a large table with intricately carved legs and eight matching high-back chairs. And taking centre stage on the right-hand wall was the most immense stone inglenook fireplace Mary had ever seen.

'This room strongly resembles the one depicted in *Jane Eyre* at Thornfield Hall.' Mary said aloud. 'The furniture, the fireplace, that grandfather clock over there and the winding stone staircase. It's just as I imagined it from reading that book.' Mary stood for a moment, taking it all in while listening to the rhythmic tick-tock of the clock, breaking the silence and resonating throughout the great hall.

A single ray of sunlight streamed through the dusty window above the great oak entrance door, casting an ethereal glow on the paintings adorning the walls around the hall, as if illuminating a long-lost memory. As she viewed each of the paintings, the portrait's eyes appeared to track her every step. She paused, her gaze resting on a picture directly ahead. Mary's eyes widened in amazement as she locked eyes with those of the mysterious woman in the portrait dressed in blue.

A sudden draught swept through the room, causing Mary to shiver as she stood listening to the continuous ticking of the grandfather clock.

As she examined the portrait of a woman and two children, a strange sense of unease came over her. The woman's golden hair fell around her face. It cascaded down her shoulders, highlighting her sapphire-blue eyes that appeared to communicate different emotions. The azure blue dress she wore brought Mary a sense of warmth, yet also a feeling of yearning to know who she was. The striking similarities between Mary and the woman portrayed in the portrait were too obvious for her to ignore.

'She has my dimpled smile!' Mary murmured to herself. 'And the locket, it looks just like the one I'm wearing that Grandma left me!' she added, her fingertips caressing the cool silver of the locket around her neck.

Who was this lady in the picture? she wondered while tracing the intricate carvings of the portrait's ornate wooden frame as she studied the portrait. What led her to experience an indescribable connection? Was it a link to her past waiting to be discovered? Was the face before her a glimpse into her own soul, a reflection of her true self beneath the surface?

'Have you seen this, Robert?' Mary asked.

'Have I seen what?' he asked.

'Look at this portrait of the lady dressed in blue!' Mary said, pointing at the painting directly before them. 'It looks like me, but it can't be me. I've never been here before in my life. I wonder who she is?' Mary uttered.

Robert approached the portrait and examined it closely. 'Other than the dress, which is outdated. Yes, you're right, it could be you,' he observed.

His puzzled expression mirrored Mary's own confusion. How could she experience familiarity in a place she had never been to before? Could the mystery of her own past intertwine with the secrets hidden within the portrait?

'I haven't been here before …' Mary whispered, as if afraid to disturb the spectral silence. 'Despite that, this place seems oddly like somewhere I've been before.'

The sense of anticipation hung in the air as if the portrait held the key to unravelling not only its own mysteries, but also those buried deep within her past.

'Are you sure that you haven't been here before?'

'No! I've never been here before…'

'Well, the woman in the painting looks just like you,' Robert said, still studying the portrait.

'I know, I know but…'

'Is it possible that you've been here before and perhaps forgotten you had? Because how else do you explain this portrait?' Robert asked pointedly.

'I don't know… I don't know.' Mary stammered. 'I can't explain it,' she added in frustration, tears beginning to well up in her eyes.

'I'm sorry,' Robert said apologetically, his arm instinctively reaching out to comfort Mary. 'It wasn't my intention to upset you. Let's explore this old mausoleum and then grab lunch at a friendly pub,' he suggested kindly.

Mary's face flushed with embarrassment and vulnerability after her outburst. She quickly shrugged off Robert's arms from around her shoulders, avoiding his gaze.

'You're right. Let's explore, starting with that big leather book on the dresser underneath the portrait.' Mary said, her fingers caressing its cracked leather cover. She wondered what secrets and forgotten stories it held within its pages that were waiting to be discovered?

Robert picked up the book and set it on the oak dining table.

'Here, take a seat and let's have a look,' he said, pulling out one of the carved oak dining chairs with red leather and a studded seat.

Robert skimmed through the faded pages of the weathered, leather-bound book. 'It looks like a journal. I can't read what it says very well, though; the ink has faded.'

'Yes. I agree with you. 'Wait!' Mary exclaimed, taking the book from Robert. 'It looks like these are recipes for remedies and … look at this one; it says something like how to make a bonnet. Oh! How I wish I could read this scribble?' Mary sighed. 'And they have the cheek to say a doctor's handwriting is illegible!' she added, laughing.

'Oh, and it is, trust me!' he said, laughing. 'Not to worry, I'll take it to Andrew, who deciphered your great-grandfather's document. He will no doubt make sense of it,' he added, his hand reassuringly resting on Mary's arm.

Mary's curiosity grew stronger. 'Oh! I can't wait to see if it will unearth any more hidden mysteries. Talk about …' A loud shrill beep, beep, beep interrupted Mary in full flow.

Robert looked at his pager. 'Sorry, I've got to telephone the office. There's a telephone in the village. Would you be all right if I left you to have a look around here? I'll be back as quickly as I can.'

'Go ahead and make your call. I'll be all right, Mary said, attempting to sound cheerful, even though her keenness to explore by herself made her uneasy. 'I'm sure there are a lot of things for me to look at here. Off you go. Take your time,' Mary remarked with a forced smile, shooing him away with her hands.

'I won't be long … don't worry,' Robert called over his shoulder as he shut the door behind himself.

Mary wandered through the grand hall, her footsteps echoing on the quarry-tiled floor. She peered into the display cabinet covered in a thick layer of dust, its glass door clouded with age. Curious to explore the cabinet's contents further, Mary grasped the brass knob and turned it to open it to inspect it more closely. She found the door was locked. Mary, determined not to be outwitted, stood on tiptoes and traced the intricate fretwork on the cabinet's top with her fingers to search for the key. Her heart pounded with anticipation.

Feeling triumphant and excited, Mary exclaimed. 'Eureka!' Holding a small brass key in her hand.

As she unlocked the cabinet, Mary's eyes were drawn to an intricately crafted silver-nibbed quill. Upon opening the cabinet, she saw its feather was a gentle shade of grey. Next to the feather pen was a silver capstan inkwell adorned with green stones set in its lid. It brought back memories of a time when handwritten letters in pen and ink were the norm, in contrast to today's prevalent use of ballpoint pens. Tucked away in the cabinet's corner, she stumbled upon a faded photograph capturing a lively family gathering. 'I wonder if these are the relatives that lived here before?' she said aloud.

Curious about the background of the place and her family's connection to it, Mary studied the photograph more closely. As she glanced around her, she suspected the picture had been taken in the great hall decades ago. Even though the room in the picture stood in stark contrast to the empty, silent great hall Mary found herself in now.

Her gaze fell upon a small prayer book that lay hidden among the treasures on the back shelf. She opened the brown leather-bound book. She carefully turned the delicate gold-edged pages until she reached an inscription: 'A precious gift bestowed upon Mary Mattleton, a symbol of hope and love on the day she entered the world. 20th May 1910'.

'Mary Mattleton!' Mary exclaimed aloud. 'Could this have belonged to Aunt Molly?' She stroked its leather cover before gently replacing it back in the cabinet and closing the door.

As Mary stood alone in the vast great hall, contemplating her surroundings. She tried to imagine the room alive with laughter and voices, as was in the photograph she'd just seen in the cabinet. Instead, only the grandfather clock's ticking broke the eerie stillness. Mary stood watching the shiny brass pendulum swing gracefully and rhythmically from side to side like a giant metronome. Despite being a beautiful relic of the past, it no doubt had its own unique story. She hated ticking clocks! The loud toll of its chime startled her. *One, two, three….* Mary looked at her watch. It was twelve o'clock. How quickly the time had passed. 'Where has Robert got to? I'm hungry.' she said aloud.

She returned to the dining room table and began scanning the yellowed pages in the well-used, leather-bound book once more. Suddenly, she heard creaking floorboards coming from above her. Startled and with her heart beating faster, Mary sat motionless in her seat. Her eyes looked upwards, following the footsteps as they crossed the room above her. The weight of solitude settled upon her shoulders, pressing down with an almost suffocating intensity, causing her to hold her breath and listen intently.

'Who are you?' A deep, guttural roar escaped from the lips of a towering figure with fiery red hair, standing at the top of the bannister-less spiral stone staircase, his presence exuding an aura of raw power and unpredictability as he advanced down the worn steps at speed.

Chapter 7

As the stranger reached the last step of the stone staircase, she was caught off guard by his sudden appearance. *What if he is a squatter?* she thought instantly. Mary stood up and braced herself for what might be coming.

As he strode towards her, Mary instinctively recoiled on detecting the pungent scent of stale alcohol and sweat clinging to his clothes. She inhaled deeply, pushing away thoughts of worst-case scenarios and focusing on staying calm. Mary gripped the edge of the table tightly, her knuckles turning white as she braced herself, determined to stand her ground. After all, she had encountered some difficult situations when working nights in the A&E department dealing with intoxicated individuals. So, she wasn't about to let this stranger intimidate her.

'I'm Mary Mattleton,' She paused, waiting for a response. 'I am the new owner of North Hall estate. Would you mind telling me who you are and what you are doing here?' she asked firmly.

The man stood motionless, his fiery red hair matted and dishevelled, hung around his weathered face, etched with years of outdoor living, towering over her, his face inches away from hers, his eyes fixated on hers in defiance.

Instinctively, Mary felt defenceless and took another step back from the towering figure before her.

'I am Jack Mattleton,' he announced, his voice resonating around the walls. 'Generations of Mattleton's have put their blood and sweat into this estate,' he proclaimed in a strong Yorkshire accent. 'My father, Leonard Mattleton, was the last in the line of his generation and has entrusted the family estate to me in his Will to carry on the Mattleton heritage.'

As Jack spoke of his family's heritage, a flicker of sympathy tugged at Mary's heart. She quickly pulled herself together. She couldn't let sentiment cloud her judgement. 'I see. But I believe Mr Hart, the solicitor, has already explained to you that he has declared your father's Will invalid for specific reasons.'

'So, what, my ma and pa didn't get wed?' Jack sneered, taking a step towards Mary.

'Oh, yes, I agree there's no stigma attached to that these days,' Mary replied, trying to maintain her composure. 'But it's not a matter of what your parents did or didn't do, it's a matter of …'

'This is me birthright,' Jack's voice cut across hers. 'Every stone, every corner, holds my family roots. I won't let anyone take it away, especially not someone like you.' His voice grew louder, filled with defiance.

Mary's composure remained steadfast, masking the turmoil within her. She couldn't let her doubts and fears show now, not when the stakes were so high. 'I understand Mr Hart has given you a copy of my great-grandfather's Last Will and Testament?'

'Aye, he give me summat. But I don't read too well.'

'Well, the Will expressly states that the estate, in its entirety, is to be passed down to the eldest son or daughter holding the Mattleton name through the bloodline.'

'Aye. That would be me pa. He was the eldest.'

'I also understand that Mr Hart explained the discovery of a document revealing that my great-grandfather adopted your father, Leonard Mattleton, who was a foundling and gave him the name Mattleton.'

Jack drew himself up to his full height. 'That may be so!'

he retorted, his voice quivering with anger and desperation. 'But! if you imagine, I'm going to stand by and allow you to waltz in here from t'other side of the world and claim what's rightfully mine – you've got another think comin.' Jack's words sliced through the air like a sharpened blade. 'I'll 'ave you know I've farmed this land alongside me, pa, since I was a boy!' he added, leaving no room for doubt.

Mary's legs trembled as she spoke, but her words were laced with determination. 'Be that as it may.' Mary stood her ground, her petite frame a stark contrast to Jack's towering presence. 'I understand the significance of the estate to you and the Mattleton family. But I am the sole surviving blood relative. I am the legitimate heir to the Mattleton estate. I am here to honour its legacy and to carry it on,' Mary declared in a calm and composed voice, her steady words cutting through the tension, contrasting with Jack's explosive outbursts, further intensifying the atmosphere.

Jack's eyes narrowed. The tension between them was palpable, like a battle of wills, as he stared at her with his cold and calculating eyes before unleashing a cutting retort. 'Over my dead body!' he boomed, his voice reverberating around the stone walls as he slammed his fist down on the dining table with a sharp thud just as Robert emerged through the door.

'What's going on? Are you alright, Mary?' Robert asked urgently upon seeing Jack's imposing figure standing over Mary and dwarfing her.

Mary rushed over to Robert, her heart pounding like a drum, her breath catching in her throat in shock at Jack's outburst. 'Robert!' Mary gasped. 'Am I pleased to see you!' she exclaimed, rushing towards him.

'What on earth has been going on here?' Robert frowned.

'It appears, although you've explained North Hall Manor's inheritance succession to Jack, and you've served notice for him to vacate the Manor, he is planning to say here, regardless,' Mary blurted out.

'I see,' Robert replied. 'Jack, what's this all about? You're not reneging on our agreement, are you?' he asked, struggling to keep his composure.

'What do this slip of a girl know about farming? She'll run the place into the ground in no time!' He sneered.

'That, my dear man, is no concern of yours!' Robert replied. 'Kindly remove your belongings by the end of the week, as we agreed. Doctor Mattleton will take up residence at the weekend.'

'Has he got somewhere to go?' Mary asked, concerned.

'I don't need thy pity, woman! Don't worry thy self; I'll be out by the weekend!' Jack barked, storming out of the door and slamming it loudly behind him.

Mary sank into a chair, her trembling legs barely supporting her weight, the room spinning around her as she struggled to regain her composure.

'Has Jack got somewhere to go?' Mary's voice trembled with genuine concern.

'Yes. Don't worry, Mary,' Robert reassured her, sitting down beside her and giving her hand a comforting squeeze. 'Jack's mother, who was a good deal younger than his late father, has been struggling to manage the smallholding Leonard left her. Jack will move in with her and take care of the farm. That should keep him occupied.'

Mary sat silently, listening to the rhythmic tick-tock of the clock filling the room, a constant reminder of the passing seconds and the weight of the situation.

'Jack is right, of course,' Mary said, breaking the silence.

'Right? Right about what?' Robert asked, puzzled by Mary's statement.

'When he said I know nothing about farming. I don't!'

'You'll soon learn!' Robert laughed aloud, looking at the horror on Mary's face. 'Seriously, there's Charlie, the herdsman who lives in the servant wing with his young son Tom. They look after the sheep and tend to the cows.'

'Tend the cows? What does that mean?'

'Well, among other things, twice a day in the summer, he's responsible for taking the cows to the barn for milking, then returning them to the fields.'

'What happens to all the milk?'

'Charlie arranges for it to be collected and sent to the local dairy.'

'He milks the cows twice a day, every day?' Mary asked, looking surprised. 'Even Christmas Day?'

'Yes! Every day, twice a day. Cows don't get Christmas Day off, silly!' Robert laughed loudly.

'Don't make fun of me, Robert. Remember, I'm used to tending to people's needs, not cows!' Mary retorted.

'I'm sorry,' Robert apologised, shaking his head. 'Look, Charlie has been around North Hall since he was a boy. His father worked here, too, until he died, so he knows everything he needs to know. But I'll provide you with a list of contacts, the vet, the mechanic for the equipment and the like. Plus, I will always be on hand to provide support with the bookwork and if you need legal advice.'

'What about help around in here?' Mary asked, looking around the hall. 'It certainly could do with a good clean if this room is anything to go on?'

'Ah, yes! I forgot to mention – Mrs Scarr, a local woman. I know very little about her. Apparently, she will come in twice a week to clean and cook, or more if you need her.'

'She does?' Mary raised her eyebrows. 'I can't see much evidence of her being in here lately, can you? The dust on that sideboard is so thick you could write your name in it!' Mary chuckled.

'I'm afraid she's another of Jack's casualties …'

'Jack's casualties?'

'They had a falling out. Jack has a quick temper, as you witnessed, especially when he's had a pint or two. Leave it with me. I'll have a word with Mrs Scarr.'

'Thank you, Robert.' Mary replied, somewhat relieved Robert would take charge of the situation.

'Anytime. Now, how much of the Manor have you seen?'

'Very little. I was in the middle of exploring when Jack interrupted me.'

'Okay, well, I'll take you on a quick guided tour, starting with the upstairs, but be warned, you'll have to look past Jack's clutter. Afterwards, I'll treat you to a meal at The Red Lion Inn in the village. How does that sound?'

'That'll be bonzer, as the Aussies say! Lead on, I'm famished,' Mary replied, following Robert up the winding stone staircase.

Chapter 8

'I love this place, Robert. How wonderful all the flowers look,' Mary exclaimed, pointing to the vibrant tubs and baskets overflowing with an abundance of blossoms outside the picturesque Tudor-style Red Lion Inn.

The sound of clinking glasses and murmured conversations welcomed Mary upon entering the inn, along with the tempting aroma of cooked food that sparked her hunger. Mary noticed several local people at the bar engaged in a light-hearted discussion. She hoped she, too, might become a member of this vibrant community.

Mary trailed behind Robert as he entered the bar, observing his struggle to manoeuvre under the low beams and occasionally hitting his head on the old timber. The publican greeted them with a warm smile and a hearty welcome.

'Ey up Mr Hart. You'll be wantin' yer usual table, I 'spose?'

Robert nodded gratefully. 'Thank you, Bill,' he replied, acknowledging a group of locals gathered at the bar as they made their way to their table.

'You seem to know everyone,' Mary said in a low whisper, her eyes scanning the room curiously.

'Yes, quite a few, I suppose. The Red Lion Inn has been the heart of this community for generations. It's where everyone relaxes and keeps up on each other's news and gossip. It's been that way since I can remember,' he replied. 'In fact, I can remember coming here with my father when I was a very young boy. In those days, though, kids had to stay on the benches out front. My dad would buy me a packet of crisps and a bottle of lemonade to keep me quiet.'

They took a seat at the table and quietly studied the menu. 'I know what I *should* have!' Mary piped up grinning. 'Now that I'm a landowner and will be no doubt be called upon to work in the fields … A ploughman's lunch.' Mary laughed, then frowned. 'What exactly is a ploughman's lunch? It's a new one of me?' she admitted with a chuckle.

Robert looked up from the menu he was studying. 'You've never heard of a ploughman's lunch?'

'No!' Mary replied, shaking her head.

'Well then, you should try one! I'll go up to the bar, put in our order for food, and get some drinks. How about a half pint of cider to go with your ploughman's?'

'If you say so.' Mary nodded and smiled.

'Won't be long,' Robert said, rising from his chair.

While Mary waited for Robert to return with the drinks, she noticed the group of locals Robert had acknowledged when they came in, talking excitedly about a recent village event. She also caught snippets of conversation from the table next to theirs, discussing the upcoming village fair. It was apparent that Robert was right. The inn was a popular spot for locals to gather and relax.

'Robert, look at those old beams. This place must be ancient?' Mary remarked as he returned from the bar carrying their drinks.

'Yes, it is old; in fact, part of this place dates back over six hundred years!'

'Six hundred years!' Mary emitted a low whistle, amazed at the age of the Inn. 'Now that is old. No buildings in Australia come close to being that old!'

'Really?' Robert frowned.

'Don't you know your history?' Mary giggled. 'Captain Cook wasn't even born then, let alone having discovered Australia! I'm interested in history. I'd like to know more about this place.'

While they waited for their food to be served. Robert told Mary about the history of the historical inn and described the local customs in the region. She listened intently, finding Robert's folklore stories captivating, especially the intriguing anecdotes of mystical creatures, secret passages, and hidden treasures.

Robert grinned mischievously. 'Legend has it you'll be granted a lifetime supply of cider if you find the hidden treasure in this inn. Fancy going on a treasure hunt?' he asked, laughing loudly and proceeding to take a large gulp of the amber liquid of his pint of cider.

'I'm not so sure ….' Mary began and was interrupted by the barman placing two oblong wooden boards overflowing with ham, cheese, pork pie, sausage roll, pickles and an apple before them. 'Wow! This is a ploughman's,' Mary exclaimed, her eyes widening. 'There's enough food to satisfy an entire battalion,' she added, laughing.

'Not at all … get it down you!' Robert laughed. 'Cheers!' he added, holding up his pint glass of cider to her.

Mary glanced out the window, her knife and fork briefly forgotten as they dangled in her hands. She contemplated the path she was about to take and the uncertainty that lay ahead. A heavy, sinking sensation had settled in the pit of Mary's stomach, weighing her down with an undeniable sense of dread despite the relaxed and cheerful atmosphere around her and the effects of the cider, which had gone straight to her head. She couldn't shake the fear that had gripped her since her visit to the ominous North Hall Manor and her meeting with Jack, despite her efforts to push her unease to the back of her mind. Had she made a mistake by leaving her life behind in Australia? Her profession, her friends and the only life she'd known, to travel halfway around the world in search of a new beginning.

Robert looked up, chewing a mouthful of food. 'Is there something wrong with your food?' he asked, his voice muffled.

Mary shook her head. 'No,' she replied softly, avoiding eye contact. 'It's very nice,' she added, looking down at the wooden board, its contents hardly touched. 'And the panoramic view from the window over to the hills is breathtaking. It's just that …' Mary's voice trailed off as she looked away from Robert and into her lap.

Robert's eyebrows furrowed in confusion. 'It's just that what?' he probed, leaning forward, looking concerned. 'Is something troubling you?' he asked.

Mary hesitated, looking into Robert's eyes for encouragement before speaking out about her fears. Should she tell him she'd imagined North Hall as a quiet retreat surrounded by hills and green pastures – that her lifestyle would be simple: farming and living a peaceful and uncomplicated life? And not, as she had discovered over the last few brief hours, an impossible number of tasks and responsibilities she was expected to take on, regardless of whether she was up to it.

'I'm worried about how I will fit in here,' Mary confessed, her fingers fidgeting with the edge of the wooden board, her appetite waning as her anxieties grew. 'After all, I'm a physician, a doctor. I spent years studying so that I could diagnose and treat illnesses and diseases in people. What impression will I make on the local people when they discover my unfamiliarity with farm life and my lack of knowledge regarding running a farming estate? I will be a laughingstock!'

'Of course, you won't.' Robert reached out, gently touching Mary's arm in reassurance.

'Yes, I will. You've already poked fun at me for not knowing that cows don't get a day off from milking on Christmas Day! I felt like a fool not knowing that.'

'I was just joking with you. I'm sorry,' Robert replied, his voice laced with regret.

'Look, let's just get one thing straight before we move on. Contrary to common beliefs – not everyone who lives in

Australia rides bareback on horses in the outback, herding cattle like they do on television! I, for one, most certainly didn't.'

'I didn't intend that … I mean, I didn't intend to upset you.' Robert's voice softened.

'No! I'm sorry for overreacting. You didn't really upset me. It's just that I'm finding myself vulnerable and out of my depth at the moment and wondering whether coming here was a mistake!' Mary admitted. 'After all, I've left everything behind in Australia, my profession, my friends, my entire life. Suppose this was a mistake coming here?'

'I'm sure it's not a mistake, Mary, and you don't need to worry about a thing,' Robert replied optimistically. 'You'll find it's a tight-knit community around here. There are plenty of people to call upon for help. Charlie will show you the ropes, and I'll be on hand for any business advice you might need. We could also benefit from your medical expertise around here.'

'I don't see how. I'm a doctor of medicine, not a vet. They aren't quite the same, are they?' Mary replied indigently.

'You're right, of course. Cows and people aren't the same, but your knowledge and skills as a physician could still play a vital role.'

'Oh! Yes! How may I ask?' Mary inquired sarcastically.

'Well, for example. It's quite a distance to the nearest maternity hospital to give birth, for instance.' Robert offered.

'Cattle don't visit hospitals to have their calves, nor sheep their lambs, Robert.' Mary replied mockingly. 'So, where does my ability as a doctor come in?'

'I know cows and sheep don't go to hospitals to give birth! I was referring to humans giving birth in the hospital, not animals.' Robert laughed aloud. 'Just last week, a farmer's wife didn't make it in time and gave birth to her baby in a layby halfway across the moors. That's where your expertise *might* be useful?'

Although Robert laughed and appeared to be light-hearted, had she detected a touch of scepticism in his voice? Or was she imagining things? Either way, despite his reassurance, Mary still faced immense pressure to succeed in her new role, leading to an internal struggle due to her lack of expertise.

'There's still another thing bothering me, though.' She added.

Robert pushed his now-finished ploughman's lunch board to one side. Surprised, he exclaimed. 'Oh? Yes … What's that?'

Mary's words tumbled out in a rush. 'I can't escape this sense of unease, Robert. It's like something is lurking in the shadows at North Hall.'

The silence that followed Mary's confession seemed to stretch on endlessly, each passing second intensifying her discomfort until Robert finally broke it with a nervous laugh.

'Are you serious?' he replied, trying to suppress his laughter.

'Yes! I'm serious! Please don't mock me …' Mary hesitated before speaking. 'There's something about the manor that unsettles me. Have you ever noticed anything untoward there?' she queried hesitantly.

'I'm sorry. I didn't intend to dismiss your concerns. In what way do you find the manor unsettling?'

Mary looked away from Robert and fixed her eyes on the view outside. How could she express the stifling uneasy feelings she'd experienced when she first entered the main bedroom at the Manor with Robert without him ridiculing her?

Mary took a deep breath and turned back to face Robert. 'Well….' she began. 'Aside from that portrait, which has left me completely baffled about the identity of the woman in the portrait. Have you ever sensed a presence in North Hall? As though you're being watched – especially in the main bedroom?' On noticing Robert's blank look, she continued. 'I can't quite explain it, but it's been bothering me.'

'You mean, is it haunted?' Robert asked. 'No, nothing like that,' he replied, brushing off Mary's concerns. 'Admittedly, these old houses can seem spooky, I suppose. Creaking floorboards, draughts and the like.'

'And what about the awful smell? I'm not certain I could live with that. It doesn't smell very healthy!'

'I agree. The air was a bit on the pungent side.' Robert laughed, holding his nose. 'It's probably a combination of years of dust and the musty old books in that old bookcase over in the corner of the bedroom and dampness. I noticed there were some damp patches above the window in the bedroom where the wallpaper was peeling off that need looking at. Plus, I bet that old threadbare carpet square right in the middle of the bedroom floor hasn't seen a vacuum cleaner in years.'

'And it was also quite dismal in there.'

'Well, for some reason, Jack had the curtains partly pulled across the window, making it dark. Perhaps that's what was making you uncomfortable,' Robert replied.

Was Robert right? Was she being overly sensitive? Or perhaps there really was something wrong with the Manor … but she would give Robert the benefit of the doubt.

'Yes! You could be right.' Mary replied slowly, nodding. 'It could have been something as simple as that, making me uneasy.' Mary answered, encouraged by Robert's light-hearted response.

'I'm sure I'm right. The sooner we get Mrs Scarr in there to give the place a good clean and have the room redecorated with a lick of paint here and there, the better. And I suggest we give that rug a decent burial while we're at it,' Robert chuckled.

As Mary's sense of ease grew, she started laughing along with Robert, envisioning a brighter future in her new home.

In any case, she didn't shy away from challenges, did she? She argued with herself. No! Despite her initial hesitation, she would embrace the unfamiliarity of her new life. She would use the opportunity for personal growth and to discover newfound strengths and resilience, all of which her Aunt Moly had taught her.

'While we are at it, I'm going to look for a new mirror for the dressing table. I noticed when I looked in it there was a small crack in the corner, and the reflections of the room were distorted.'

Chapter 9

Mary's emotions were running high as she carefully packed up every corner of her Aunt Molly's house. Each room held a piece of her heart, full of precious memories and emotions. She picked up the bottle of her aunt's 4711 Eau de Cologne from her dressing table. Tears pricked the back of her eyes as she inhaled its familiar scent. She brushed her fingers against the worn velvet-covered armchair in the living room as she passed. Its softness reminded her of countless evenings snuggled up in it with her aunt, sharing secrets and dreams.

The house and its contents had become a safe haven for her since her aunt had taken her in following her parent's accident. Not just the house, but the garden, as well. The work they had done out there had been a labour of love for Mary and her Aunt Molly and stood as a testament to their unbreakable bond. Each tree, once a mere sapling, now stood tall and proud, acting as a towering protector, offering shade and shelter along with the plants she'd watched flourish over the years.

'I never realised how much this house had become a part of me until this moment. It will be harder to leave it than I imagined.' Mary said to herself, her voice barely audible above the creaking of the floorboards as she took one last look around the house.

The empty rooms, once filled with treasured mementoes and familiar images, now stood as a blank canvas. The silence served as a haunting reminder of the void in Mary's heart caused by her aunt's death, longing to be filled once more. And now, no matter how bittersweet, the moment had come to move on. A fresh chapter awaited her in a faraway country.

As Mary closed the door behind her, a sense of finality came over her. 'It feels like I'm leaving a piece of my heart behind,' she remarked as she stepped outside onto the covered verandah.

Tears welled up in Mary's eyes as she ran her fingers along the old wooden verandah rails. She could almost feel the imprints of her aunt's touch filling her heart with a longing for the days gone by and the enduring bond they had between them. There had been many happy hours, countless conversations, and shared laughter spent on the verandah with her aunt on summer nights when it was too hot inside to sleep.

Mary lifted her face to feel the gentle breeze which rustled the leaves of the gum trees surrounding the house, creating a soothing melody that seemed to bid her farewell as she viewed her packed boxes, neatly stacked in the corner. They held fragments of her life and were ready to embark on a journey with her across the water to Yorkshire to start a new beginning.

'If only I could stay here forever, Aunt Molly, but it's time to let go and follow my own path,' she said as she left the house for the last time, tears filling up in her eyes.

***

Was it only six months ago when she landed here in London for the first time? Mary reflected as the plane touched down on the tarmac. That journey had seemed incredibly long and had left her completely exhausted by the end. The trip this time had been noticeably better. As a woman of property, she'd justified indulging in travelling in business class from Australia to London. And what an enormous difference it was to stretch out and sleep, Mary acknowledged to herself as she descended the plane's steps, her feet touching the solid ground with a sense of relief and liberation.

After collecting her luggage and passing through passport control unscathed, Mary manoeuvred her luggage trolley with a newfound sense of accomplishment along the bustling walkway, alive with the rhythm of hurried footsteps and the symphony of rolling luggage moving towards the arrivals lounge at London Heathrow Airport.

The clock on the wall showed it was a little past seven in the morning, and the first light of dawn was barely breaking on a chilly March Sunday morning. Mary had expected the airport to be quiet at that early hour, assuming that most people would still be lost in their Sunday slumbers. However, as she stepped through the doors of the arrivals lounge, with its towering glass walls, high ceilings and bright fluorescent lighting, Mary found herself surrounded by a sea of expectant faces and a loud, confused mixture of voices and sounds from the hordes of people all eagerly waiting behind the barrier, brimming with excitement and anticipation. Some were waving placards with names on them, while others held banners and balloons. Her eyes darted anxiously from face to face, searching for Robert's familiar face. He had volunteered to make the four-hour trip from Yorkshire to meet her, sparing her from taking the train with her luggage.

'Mary! Mary,' she heard a voice calling out over the chaotic noise coming from the crowd of people and the clatter from the luggage trolley wheels. She turned toward where she believed the voice was coming from, searching for Robert's face.

'Mary! Over here …'

Relief washed over Mary like a warm wave, dispelling her anxiety when she finally caught sight of Robert's tall, muscular body, his smile a beacon of comfort in the midst of the frenzy.

'Robert!' Mary called out as she spotted him grinning and waving frantically at her. 'Thank heavens I found you amongst all these people!' she exclaimed, pushing the luggage trolley and almost running towards him.

'It's great to have you here, Mary,' Robert replied, giving her a broad smile. 'Here, let me take your trolley. My car is this way. Follow me,' Robert said, gesturing towards the walkway lined with shops and cafes ahead and setting off at a brisk pace.

Mary lagged behind him, not even attempting to keep abreast, as he strode on ahead of her at great speed. She was relieved to be off the plane and was enjoying the opportunity to stretch her legs and get some fresh air, and she was in no hurry to catch up with him.

'Can we stop somewhere on the way for breakfast, perhaps?' Mary asked as they reached Robert's car. 'I'm famished,' she added, her stomach growling.

'I thought you flew over in business class this time. Did you miss out on the fancy breakfast?' Robert said, teasing.

'No, I could have had breakfast, but I was still half asleep, so I gave it a miss. But now I'm hungry!' Mary replied. 'Sorry,' she added, pulling a face.

'No need to apologise. I'm hungry as well. It seems a long time since I last ate a McDonald's breakfast at the services on the M1 on the way down here,' Robert announced, chuckling.

'You had Maccas for brekkie? Sounds ripper.' Mary playfully imitated a strong Australian accent.

Robert chuckled. 'I see you've not lost your Aussie twang, then?'

'Oh! Do I really sound Australian?' Mary asked, frowning.

'Yes. Now and then, you do…'

'It's fortunate Aunt Molly isn't around then. She was very well-spoken and was always correcting my speech.'

'And it's a good thing I brought the Jaguar with me today with all this luggage of yours,' Robert said, skilfully trying to fit Mary's large suitcase into the boot. 'But you still might have to travel on the roof rack at this rate.'

Mary laughed aloud as she sank into the plush red leather seat of Robert's classic Jaguar. 'Home, James, and don't spare the horses!' she said, slapping the dashboard.

'Your wish is my command,' he replied light-heartedly. 'Let's leave the chaos of London behind and embark on a culinary adventure. I know of a cosy little place near St Albans that serves an excellent breakfast.'

As they left the hustle and bustle of London behind them, Mary watched as the landscape transformed from high-rise buildings standing cheek-by-jowl into the English countryside with the fields stretching out before them, scattered with grazing sheep, rolling hills and quaint villages. Mary leaned back in her seat, her eyes scanning the passing scenery and her fingers tapping nervously against the armrest as a mixture of anticipation and anxiety about her uncertain future washed over her. *So, this is to be my home from now on,* Mary mused as the car sped along.

'This all seems so surreal,' Mary piped up, breaking the silence.

'Surreal? How so?' Robert inquired, glancing at Mary.

Mary paused momentarily. 'Well, the idea of being here in the car with you on my way to my new home in North Hall Manor. My worldly possessions packed up in boxes in a container on a ship somewhere in the middle of the ocean on their way over here to join me.' Mary paused. 'I hope I've not made a big mistake!' Her words lingered, a hint of uncertainty shrouding the future.

'I'm sure you've made the right decision to move here,' Robert said, reaching over and lightly touching her hand to reassure her. 'Why do you think you might have second thoughts about this move?'

'I don't really …' Mary slowly shook her head. 'I mean, I have no idea why I said that. It's an opportunity every girl would dream of. A beautiful house to live in surrounded by wonderful open countryside and the chance to get to know family I didn't know even existed. But …'

'But?'

'Ignore me!' Mary chuckled. 'I'm just tired from the flight. Tell me what's been happening at the Manor in my absence.'

'Where to start? There's been so much going on these past six months or so since you've been away.' Robert's voice carried a hint of excitement as he continued, 'The Manor has undergone a fantastic transformation. It's almost like stepping into a whole new world. We have completed most of the work you ordered. You'll likely see a vast improvement!'

'I can't wait to see it!' Mary's curiosity piqued as she asked, 'Have you seen much of Jack lately?'

'Oh! He's been around a few times,' Robert replied dismissively.

'Oh dear! Is he still angry about losing the Manor?'

'Look … You're not to worry about that, Mary. Remember, you are the rightful heir to North Hall Manor,' he replied assertively.

'I know, but …' Mary's voice trembled with a blend of confidence and doubt, her mind still grappling with the burden of her inheritance as she attempted to suppress her lingering insecurities.

'No buts! Now, let me see… ah yes! Here's the turning …'

As they turned off the main road and entered the sweeping drive ahead, Mary gasped in awe upon seeing the majestic ivy-clad, stone-built building standing proudly at the far end of the drive.

'The Barley Mow?' Mary's brow furrowed with curiosity at seeing the sign on the building. 'That's a strange name. What does it mean?' she asked.

'It means a stack or sheaf of barley, which is what they use over here to make beer.'

'And back home. But I've not heard the term *barley mow* before. You Brits use the strangest of words. I'm going to have to get myself a translator.' Mary laughed aloud.

Upon entering the centuries-old building, Mary's eyes were immediately drawn to the exposed beams that crisscrossed the ceiling. Their weathered appearance added a rustic touch, while the blazing log fire in the grate added a cosy, homely atmosphere.

'This is a nice place, Robert and I'm famished!' she remarked, smelling the tantalising aroma of sizzling bacon mingling with the rich smell of freshly brewed coffee. It instantly awakened her senses, transporting her back to the traditional English breakfasts she had enjoyed the last time she was in England.

'It's good to be home!' she found herself saying aloud, a lump forming in her throat.

Chapter 10

10th April 1982

Oh! God, I'm tired. What with the mattress being so lumpy and that damn clock kept ticking and chiming all night, I barely slept a wink! I gotta say, though, things looked much better when I pulled back the curtains this morning compared with when I glanced out last night when I couldn't sleep. The air is super clean and refreshing here, and everything is so green and colourful in the garden below. I will have to ask somebody what the flowers are called. Especially the little yellow ones with trumpet-shaped flower heads. The hills and fields I can see from my window look so lush, unlike the dry and empty landscape back home. I hope I get the chance to explore sometime soon. I realise it's been some time since I've written in my journal; maybe after I've explored further, I'll have more to write about.

Mary closed her journal, put down her pen, and stretched out her arms, yawning. A testament to her sleep-deprived state after tossing and turning most of the night. Maybe it was because of jet lag. But more likely the uncomfortable bed, she decided. Each time she shifted positions, the mattress pressed uncomfortably against her back as if a handful of rocks had been dumped under the sheets. Plus, it was also impossible for her to disregard the grandfather clock downstairs ticking loudly. Its constant tick-tock served as a continual reminder time was slipping by with each passing hour and that she was still wide awake. Mary tried counting each chime, as one might do sheep, as the sound pierced the silence like a sharp needle as it chimed on the hour every hour. Yet sleep still eluded her.

However, the discomfort of the bed and the ticking of the clock only served to strengthen Mary's resolve, which had lived with her for as long as she could remember. The desire to find a place where she truly belonged. This resolve had been her constant companion and had driven her to take risks to face new challenges in the past.

Mary took in a long breath. 'However difficult it's been in the past, that's all behind me now, and it's time to move on!' Mary whispered a silent promise to herself while she was getting dressed.

She noticed Elsie Scarr was in the great hall below, cloth in one hand and a tin of polish in the other, vigorously polishing the dining table, giving off an air of energy and activity as she descended the spiral stone staircase.

'Good morning, Mrs Scarr,' Mary greeted her cheerfully.

'Mornin miss, grand day. Do you want summat fer breakfast?' she asked in a broad Yorkshire dialect.

'Thank you for your offer, but I don't want to disturb your cleaning,' Mary replied. 'I can get it myself,' she added, making her way towards the kitchen door.

'Nay, lass,' said Mrs Scarr. 'No bother, I was ready for a brew meself.' Mrs Scarr replied, following Mary into the kitchen. 'Sit yourself down, and I'll rustle you up some breakfast to go with it.'

Mary sat down by the fireplace. Its blazing fire created a cosy atmosphere on what was a cool spring morning. She leaned closer to the fire while observing Mrs Scarr scurrying around in the kitchen. Mary was touched by Mrs Scarr's genuine warmth and friendliness, insisting on preparing breakfast for her. Her nurturing nature reminded Mary of Aunt Molly as she watched the plump, ruddy-faced Elsie Scarr bustling around the kitchen, ferreting in cupboards until, finally, she exclaimed, 'There tis. I knew there was one somewhere!'

Mrs Scarr brandished a large cast iron frying pan, which stood as a proud relic of generations past, its exterior tarnished by years of use. Its shiny interior reflected the dedication and care she had given it by scrubbing it clean after each meal. Soon, the aroma of sizzling bacon and sausages filled the kitchen, along with the rhythmic tapping sound of her wooden spoon against the large black porridge pot.

Mary gasped in surprise as Mrs Scarr placed a steaming bowl of creamy porridge on the kitchen table before her.

'Help yourself to cream and sugar,' she announced, pointing to the jug and bowl in front of her.

As soon as Mary had finished her porridge, Mrs Scarr removed the empty bowl, replacing it with a plate piled high with a mouthwatering assortment of crispy lean bacon, golden-brown sausages, perfectly fried eggs, juicy tomatoes and, hearty slices of black pudding.

'There, lass, get that down you,' she said in a warm and hearty tone, beaming with pride and contentment, a testament to her satisfaction in her work and her eagerness to please.

'Thank you. That's very kind of you!' Mary exclaimed, her eyes widening in delight as she looked down at the mountain of food on her plate, wondering where to start.

'If that's all, lass, I'll get about me cleanin' now,' she announced, picking up her box of cleaning materials.

Fit to bursting, Mary pushed her nearly empty plate away from her and was about to settle back in the chair as the shrill ring of the telephone pierced the air. Startled, Mary sprang to her feet and hurried to answer it, her footsteps echoing through the great hall.

'Hello. North Hall Manor.' Mary's voice resonated around the hall with an air of pride and ownership.

'Good morning, Mary,' Robert's voice exuded warmth and familiarity. 'It's Robert. Robert Hart. How are you this morning?'

Pleased to hear Robert's familiar voice, she replied cheerfully. 'I am very well, thank you, Robert, and you?' Inwardly laughing to herself at how suddenly she sounded so *British*.

'I'm coming over your way this morning. There are still some important documents that require your signature. Once we're done, I propose we have lunch at a lovely inn I know of that is high up on the moors. How does that sound?'

'That sounds lovely. Thank you, Robert. I'll look forward to it.'

After hanging up the phone, Mary found herself skipping up the stairs, eager to see Robert, but at the same time, she was unsure about what she should wear. The mode of dress was so different here than back home. She was torn between the cosy oversized jumper and slacks, which she'd dressed in for comfort and warmth earlier when she got up for breakfast. Or maybe she should change into something more stylish to make a good impression on Robert.

Mary opened her wardrobe doors and scanned the contents.

'I have nothing to wear!' she exclaimed, her voice betraying her frustration and desperation as she surveyed her near-empty wardrobe and quickly realised that there wasn't much to choose from. All that was left of her once extensive wardrobe were empty hangers. 'Most of my clothes are packed away in boxes.' Mary lamented.

Upon reaching the last dress on the rack, her eyes suddenly caught sight of an unfamiliar blue garment tucked away in the corner. Mary extended her arm fully and reached down into the back of the wardrobe to retrieve it.

As she gazed upon the azure blue hue of the dress, its

shade reminiscent of the sky on a clear day, with its intricate lace collar. Mary experienced a sensation of being transported to a different time, as if the dress had a connection to a forgotten past or a distant memory. The garment appeared to hold a secret story, hidden and waiting to be revealed, a mystery from a past long gone. Then it came to her as she held it out at arm's length. She instantly knew what it was – it looked like the same dress the woman pictured in the great hall was wearing.

Still gazing at the dress, she heard Mrs Scar's voice calling her from downstairs.

'Mr Hart is here, miss,' Mrs Scarr shouted from the bottom of the stairs, interrupting Mary's thoughts.

'I'll … I'll be right there,' Mary replied, flustered. Without wasting time, she threw on the nearest dress and cardigan, twisted her hair into a bun, and then hurried downstairs.

Upon descending the stairs, Mary detected the smell of polish and a strong smell of detergent. She smiled. Mrs Scarr had spent the morning cleaning and polishing the furniture and scrubbing the tiled floor till it all gleamed. Once more, the impressive great hall dazzled with its elegance and grandeur, decorated with portraits and beautiful tapestries.

Robert was sitting at the dining table. On seeing Mary descending the stairs, he stood up.

'Hello, Mary,' he greeted her, smiling warmly. 'I hope I'm not disturbing your day. It's just that …'

'No, no … Please, sit down and make yourself comfortable,' indicating to the chairs around the dining table. 'I had nothing pressing on today other than finding my way around here, of course.' Mary replied, chuckling. 'And that's going to take a month of Sundays, no doubt!'

Robert produced a pile of documents from his briefcase. Mary pulled a face and glanced at the clock. They would have to go through the papers quickly if they were to go for lunch as well. She inwardly groaned to herself.

'That looks like a lot of paperwork for me to sign, Robert. I was under the impression that you had promised me a ride out and lunch. Was that just a ruse to get me to sign your documents?' she asked with a mischievous smile.

Robert laughed. 'Don't worry, it's only three signatures to authorise you as a signatory at the bank. Nothing more painful than that, I promise.'

'Okay then, you're off the hook this time. Where do I sign?'

Chapter 11

As the car climbed the steep moorland road that stretched out endlessly before them. Mary caught a glimpse of the seventeenth-century Tan Hill Inn slowly emerging into view on the horizon. It stood perched on top of the hill like a solitary guardian, its weathered façade adorned with ivy framing its many windows.

On reaching the Inn, Robert parked the car, got out, and donned his worn leather jacket that matched his sturdy boots. Mary noted he looked every bit like an adventurer in the rugged setting. A gust of wind hit Mary as she stepped out, causing her teeth to chatter uncontrollably. She hurriedly wrapped her woollen cardigan tightly around her shivering frame for protection against the biting winds as she stood gazing at the untamed beauty of the surrounding moorland, with its rugged terrain stretching out before her.

'Wow!' Mary exclaimed. 'You weren't kidding when you said it was like being on top of the world, were you?' she remarked to Robert, her voice filled with genuine astonishment. 'The view from up here is breathtaking!' Mary continued, her eyes sparkling with awe as she watched the silhouette of a lone hawk soaring through the sky.

Robert nodded. 'I knew you would love it. There's something magical about this place, isn't there?' he replied with pride in his voice.

'There certainly is. But let's go in. I can't remember the last time I've been this cold!' Mary exclaimed, shivering and throwing her arms around herself. 'And hurry before I turn into an icicle!' she said in jest.

Robert took Mary's arm. 'You're right. It always feels about ten degrees colder up here. Come on, let's see if they have a roaring fire and a pint of ale waiting for us. I wonder what's on the menu today. I hope it's something good and hot to warm us up.'

The Inn's interior, with its rustic wooden beams and antique tapestries, appeared to have withstood the test of time. A log fire was burning in the fireplace, and the aroma of home-cooked food permeated the air. Vases of wildflowers adorned the wooden tables, lending a natural touch to the cosy setting. Robert guided Mary to a table by the window, which had a stunning view of the moorland and rolling hills stretching to the horizon.

'What's it to be?' Robert asked, looking up from the menu in his hand.

'Well …' Mary paused. 'As much as it all looks to be very tempting, I'm still quite full of the breakfast Mrs Scarr served me this morning. Perhaps I'll have something light, like a sandwich?'

Robert pulled a face. 'A sandwich?' he exclaimed. 'Nothing else?' he asked, aghast.

'Just a sandwich, please.' Mary replied with a smile.

After placing the menu back down on the table, Robert announced. 'Well, I'm having the stew,' and then, looking directly at Mary, he declared. 'You don't know what you are missing,' he said, grinning.

A young brunette waitress gracefully weaved her way through the tables towards them. 'What can I get for you today?' she asked with a friendly smile.

While Robert was giving the waitress their lunch orders, Mary stared out of the window. She was suddenly hit with nostalgia and apprehension. Was it looking at the vast expanse of the moorland that caused her to reflect on what she had left behind in Australia and the uncertainties she had faced since coming to Yorkshire? Or was it the dress she had stumbled upon in the wardrobe that morning? Indeed, there was no doubt that the presence of the dress had left her with several unanswered questions, intensifying the already unsettling uncertainties she had experienced since she arrived at North Hall.

'The view from up here is amazing, wouldn't you agree?' Robert asked.

Mary nodded. 'Yes ...' she replied quietly, her eyes still fixed on the moorland. The beauty of her surroundings only served to deepen her sense of unease.

'What is it, Mary? You seem far away today?' Robert's concerned voice cut through the lonely silence. 'Is there anything wrong?'

Pulled back from the depths of her thoughts. 'I'm sorry, Robert, I was miles away. What did you say?'

'Are you all right, Mary? Is something bothering you?'

Despite the warmth of the crackling fireplace, a chill crept up Mary's spine. The cosy ambience clashed with the unsettling thoughts that had consumed her. Wanting to escape the cold that was creeping into her bones, she wrapped her cardigan tightly around herself.

'I'm fine,' she replied, forcing a weak smile. 'I'm probably just tired. I didn't sleep at all well last night.'

'Oh? If you weren't warm enough, I'm sure Mrs Scarr could find you more blankets, or maybe ...'

Mary interrupted. 'No! It was nothing like that,' she said, with a shake of her head. 'I don't need more blankets. I need answers!'

'Answers to what? What's troubling you that is keeping you awake?'

'Promise you won't laugh?' Mary asked guardedly.

'Of course I won't ... Go ahead, tell me what is bothering you.'

Mary paused. 'I'm not usually given to being overdramatic…'

Robert nodded. 'I agree. The little I know of you, I'd put you down as a very down-to-earth person. So, what's troubling you?'

She drew in a long, slow breath, letting the air out slowly while she looked away to gather her thoughts. 'Well … Besides the constant ticking and chiming of that cursed clock in the hall, plus the lack of sleep, I can't shake off an unsettling sense that something is terribly amiss in North Hall,' Mary confessed.

'Something amiss? In what way?' Robert asked, his brow furrowing.

'The place makes me uncomfortable. And I hear unexplained noises.'

Robert furrowed his brow. 'Mary, it's an old house. There's bound to be some creaking of floorboards,' he replied with a hint of frustration.

'No, there's more to it than that,' Mary said, her voice growing more urgent. Her agitation was apparent as she shifted in her seat. 'It's something deeper, something I can't quite put into words.'

'Please try.' Robert leaned forward in the chair. 'I'm listening. Tell me what's bothering you.'

Mary hesitated briefly, unsure whether to tell Robert about the flicker of movement that she had seen in the dressing table mirror and the coldness that had suddenly crept into the room the night before. Would he wonder about her state of mind?'

She gathered her courage and spoke rapidly. 'Well … I have this strange sensation I'm not alone. That I am being watched all the time,' Mary replied, her words tumbled out. 'Especially in my bedroom,' she added softly, with her head down and her hands fidgeting with her cardigan.

Robert maintained a stoic expression, his eyes narrowing

with curiosity before replying. 'It's not just your imagination playing tricks on you, is it? Like any other old house, the Manor has its fair share of creaking noises.'

Mary replied forcefully, her voice rising with frustration. 'No! It's not all in my imagination – definitely, it's not! Explain this if you can …'

'Okay, I'm listening.' he settled back.

Mary inhaled deeply. 'I am a heavy sleeper once I get to sleep. Which in that bed in the Manor isn't easy,' she confessed with a sigh.

'Why? 'What's the matter with the bed?' Robert asked.

'It feels as though it's got rocks in the mattress!' she said and laughed. 'As I said, I'm a heavy sleeper … I can sleep through the mightiest of storms back home, and there can be some real hum dingers at times.' Mary laughed nervously. 'So, I'm not prone to be woken easily. However, last night, I suddenly woke up from a deep sleep on hearing someone whispering my name.'

'Perhaps you were dreaming? You've been through a lot lately, especially settling into a different country.'

'No! I'm certain there's more to it than that. I'm sure after I heard my name whispered, I also heard people having a conversation. I couldn't make out what they were saying. It was just a mumble.'

'Sometimes, when we are over-wrought and in strange surroundings, we can imagine all sorts of things,' Robert offered.

'I might be in strange surroundings, and maybe I am a little tired, too, but I don't believe I'm over-wrought and imagining things,' Mary said firmly.

Robert dropped his head to one side. 'What actual evidence do you have that there is something wrong in North Hall, though?'

Mary sensed the atmosphere between them was getting tense, and doubts were creeping into her mind as the conversation went on.

'Well …' She drew in a long breath. 'I certainly didn't imagine the dress I found in my wardrobe this morning, which most certainly doesn't belong to me,' Mary replied with determination.

'Dress? What dress are you referring to?'

'I found the same blue dress worn by the lady in the portrait in the great hall tucked away in my wardrobe when I was looking for something suitable to wear to go out with you this morning.'

'The same dress? Surely not?'

'Yes, the exact same blue dress!'

'Are you certain the dress you found in the wardrobe is the identical dress to the one in the picture?' Robert pressed. 'After all, a blue dress is a blue dress?'

'No!' Mary exclaimed. 'I swear, the one I found is the identical blue dress the woman is wearing in the portrait.'

'So, the simple answer is then, it must belong to a member of the previous family who left it in that case?'

'No! I asked Mrs Scarr. She swears she cleared the wardrobe out when she knew I was coming! And that's not all …'

'What's not all?'

'The mirror …' Mary said in a loud whisper, lest their fellow diners might hear.

'The mirror?' Robert frowned.

'The one on the dressing table. It's hard to put into words, but there's something strange about it. Each time I look in it … I get an odd sense of unease.'

'Cos you don't like what you're wearing, or maybe your hair is all wrong?' Robert laughed aloud.

'Don't mock me, Robert. I'm being serious!' she replied sternly.

Robert's laughter faded, his face softening with concern. 'Sorry. I was trying to lighten the conversation. Forgive me.'

Mary nodded, giving him a faint smile, wishing she'd not started the conversation.

'Look, I'm sorry for being facetious!' Robert continued. 'Please, do go on. I'm intrigued. What do you see in the mirror that makes you uncomfortable?'

Mary anxiously twirled a strand of her hair around her finger. 'I know this sounds odd, but when I look at my reflection, I see a distorted image of my face. Like those mirror attractions you find at the carnival.'

'That's probably because of the imperfection in the glass we found, remember? It's nothing to worry about. We can easily replace the glass,' Robert reassured her, patting her hand gently.

'There's something else going on there… the reflection of the room behind me is not as it should be …'

'Not as it should be?' Robert threw his hands up. 'Now I'm lost!'

'Well, instead of seeing what I expected to see behind me, my chair and the fireplace reflected in the mirror. I see a blurred vision of a different room.'

'A different room? What room? The Palace of Versailles, perhaps?' Robert asked, smirking.

'I knew you wouldn't believe me!' Mary replied as tears were welling up in her eyes.

'I'm sorry, Mary, I don't mean to tease you, but you've got to admit it does all sound a bit far-fetched, doesn't it?' Robert said, trying to reason with her gently.

'I know it sounds unlikely! But I am telling you what I saw!' Mary replied, raising her voice in frustration.

Robert stared at the sense of isolation and vulnerability etched on Mary's face. 'It's not that I'm unwilling to believe you, Mary. The truth is, I'm having problems processing it all. But, please, do go on. What room do you see when you look in the mirror?'

'I can't quite make out which room it is. As I try to look closer, I sense the mirror is trying to draw me in with some magnetic force, and it scares me, so I pull away.'

'I'm still convinced it's because of the damage to the mirror. I'll get someone to come out and measure for a new one. Don't worry, I'll take care of it,' Robert replied assuredly.

'I know this may all sound fanciful to you, but …' Mary paused and inhaled deeply, wondering if she should go on. 'I can't escape the notion that there's something more behind that mirror. That it contains some hidden secrets.

Robert's patience seemed to wane. 'It's just an old mirror, Mary, and its glass needs replacing, nothing more than that. Trust me,' he replied, his voice tinged with exasperation.

Mary's frustration escalated as she remained unconvinced by Robert's explanation.

'Last night, I saw a fleeting image of a figure.' Her voice quivered. 'I had the impression that it was watching me. Like it was waiting for me …' her voice trailed off as the waitress set down their food order.

'One stew, one sandwich,' the waitress announced.

'Ah, good food – thank you!' Robert replied, picking up his knife and fork.

'Enough of this supernatural, things-that-go-bump-in-the-night talk. Eat up your healthy-looking sandwich while I tuck into this delicious-looking stew,' he added, his cutlery poised over an enormous plate of steaming hot stew, mashed potatoes whipped to perfection, and a mound of bright green cabbage.

Mary smiled with amusement while she watched him devour his enormous plate of food while she took a bite of her sandwich.

Lost in contemplation, Mary let out a sigh. She was caught between Robert's rational perspective on the mirror incident and her own conviction in the inexplicable occurrences she'd observed. How could she convey to Robert the sense of foreboding she'd sensed the night before when she didn't understand it herself?

Chapter 12

11 April 1982

I went to the Tan Hill Inn with Robert today. It was way up high on the moors. Robert claimed it's the highest public house in the country, a staggering 1,700 hundred feet above sea level. It felt like when we finally reached the summit, the views completely blew my mind. Robert warned me it was like standing on top of the world, and it was. I was chapter surrounded by clean, crisp air and a peaceful silence. The landscape here is so different from the wide-open spaces of the Australian outback. Instead of endless plains, here, there is a tapestry of colours and textures, with trees, hills, and valleys interwoven among craggy cliffs and jagged rock formations. As I stood there taking in the view, it was almost as if all the worries and anguish from packing and relocating here that had consumed me for months had melted away, leaving me with a profound sense of tranquillity and renewed vigour. I hope Robert will show me many more places like this. Although he's my solicitor, I find myself hoping that our connection might extend to friendship. One thing that I have been longing for since I've been here is the company of my friends back in Australia. Still, it is early days. While I respect Robert's boundaries and refrained from asking too many personal questions during our time together today, I was inevitably curious about the man behind the solicitor. The few glimpses he shared about his personal experiences only made me more curious and eager to learn more. Of course, I respect his privacy, and I would not dream of prying into his private life – just yet!

Mary put her pen aside and closed her journal. She glanced at the clock.

'It's late, yet I'm still wide awake,' she said with a sigh. 'Perhaps some hot milk might help?'

Laughing to herself, she recalled the many times she'd prescribed the very same remedy to her insomniac patients rather than prescribing sleeping pills. Not that she had tried the hot milk remedy herself, as she rarely had problems getting to sleep.

'Now might be a good time to check if it actually works,' she said brightly, getting to her feet.

Cautiously, Mary descended the narrow, winding stone staircase, its steps worn smooth by years of use. In the dim light and without a bannister, the uneven steps made them even more challenging to navigate. On entering the kitchen, she gazed through the window at the full moon against the backdrop of a pitch-black sky, which bathed the kitchen in a soft, silver light, casting eerie shadows dancing across the kitchen walls adorned with antique copper pots and other relics of a bygone era.

Mary suspected that not much had changed in this kitchen over the years as she reached into the cupboard where Mrs Scarr kept the pans. She retrieved a small saucepan, poured in the milk and, placed it on the range. While waiting for the milk to heat, Mary stepped outside the back door and inhaled a breath of the frosty night air. She hastily adjusted her dressing gown around her as she studied the stars before hurriedly returning to the kitchen and rescuing her milk, which was bubbling and hissing and about to boil over on the stove.

With her cup and saucer of hot milk in her hand, Mary walked back through the great hall on her way back to bed. Standing in the moonlight, she paused at the portrait of the woman in the blue dress. Despite Robert's earlier remarks, Mary remained convinced that the woman was wearing the same dress she had discovered in her wardrobe, deepening the mystery of where the dress came from. *What was the connection between her likeness to the woman and the discovery of the dress?* she mused.

Back in her bedroom, Mary lowered herself into the easy chair by the fire and rearranged the soft cushions around her. With her hands around the cup, she drank some of her milk, sounding a satisfied 'Ahh' as she gazed into the fire, focusing on the last remaining ember glowing at the back of the grate. Her thoughts wandered back to the blue dress. What secrets did it hold? Why was it in her wardrobe? Who was that person in the portrait that looked so much like her?

Curiosity getting the better of her, Mary went over to her wardrobe, took out the dress and, held it up against herself. *I wonder if it would fit me.* She pondered as she tried it on. It was her exact size.

Mary stood before her dressing table mirror, mustering up the courage to draw back the velvet curtain she'd thrown across it the previous night after she thought there was something in the mirror watching her. She hesitated, with her fingers poised and curled around the red velvet curtain. A sudden chill filled the room, causing her to shiver. The candle on the dressing table flickered, casting eerie, distorted shadows around the walls that appeared to mock her hesitation. The relentless, loud ticking of the old clock downstairs amplified Mary's growing unease. It marked each second until the clock would chime ….

One...Two...Three... Four...Five...Six .... With each passing chime, the tension within Mary grew.

Seven...Eight...Nine ...Ten .... Slowly, Mary pulled back the curtain. She gasped in surprise as she caught sight of herself, dressed in the blue dress, her blonde hair hanging loosely down over her shoulders. Her reflection mirrored that of the woman painted in the portrait, almost as if they were one and the same. Mary touched her reflection in the glass just as the clock chimed twelve.

A flicker of movement in the mirror caught Mary's eye. Shadowy forms gradually emerged, enticing Mary to look deeper into the mirror.

Mary saw the familiar reflection of her bedroom with the floral-covered easy chair and, alongside it, the small, round wooden table with her cup and saucer from which she'd drunk her milk. The warm, inviting colours in the reflection slowly gave way to a chilling, monochromatic scene as she continued to stare into the glass. It was as if life was being drained from the world beyond the mirror. Then, in an instant, the reflection shifted from her bedroom to the downstairs kitchen. It revealed a gathering of people around a table. The transformation held Mary's gaze, capturing her attention like a hypnotic spell, yet giving her the urge to traverse an unseen barrier between the two realms and delve deeper into the unknown.

It was like stepping into a parallel universe where the past and present intertwined. *Am I dreaming?* She puzzled, finding herself with her back against the kitchen wall, observing the group of people she'd seen reflected in the mirror, not understanding how she got there. Still, what she was looking at appeared real enough. She reasoned with herself. Mary studied the table adorned with a red chequered tablecloth overflowing with an array of mouthwatering platters of food, leaving little space for any additional dishes.

Mary was transfixed and had a strong desire to learn

more about the people gathered around the large, scrubbed wooden kitchen table. Her eyes moved swiftly from one face to another around the table as she listened to the lively interactions and laughter. Mary experienced a potent mixture of longing and sadness. The sight of the family reminded her of her own family that she had lost and longed to be part of again. Her eyes rested upon a fair-headed woman with long wavy hair who, she guessed, was about her own age, sitting next to a small boy. Mary studied the woman's face closely. She thought her face looked familiar, but she couldn't place who it was. Her thoughts were interrupted.

'Ey up! Did you 'ear me, Molly?' piped up a Yorkshire-accented, jolly-looking, ruddy-faced male.

A young, curly-headed, fair-haired girl replied, 'Sorry, Pa, what did thee say?'

'Bloomin' 'eck Molly, have thee got cloth ears or summat? Muther wash out young Molly's lug 'oles tonight, will thee,' he exclaimed, letting out a belly laugh. 'I said pour us a brew, lass. And make it a strong one; can't be doin' with no weak stuff.'

The man's words hung in the air while the child looked earnestly in Mary's direction. Was the girl aware of her presence? Mary's heart pounded as she anxiously awaited any sign that the curly-headed girl might acknowledge her existence.

'Sorry, Pa,' the child replied brightly, placing a large enamel mug of steaming hot strong tea on the table before him. 'I'll go outside to feed t'lambs. Are thee comin' Thomas?'

The boy shook his head. 'Nay. I don't feel well.'

'There's always summat wrong with you!' the girl said, flouncing through the doorway and brushing past Mary without acknowledgement.

Chapter 13

The following day, Mary lay in bed, deeply absorbed in her thoughts, as she attempted to unravel the mystery of her sudden appearance in the downstairs kitchen in a different time-period the previous night, wearing the mysterious blue dress that had inexplicably materialised in her closet.

'Were the people I saw real, I wonder? Or was I dreaming?' Mary asked herself aloud.

'If I wasn't dreaming and did see that family sitting around the table in the kitchen, why did that woman look familiar?' Mary pondered.

'Could there be a link between last night's phenomenon and the mirror on the dressing table?' Mary asked herself, glancing over at the mirror. 'I remember reading a book that claimed it was possible to get a glimpse of an alternate reality. Could the mirror be a way to access another reality?'

Mary pulled the blankets up under her chin and tried to get back to sleep. 'I am beginning to feel as though I'm trapped in a never-ending maze of unanswered questions,' she confessed, frustrated.

Fully awake, Mary got out of bed and drew back the heavy velvet curtains. The blinding brightness from the sun poured through the window, causing her to squint and shield her eyes with her hand. She lingered at the window, mesmerised by the spectacular view of the rolling hills in the distance and the fluffy white cloud formation that hung over them. At the same time, her mind continued to seek answers to what she had remembered about the night before.

The scent of sizzling bacon and warm bread mixed with the rich smell of freshly brewed coffee wafted up from the kitchen. Mary hurriedly got dressed and went downstairs.

Mrs Scarr greeted her as she entered the kitchen. 'Morning miss, sit your sen down. There's fresh coffee in the pot. Help yourself.'

'Good morning, Mrs Scarr,' Mary said, pouring the steaming hot coffee into a pink rosebud china mug.

Mary sat down at the large scrubbed kitchen table and looked about the room. How different it had looked in the mirror's reflection on her dressing table the night before, devoid of colour and life, before morphing into this kitchen in a different era.

She pictured the family sitting at this very same table in her mind. Their faces lingered like a distant dream, a thin veil that separated reality from a different realm. Had she travelled to a parallel world? Mary wondered. Did those apparitions contain the key to her past, offering a tantalising glimpse into the family she believed she had lost?

'Thank you, Mrs Scarr,' Mary said, her eyes widening as she gazed down at the hearty traditional Yorkshire breakfast laid out before her. It wasn't just the food. It was the care and thoughtfulness of the meal. She missed the sense of being cherished, absent since Aunt Molly's death.

'You're welcome, lass. I hope it's to your liking?' Mrs Scarr asked.

Mary bit into the crispy bacon, its smoky flavour engulfing her taste buds. 'It's all delicious, Mrs Scarr, thank you!' she said, her voice filled with genuine gratitude.

Mrs Scarr chuckled, her eyes crinkling with warmth as she replied, 'Glad ta see thee enjoying it, lass. There's nowt like a good Yorkshire breakfast to start t'day right I say.' She added while her over-generous form leaned over the sink of dirty pots and pans, diligently scrubbing each one clean.

'How long have you been working here?' she asked,

tucking into a forkful of sausage and bacon dipped into the bright yellow yolk of the fried egg.

'Oh, nigh on fifty-five years, I'd say,' Mrs Scarr said, chuckling.

'You have been here for fifty-five years? You don't look old enough!' Mary replied light-heartedly.

'Nay! Get away with you,' Mrs Scarr laughed, dismissing Mary's remark with her hands. 'I'm as old as those there hills, yonder! I'll be three score years and ten, as the good book says, next birthday!'

Mary looked blankly at Mrs Scarr. 'Three score years and ten?'

'Seventy! I'll be seventy next birthday!'

'Goodness me!' Mary exclaimed. 'You must have seen a lot of changes here at this place over the years?'

'Aye, miss. I've seen many changes, that's for sure. More than I care to remember,' Mrs Scarr replied with a wistful smile. 'But one thing remains the same.'

'Oh? What's that?'

'The joy of serving a hearty breakfast. Now eat up.'

'I will indeed,' Mary replied, her knife and fork poised over the plate. 'Tell me, Mrs Scarr, I hope you don't believe I'm being nosey, but what brought you here to the Manor at such a young age?'

A blush of embarrassment crept up Mrs Scarr's cheeks. 'Well … it was a bit complicated, see …'

Sensing that perhaps she may have crossed the line, Mary added quickly, 'I'm sorry, Mrs Scarr, that question was rather bold of me. Please forgive me.'

'Nay lass. I've a mind to tell thee,' Mrs Scarr said, drawing a chair out from under the table. 'It was our Jack that brought me.'

'Jack? What's Jack got to do with you?' Mary asked.

'Well … he's my son, thee knows?'

'Jack? Jack is your son?' Mary asked in astonishment.

'Aye, lass, he's my son right enough. Although he takes after his pa more than after me,' she replied in a disapproving manner.

Mary hesitated for a second, allowing Mrs Scarr's revelation to sink in. 'Please, Mrs Scarr, don't take offence at my next question.' Mary paused briefly, carefully trying to string her next question together. 'I gather you must have been quite young when you found you were expecting Jack?'

'Barely fifteen. Pa gave me a whippin' after he learned. He threw me out on my ear he did!' Mrs Scarr replied, moving her head from side to side.

'How terrible for you!' Mary said, nodding sadly and lightly touching the woman's hand. 'The father of your baby? Did he know you were pregnant?'

'Aye. That's why I came here.'

Mary frowned. 'I don't understand?'

"The baby's pa took me in. That's what brought me here.'

Mary frowned. 'I'm sorry, Mrs Scarr, I'm still not sure I understand.'

'Leonard Mattleton is, or was, Jack's pa!'

Mary's eyes grew wide, and her jaw dropped. Had she heard correctly? Leonard Mattleton was Jack's father? Time seemed to stand still as Mary's thoughts raced, realising the implications of this revelation. She was no prude, but Mrs Scarr would have been underage when she fell pregnant, and not forgetting Leonard Mattleton would have been around twice her age when he took her to his bed. The very idea seemed inconceivable.

'Did you not know? Didn't that fancy solicitor not tell you?' Mrs Scarr asked.

'No, I had no idea,' Mary replied, still struggling to process the information. 'Mr Hart didn't tell me that Jack was your son. Nor that Leonard Mattleton was his father.'

'Nay matter. Most folks around here don't know either. Leonard said to keep it quiet. He said I'd be sent away if I told anyone, and me babby would be taken away from me.'

Mary paused for a moment, lost in her own thoughts on what Mrs Scarr had said. So, Leonard Mattleton, the man who once held this house in his grasp, also hid his shame behind closed doors. That was, until now! 'But Jack lived with you in the Manor until now, though?' Mary asked.

'Aye. Jack grew up here in this house. He and his pa were as thick as thieves. Leonard took my son from me and shaped him into his own image.'

'Weren't questions asked as to whose Jack's father was?'

'Aye, some asked. Leonard spun some cock and bull story. Then, as soon as Jack didn't need no more mothering, they sent me away to the farm and only allowed me back now and then to clean the place up and do their washing and cooking for them.'

'But what about schooling? Did Jack go to school?'

'Oh, aye! He went to school – when Leonard wanted him out of his hair so he could get up to no good, I'll be bound.' She paused. 'Our Jack was always in trouble with his teacher, Mrs Hardisty, though. She'd often clip him around his ear or wrap him over his knuckles with a ruler to toe the line. Alas, he never did, so when he reached eleven, instead of going to big school, he stayed home with his pa.'

'Has it always been just Leonard and then Jack living here after he was born? Do you remember?'

'Nay! It was a lovely family home afore that. Leonard's ma and pa, along with his younger brother James Mattleton, his wife Sybil, and their two young uns, were living here, I remember.'

'And Leonard? Did he have a wife and family?' Mary asked.

'Nay. He never married. He had plenty of mistresses, though,' Mrs Scarr sniggered, touching her nose with a finger. 'Old Mrs and Mrs Mattleton, Leonard and James' ma and pa had the big rooms on the east side of the house, where your rooms are now.'

'It was quite a large family, then?'

'Aye, and a well-respected family, you know. Ol' Mr and Mrs Mattleton were good employers. My ma used to do sewing for old Mrs Mattleton. Ma would take me along with her some days, and I played with the young Mattleton girl who was about the same age as me. Mary, same as you, but they always called her Molly.'

'Molly? Do you mean Molly Mattleton?' Mary asked in astonishment.

'Aye, that's right. I also remember the littlest one, Thomas. He was about a year or two younger than Molly. He was a lovely little lad.' Mrs Scarr sighed.

'Thomas? So, would that be Thomas Mattleton?' Mary asked eagerly.

'Aye, lass. That's reet, did you know him?'

Mary shook her head and responded, 'Not exactly. Please tell me more about the household, Mrs Scarr,' Mary urged, curious and wanting to know more, reaching a fever pitch.

Mrs Scarr reclined in her chair, her eyes closed, appearing to be lost in a world of memories as she relived her cherished youth. She reminisced about her time with Molly, where they played games and hid in the passage concealed behind a bookshelf in the library. The times they helped with feeding the orphan lambs. When they fetched and carried provisions from the kitchen to the farm labourers at harvest time.

The look on Mrs Scarr's face suddenly changed. With a mixture of sadness and resignation, she recalled the fire that caused a rift that tore the family apart.

'So, it was Leonard's lies that drove out James, his younger brother, and his young family. The Manor wasn't the same after that,' Mrs Scarr added, sighing.

'What happened to James and his family? Tell me, please.' Mary asked.

'No one knew for sure. Some say they sailed away on a big boat …'

Could it be that Mrs Scarr's revelations held the key to unlocking a long-awaited truth? Was this *her* family Mrs Scarr was talking about? She wondered. She must speak to Robert to learn what he knew.

'You claim the Manor wasn't the same after James Mattleton and his family moved out. What do you mean?' Mary asked.

'It became tainted by secrets and lies after old Mr and Mrs Mattleton passed away. That's what I mean. Outside, the buildings fell into ruins. Not a one wanted to come and work here on the farm. It was all Leonards' and Jack's doing! I'm reet glad you are here now to save this old place …'

'I will do my best, Mrs Scarr…'

Little did Mary know, Mrs Scarr's shocking revelations were only the beginning, the mere tip of an iceberg hiding deeper secrets buried deep within its walls, yet to be unveiled. The Manor was a ticking time bomb waiting to explode.

Chapter 14

'Ey up! Young Thomas, stop lolling about and 'elp Ma clear the table.'

The older woman's voice pierced the air, sharp and cutting, causing Mary to jump and the young boy, who had been slumped down in his chair, to sit up straight.

Mary froze as the event appeared to play out like a recurring dream. She had somehow found herself back in the kitchen, with her back firmly pressed against the worn-out, peeling wallpaper hidden in the shadows. The people gathered around the kitchen table were the same as she had seen last time.

The young, fair-headed woman was the first to rise from the table. She swiftly gathered the plates and cutlery, creating a lively soundscape of clattering plates and the clinking of cutlery as she placed them in the stone sink under the window.

'But … but I'm not well …. me 'ead 'urts and me throat is sore,' the young boy whined.

'There's nowt wrong with you that a clip round the ear won't put reet,' the older woman said as she got up from the table. 'Up you get now! Then, fetch a bucket of coal for the fire,' she added, giving the boy's ear a slight tweak before sauntering out of the room, her ample breasts swaying like the pendulum in the grandfather clock with each step.

'Och! That 'urt Gran!' the boy squealed.

'Aww, get away with you!' she said, glancing back over her shoulder with a tinkling laugh.

'Mind what your gran says, young Thomas?' the older man said, wagging his finger as he rose from his chair and followed the woman down the passageway. His heavy footsteps reverberated on the flagstone floor as he went.

'Aye, Grandpa!' Thomas mumbled his reply, his head bowed low.

'James …' the young woman addressed the tousled blond-haired young man with piercing blue eyes sprawled in his chair, smoking a pipe and reading the newspaper. 'When's that brother Leonard on yours going to show his face back here and help you? What with calving and lambing, you can't do it all!'

James scratched his head. 'Ah don't know, Sybil,' he replied, glancing up at the clock. 'But it's time for me to go back to work,' he added, pulling his braces up over his shoulders and putting on his well-worn boots over his mud-stained trousers.

Mary slipped out of the back door, her eyes darting nervously, searching for anyone who might see her. She stood watching James striding off into the distance, with his black and white dog following him at his heels until they vanished from sight.

As she looked across the yard, she noticed that one of the barn's enormous old wooden doors was open. Sunlight was streaming through a large window on the far wall, revealing a glimpse of the cavernous inside of the barn, which was packed with towering stacks of hay bales. Mary was tempted to take a closer look.

On entering the barn, a comforting and rustic sweet smell of hay and the earthy scent of animals permeated the atmosphere. At the back of the barn, Mary could see the young girl she'd seen earlier in the kitchen sitting on a wooden stool. She was cradling a small, white lamb in her arms, its tiny mouth eagerly latching onto a bottle of milk and making faint suckling noises as it gulped the milk. Mary stood and watched the girl, transfixed.

The girl suddenly looked up. She looked directly at Mary and snapped. 'And who might you be?'

'You can see me?' Mary asked with an element of surprise in her voice.

'Course I can! I got eyes, ain't I?' the girl replied haughtily. 'I saw you in the kitchen afore. So, who is you?' she repeated.

'I'm Mary. What is your name?'

The girl gently placed the lamb down among the hay in the pen, brushed the hay off of her skirt, and turned to Mary.

'I was baptised Mary too, but everyone calls me Molly,' she replied. 'I see souls of the living and the departed,' Molly said. 'But I don't remember seeing you afore.'

'You see people's souls?'

'Aye. Gran says I was born with The Sight,' Molly replied.

'You were born with The Sight? I'm sorry I don't understand?'

'It's a special gift, Gran says. I sees and talks to people who have died.'

Molly's explanation suddenly made everything clear, and slowly, things started to fall into place. Aunt Molly believed she had a gift, which she called *second sight*. Mary remembered her aunt explaining it to her as a child. Just as Molly claimed, she possessed *The Sight*. They were one and the same!

Somehow, whether or not in a dream, she'd travelled to a parallel world where this young girl was her Aunt Molly, who had raised her after her parents passed away. And the other people around the table must be her family. Molly's parents were her grandparents, and the older couple, whom she barely remembered, were her great-grandparents. Which meant the young boy, Thomas, her father. Mary frantically searched for a way to explain her existence to Molly. She didn't want to alarm the girl by telling her she came from another time, but how else could she explain her being there?

'Molly, I'm not dead? I'm from a parallel world.'

'You says daft things, 'course you're dead!' Molly cut in.

'It's difficult to explain, but maybe I am dead of sorts to you in your lifetime because I've not been born yet,' Mary replied. She could see the young girl looked confused and quickly changed the subject. 'How old is the lamb?' she asked, deciding not to go into any more detail and hoping she'd satisfy Molly with her answer.

'This one be two weeks or thereabouts. It's one of t'orphans.'

Mary leaned over the pen and gently stroked its muzzle. 'I, too, am looking after some lambs at the moment. They are about the same age.'

'Thems really me brother Thomas', but he's too lazy to feed em.'

'That's brothers for you!' Mary laughed. 'How old is Thomas?'

'Oh! He's still a baby. He's eight.'

'So, how old are you, Molly?'

'I'm ten, I'll be eleven next birthday, and I'll be going to grammar school. I can't wait!' Molly exclaimed.

'What's so good about grammar school?' Mary asked, caught up in Molly's excitement.

Molly leaned over the pen and grabbed another lamb, thrusting the bottle of milk into its mouth. 'Well, I won't have to walk with me little brother to school for a start. My school is in the next town, and I'll be catching the bus. Thomas will have to do his part round here like feeding these lambs,' Molly said, looking down at the lamb she was feeding. 'I will be too busy doing homework when I get home.'

'Molly! Molly! Where are you?' a voice was calling outside.

Molly swiftly dropped the lamb back into the pen and ran outside. Mary followed.

'What is it, Ma?' Molly called, running towards her mother.

'Quickly, go fetch Pa from the fields and ask him to get the pony and trap out and go into town to fetch the doctor.'

'Why? What's happened, Ma?'

'It's Thomas. He has collapsed. He can't breathe properly and is burning up, and he has come out in a rash. I'm worried. Hurry, go tell Pa!' she said quickly without taking a breath.

'Molly, I'm a doctor. Take me to Thomas, please.'

Molly shook her head. 'Ah can't, Ma says, to hurry to fetch Pa!'

'I know, but please take me to your brother first.' Mary begged.

'All right, follow me, but hurry!' she replied reluctantly.

Mary's heart sank upon finding Thomas lying on his bed, his eyes wide open in terror, struggling to breathe. She noticed a bright red rash forming on his body, which was partly covered by a sheet. As Mary understood the seriousness of his condition, she bent over him and reached down to touch his forehead. Her hand passed through it. It was no good; despite being confident she knew what was wrong with him without being able to touch him, how could she examine him? All Mary knew was that he needed medical attention fast.

'Please, Molly, hurry back. We can't lose him,' Mary muttered under her breath as a sense of urgency overwhelmed her with Thomas's fading strength, his every breath a struggle.

Thomas's mother returned to the room with an enamel bowl of water. She sat down next to the bed, her tear-stained cheeks mirroring the despair in her eyes, her face full of anguish as she sponged down Thomas's body with the water.

'Don't leave us, our Thomas, don't leave us!' she implored, placing a cold flannel on his forehead.

The light was fading fast, and anxiety was gnawing at Mary's mind with each passing moment, wondering when the doctor would arrive.

Finally, a large, ruddy-faced man carrying a small black bag rushed into the room, closely followed by James and Molly.

'Now then, young Thomas. What's going on with you?' the doctor asked briskly, pulling back the sheet that was covering him and then proceeding to feel around his glands and peer into his mouth.

'Aye, it looks like he's got a bit of a sore throat, but I'm certain an aspirin, plenty of fluids, and a couple of days in bed and he'll be reet as nine-pins,' the doctor announced, replacing the sheet and stepping back from the bed. 'Reet, I'm a busy man, so I'll take me leave.'

'I was worried we were going to lose him, Doctor!' Sybil said, her voice trembling.

'Nothing of the sort, Mrs Mattleton,' the doctor replied brusquely. 'Just a touch of a sore throat, no doubt, caught a chill. You know what boys are like walking around half-naked or sitting around in wet clothes? Aspirin, lots of fluids, happen one of your thick soups and bed rest, and you'll see he'll soon be up and about. Good day, Mrs Mattleton,' he added, tipping his hat as he turned and left the room.

'Thank you, Doctor,' James said. 'We'll see you out.'

'Yes, thank you, Doctor. This way,' Sybil added. 'Come, Molly,' Sybil beckoned to her. 'Leave Thomas in peace.'

'Wait! Molly!' Mary called out to her as she was leaving the room.

Molly turned. 'You still here?' she asked.

'Yes. Tell me, how long has Thomas had a sore throat?'

'I dunno. Thomas complained of a sore throat t'other day, I reckon,' Molly replied.

'And what did your mother give him for the sore throat?' Mary pressed.

'Nowt, she's busy. She ain't got no time for mollycoddling!'

Mary returned to Thomas's bed. 'Molly, this is important. Get Thomas to open his mouth wide so I can look at his throat.'

'If you wanna see, you do it!' she replied. 'I've got to feed the lambs now Thomas has taken to his bed! Molly pulled a face and frowned as she was just about to leave the room.

'Please, Molly. I can't; he can't see me, and I can't touch him. So, it would help if you asked him to open his mouth. It's important.'

'Oh! All right,' she replied reluctantly. 'Open your mouth, our Thomas!'

Thomas groaned as he partly opened his mouth.

'Wider,' Mary said. 'Ask him to open it wider, please, Molly.'

'Wider you gormless lummox!' Molly instructed, poking his arm.

Mary peered inside Thomas's mouth. 'It's far worse than I feared,' she muttered in hushed tones, her brow furrowing at the gravity of the situation. 'Molly, I believe Thomas has rheumatic fever. Left untreated, it could be fatal.'

'What does fatal mean?'

'He could die …'

Chapter 15

14 May 1982 (late at night because I can't sleep)

It's been quite the emotional rollercoaster day today, to put it mildly. Finally, after waiting for weeks, I took delivery of my long-awaited new car today. Hurrah! I will now be able to get around under my own steam, starting with driving to meet Robert for lunch at The Red Lion. I was really looking forward to not only showing off my new car but also catching up with him, as I hadn't seen him in a while. Then I go and spoil things. In retrospect, I realise how childish I acted, storming out of the pub like an angry tornado. Oh! Why can't I learn to keep my mouth shut? It was all my fault; I knew how sceptical he was. But no, I went on and on about all the weird stuff happening here. It's moments like these that make me question my own maturity and ability to handle conflicts. He will probably never speak to me again after today, and who can blame him?

I am perhaps beginning to understand what people must have thought of Aunt Molly when she openly admitted seeing and hearing people. Probably very much like Robert's reaction today. Thankfully, I've been sleeping through the night recently, so it's been a few days since I've seen or heard from Molly and her family. Could Mrs Scarr's home remedy of warm milk with a spoonful of honey be working? She really has taken me under her wing, bless her with her mothering, feeding me up and giving me advice, yet not interfering. I am growing very fond of her. Wish I could say the same for her son, Jack!

With her pen still in her hand, Mary stared off into the distance, replaying her confrontation with Robert in her mind.

'Yes! On reflection, I did act rather hasty and immature, leaving The Red Lion in such a rage like that,' Mary argued with herself aloud. Hesitating, she added. 'But there again, I was justified, wasn't I? He wound me up, didn't he?' she giggled.

***

'Are you sure you weren't imagining it? Could it have been a dream or a nightmare, even?' Robert commented after she shared her experience of being transported back in time a few weeks earlier.

'No! It certainly wasn't a dream or a nightmare.' Mary bristled with indignation.

'I'm sure there must be a simple explanation then,' Robert replied tentatively.

'I've told you before, there's something strange about that mirror on my dressing table,' Mary whispered, her voice barely audible lest the diners around her heard. 'I can sense it, Robert. It's like there's a parallel world inside that mirror waiting to be discovered,' Mary said, her voice laced with equal parts of fear and curiosity.

'Something inside the mirror? Pardon me for saying it, but that all sounds a bit fanciful, to be honest. I'm not sure I believe in spirits, ghosts, and things that go bump in the night,' he said and laughed.

'Okay. Laugh if you must, but I am positive that the family Mrs Scarr told me about that lived here when she was a girl could be my family.'

'If hypothetically speaking, you saw someone, which I'm not saying you did, it would be somewhat of a coincidence that they were your family, wouldn't it?'

Mary experienced a deep longing gnawing within her as she pictured the family she'd seen around the table. Their presence, while offering uncertainty, also somehow provided her with solace.

'No! I believe the family I saw was my family as they were in the days leading up to their departure for Australia – the family that, until now, has been lost to me.' Mary's words poured out rapidly, remaining steadfast in her beliefs.

'You really mean that?' Robert asked, his voice laced with disbelief. 'Your long-lost dead family are ghosts living in the kitchen? Stuff and nonsense!' he added, with an air of mockery and laughing aloud.

Crushed by Robert's scepticism, clashing with her own unwavering belief, Mary felt a tension between them like an invisible barrier. 'I didn't say they were ghosts,' she snapped.

'Well, how else could you describe what you saw?' he retorted.

Her voice faltered as she replied, uncertain of the answer. 'I don't know… I don't know …'

'Look, sorry, Mary. I didn't mean to upset you,' Robert said, his voice filled with genuine remorse. 'But I am finding it hard to take all this in.'

She looked long and hard at him before replying, 'I know the whole thing appears to be far-fetched, and normally, I'd be the first to agree with you.' She paused. 'I can hardly grasp the reality myself. But I honestly believe I have been guided here for a purpose and that perhaps I even have the gift of second sight, just as my Aunt Molly had.'

'Second sight? Crystal balls, Tarot cards and all that?' Robert scoffed, his voice dripping with sarcasm.

'That is a typical uneducated response of what extra-sensory perception and precognition are about, and quite frankly, I'm surprised to learn how blinkered you are!' Mary exclaimed.

'Oh! But Mary, you can't really believe in all that mumbo jumbo, can you?' Robert said, his loud laughter echoing around the pub.

Mary got up from her chair, forcefully pushing it away from herself, scraping it noisily across the tiled floor, which reverberated throughout the otherwise quiet corner of the pub.

'I'm not staying here to be ridiculed.' Mary's voice quivered in anger, flinging her napkin onto the table with such force that it sent her glass of red wine flying, spilling its contents over the tablecloth and down Robert's white shirt before flouncing out of the inn.

'Mary, Mary, come back! I was only teasing. Come back please, I'm sorry…'

Robert's words had fallen on Mary's deaf ears. His insult to her intelligence had left her seething with anger and resentment. She climbed into her new blue mini, turned the key in the ignition, revved the engine, and roared off down the road, clenching the steering wheel tight with both hands.

The encounter with Robert had set her on edge. 'How dare he treat me with contempt and ridicule me?' Mary uttered through gritted teeth before slamming on her brakes to avoid a sheep that was about to wander across the road in her path. 'After all, I'm not some silly little bimbo. I'm a highly qualified doctor of medicine,' she fumed.

Preoccupied by her thoughts, Mary suddenly realised she'd reached the crossroads at High Abbotside. She decided it might be safer to take the longer route along the lower road, which led to the manor. The quicker route through the moors and the Buttertubs Pass was frightening enough as a passenger, let alone driving herself over it in the mood she was in. That road required complete focus to navigate the winding, steep, and uneven road, not to mention the sheer drops of Buttertubs Pass.

'No! I don't think so ...' She announced in a loud voice, changing direction, leaving the moors behind.

Mary felt a flood of shame sweep over her as she drove home the long way to the Manor. She knew deep down that she had overreacted with Robert. However, his reactions had also sparked doubts and concerns in her mind. Her belief that she had seen her family in another realm was wavering. There could be a simple, logical explanation for what she'd thought she'd seen, as Robert had pointed out. 'After all, from an outsider's perspective, logically, it did all seem rather far-fetched,' she muttered. 'I hope this hasn't jeopardised our friendship,' she whispered to herself.

As she drove up the driveway to the Manor, Mary noticed Jack's Land Rover in the driveway. 'That's all I need!' she yelled, striking the steering wheel with her hand. She got out of the car, shutting the car door noisily behind her.

She walked purposely along the path leading to the back door, the gravel scrunching beneath her feet. As she prepared to confront Jack, Mary felt an overwhelming sense of unease, as if she were entering the lion's den.

On reaching the back door, she found it wide open; she stepped into the kitchen, and there was no one in sight. 'Hello. Is there anyone there?' Mary shouted, her words filling the room.

There was no reply. Mary walked from the kitchen into the great hall. 'Hello. Is there anyone there?' Mary called out once more. Yet again, there was no response. Mary suddenly heard a noise coming from the library. Her footsteps echoed over the stone floor as she walked over to the other side of the hall to investigate. She found Jack in the library, crouched down by the fireplace with a hammer and chisel in his hands, attempting to remove one of the stones from behind the inglenook fireplace.

'What on earth are you doing?' Mary exclaimed, surprised to see him.

Jack turned round in astonishment. 'You made me jump, creeping up on me like that!'

'You've no right to be here! How did you get in?'

'How'd you suppose? Ma let me in.'

'I see,' Mary replied, gritting her teeth. 'Well, you can stop what you're doing and tell me why you are here,' Mary said, standing her ground.

Jack stood up, rising to his full height, stepped forward and faced Mary square on. 'I'm here to get something that's rightfully mine,' he replied, his fist clenched by his side and his face almost touching hers.

The rhythmic ticking of the clock filled the otherwise silent room as Mary locked eyes with Jack. There was something about this man which unnerved her. Mary took a step back.

'There is nothing in this house that belongs to you, so I would ask you to leave, please, before I have you forcefully removed!' she replied, her voice faltering.

To Mary's surprise, Jack tossed the tools he was holding into the canvas bag at his feet. Then, picking up the bag, he turned on his heels and marched towards the door. 'I'll be back, mark my words!' he said ominously over his shoulder.

Mary stood, her legs trembling, and watched as his car roared down the driveway before returning to the kitchen to make herself some tea.

'Was that Jack's car I heard going down the driveway?' Mrs Scarr asked her as she walked into the kitchen.

Surprised to see Ms Scarr, who seemed to have appeared from nowhere, Mary replied. 'Yes, yes, it was.'

'I was just about to make some tea for him. Would you like a cup of tea, lass? You look a bit pale.'

Mary pulled a chair away from the table and slumped down heavily. Her encounter with Robert earlier and now with Jack had left her drained. 'Thank you, Mrs Scarr, yes, that would be very welcome.'

'Help yourself to some oat cakes. I made a fresh batch this morning. Here, spread some of my homemade butter on them. That will put the colour back in your cheeks.'

As Mary nibbled at one of Mrs Scarr's oat cakes, she remembered Mrs Scarr's story about the children who lived there years ago, hiding in the secret passage behind a bookcase in the library when they played hide and seek. 'Thank you, Mrs Scarr, these are delicious.' Mary began after finishing her tea and oat cake. 'Tell me,' she continued. 'That secret passage in the library, where you and the children used to hide, is there also a secret place behind the fireplace?'

'Not as far as I knows, lass,' she said, shaking her head. 'Why do you ask?'

'Oh! No real reason,' she replied, rising from her chair. 'I'm going up to my room to read, then have an early night. I won't need supper tonight. Thank you, Mrs Scarr. Good night.'

Back in her room, Mary picked up her pen and continued to write in her journal.

What am I going to do about Jack? I can't ask Robert's advice now after our fallout, damn it! I might have handled things differently and been more careful with what I shared with him until I was sure of my facts …. I regret telling him now.

Mary abruptly stopped writing, letting out a heavy sigh as she set her pen down. She stood and paced back and forth in her room, her steps quickening with each turn, as if trying to outpace the mounting tension within her and, at the same time, casting a look at the dressing table mirror. Was the mirror a portal that she could use to reach a parallel world and be with her family? Was what she believed she'd seen a few weeks ago a dream or a figment of her imagination?

The rhythmic ticking downstairs grew louder with every passing second, heightening the sense of urgency for Mary to choose her next move.

Chapter 16

Mary awoke from a sound sleep to find Mrs Scarr standing over her bed. 'Morning miss. You're are wanted on the telephone.'

'What … what is the time?' Mary asked, her voice heavy with sleep, struggling to grasp the concept of where she was or if she'd entered a waking dream.

'Why, it's nigh on nine o'clock, miss?' she replied, crossing over to the window and vigorously yanking back the heavy curtains, filling the room with bright sunlight, causing Mary to shield her eyes.

Reluctant to leave the warmth and cosiness of her bed, Mary snuggled under the blankets. 'Who on earth is calling at such an ungodly hour?' Mary asked grumpily.

'It's your solicitor, Mr Hart. Do you want me to take a message?

Mary sat up in bed. 'Oh, no. I'd better take the call. Let him know I'm on the way, please, Mrs Scarr,' she replied, jumping out of bed and grabbing her clothes from the chair in the corner. Perhaps he was ringing to apologise for yesterday, and so he should! Or maybe he was waiting for her to apologise to him for her outburst. No chance of that!

As Mary was putting on her clothes, she realised she didn't remember getting undressed the night before, let alone going to bed. The last thing she remembered was drinking Mrs Scarr's warm milk and honey and deciding whether to uncover the mirror. Her glance shifted towards the mirror. It was uncovered. When had she uncovered it? Perhaps Mrs Scarr's remedy was a potent sleeping draught and had knocked her out? Mary continued to pull on her clothes quickly, her fingers fumbling with buttons and zippers as her curiosity about why Robert was ringing her grew.

She quickly made her way down the stairs, carefully manoeuvring the bannister-less hazardous curve of the staircase halfway down.

On reaching the bottom, Mary paused briefly, taking a deep breath to steady herself before picking up the telephone. 'Hello, Dr Mattleton speaking,' she answered in her best telephone voice, then chuckled to herself at how officious she must sound.

'Good morning, Mary! How are you this morning?'

On hearing Robert's familiar voice, all thoughts of being cross with him dissolved and were replaced by a flood of warmth and familiarity. 'Good morning, Robert. I'm well. Thank you. What can I do for you?'

'I have some more documents I need you to sign.'

Mary inwardly groaned. 'More documents?'

'Yes, but nothing too complicated!' Robert said and chuckled. 'However, they contain some important information that you should be aware of. When will it be convenient for me to pop over with them?'

Mary hesitated. There was no hint of incrimination in Robert's voice, leaving her unsure of his feelings towards her after her outburst the previous day. *He might have forgiven me*, she mused. *Or perhaps he's just being polite and maintaining an air of formality*. She was learning the Pommes were good at that! Either way, it seemed she was about to find out.

Mary could hear the faint clatter of pans and the rhythmic chopping of vegetables drifting in from the kitchen, indicating Mrs Scarr was preparing their upcoming lunch.

'I'm free today. Would you like to come for lunch?' Mary

asked, a hopeful smile spreading across her face. 'I'm sure we're giving Mrs Scarr ample time to craft one of her culinary masterpieces.'

'Yes! That works well for me. Thank you. I always enjoy Mrs Scarr's culinary masterpieces.' He replied lightheartedly. 'I'll come over around eleven, and we can sort the paperwork before lunch,' he added.

'Perfect! See you at eleven.' Mary was about to put the phone down. 'Oh! And Robert. Are you still there?'

'Yes.'

'Bring along a masonry chisel and hammer, would you please?'

'Pardon?'

'You heard,' Mary said and giggled mischievously.

'What on earth do you want them for?' Robert asked.

'All will be revealed when you get here. Till eleven.' Still chuckling to herself, Mary replaced the receiver, envisioning Robert's reaction to her strange request as she went off to find Mrs Scarr to let her know there would be a guest for lunch.

Mary looked at herself in the full-length mirror after putting the finishing touches on her makeup and tucking her cream blouse into her cream-tailored slacks, which hugged her long, slender legs, accentuating her graceful figure. The grandfather clock began to chime, *one, two, three.* She caught sight of the clock on her bedside table as she reached for her hairbrush. Oh goodness, eleven o'clock already! She thought to herself. Her hair would have to remain as it was, hanging loose; she didn't have time to find a hairband or pins to pull it back like she usually did.

'Anyway, Robert once remarked that my hair looked better hanging loose. He said it made me look less stern. Perhaps that's not a bad thing for today's meeting with him,' she said aloud to herself. 'Not bad, if I do say so myself!' she said, looking at her reflection in the mirror. 'Yes! Quite passable for a thirty-two-year-old – no, wait, almost thirty-three-year-old,' Mary added with a nod, her hands on her hips.

The hall clock finished chiming eleven, alerting her she was already late. The clock always ran two minutes slow, no matter how often she corrected it. She'd better get a move on if she didn't want to get off on the wrong foot again with Robert Hart.

Upon reaching the bottom of the stairs, Mrs Scarr was already at the front door, welcoming Robert inside.

'Hello Robert, do come in!' Mary called out excitedly, rushing towards him. 'Please, do come and sit down. I've set up the furthest end of the table for us to eat,' she said, gesturing towards the crisp white tablecloth at one end. 'And this end for us to work. 'It's probably what you Brits call a working lunch, right?'

'An impressive level of organisation, Doctor Mattleton,' Robert said, a touch of amusement in his voice as he surveyed the meticulously prepared table. 'I'm in good hands, it seems.'

'Please, do take a seat down at the business end.' Mary chuckled, pointing to the end of the long dining table nearest to them.

'Mrs Scarr, will you bring us some coffee, please? Meanwhile, we can review the papers you want me to look at and get that bit out of the way?'

Robert sat down and pulled a thick pile of paperwork from his briefcase. Mary's eyes widened. 'That looks like the manuscript of *War and Peace*!' she said in astonishment.

Robert laughed out loud. 'Trust me, it's not and, we only have to concentrate on the first couple of pages and sign the last one. I'll give you a rough outline of what the rest of it is all about, and I'll leave it with you to read at your leisure. Okay?'

Mrs Scarr set down a tray of coffee in front of Mary.

The smell of freshly brewed coffee filled the air. 'Phew! Save by coffee, thank you, Mrs Scarr, I'll pour,' Mary said as she began pouring out the steaming fresh coffee into the bone china cups.

'Now, where were we?' Mary asked.

'Basically, these are title deeds for the land and buildings that have been transferred to you upon the death of your grandfather, James Mattleton. He inherited them from his father. Of course, if your father, Thomas Mattleton, was still alive, he would have been entitled to the life interest of these properties and land. However, since he is deceased, his interest in the estate passes to you. Do you understand?'

'Yes. I believe so. But perhaps you'd explain the life interest part, please.'

'In other words, you can utilise the property and estate throughout your lifetime. You may not sell or mortgage any part of the land, and in the event of your demise, the land transfers to your nearest family member, who is named Mattleton, or is a direct offspring.'

As Mary silently scanned through the overwhelming stack of papers, she felt the burden of responsibility settling on her shoulders. The never-ending ticking of the grandfather clock, which had become a constant source of irritation, only added to her growing anxiety.

She occasionally paused, her brow furrowing in confusion. 'I'm not quite sure I understand this. Could you explain that part again, please?' she'd asked when having trouble comprehending the legal jargon.

Patiently, Robert went through legal outcomes once more. Finally, she looked up and addressed Robert. 'Okay. I think I understand the key points of this. Where do I sign?'

Robert carefully flipped through the hefty bound document until he reached the back page. 'Please sign your name on the dotted line right here if you would,' he replied, handing her a pen. 'Then I'll witness it. Unfortunately, we do have a slight problem. The Mattleton Seal, a crucial element to seal your signature, seems to have gone missing. But we can come to that later.'

'Okay, now the formalities are over, and we've still got a bit of time left before lunch. Let's head into the library and do some exploring,' Mary said, rubbing her hands together.

Robert scratched his head, perplexed.

'Did you bring the tools like I asked?'

Robert reached into his briefcase and held out a chisel and a hammer. 'If you mean these, then yes, I did, but …'

Mary's eyes sparkled with excitement. 'Perfect! Follow me,' she said, marching off down the corridor to the library.

The library was one of Mary's favourite rooms. Not only did it get the morning sun, a perfect place for her to write letters to friends in Australia, but it was also in sharp contrast to the formal furnishings of the great hall they had just left. The oversized, comfy armchairs scattered around the room offered a cosy and intimate space to sit and read the many leather books on the shelves that extended up to the ceiling.

Mary approached the stone inglenook fireplace with its intricate carvings on the surrounds of the partially enclosed hearth area and stone seating on either side of the fire basket, affording an ideal place to sit and get warm.

She felt around the stones with her fingers, where she'd noticed Jack was the day before she called out to Robert. 'Here!' she exclaimed urgently. 'Bring the tools!'

Robert came over to join her. 'What do you want the tools for, may I ask?' He looked puzzled.

'See that stone there? The big protruding one. It's loose. Could you loosen it some more and remove it so we can see what's behind it?'

'Are you serious? We can't just start removing stones from a historic fireplace!'

'Yes, yes, I'm serious! Please do it!' Mary exclaimed, her face flushed with excitement.

Robert, standing at over six feet tall, had to stoop down to enter the fireplace before cautiously chipping away at the stone with the chisel and hammer until it came loose. He pulled out the stone and peered inside the hole.

Mary hopped from one foot to the other, almost unable to contain her excitement, as she tried to catch a glimpse of what was inside the hole. 'Is there anything inside there?' Mary asked, excitement creeping into her voice.

Robert reached inside the hole. 'Wait a minute, I can feel something but …'

'But? But what?' Mary asked, peering around him to see if she could see what was in the hole.

'I can't quite reach it. Hang on. Yes, got it!' Robert exclaimed, pulling out a red leather-covered box with the initial M in gold lettering on it.

Brushing the dust off the box, Robert studied it. 'Here, you open it. After all, it's your property,' Robert said, smiling and passing it to Mary.

Mary carefully released the clasp on the box and slowly opened the lid. Nestled inside the cream silk-lined box was a gold-coloured metal seal.

'Here … is this something you're looking for?' she asked, handing Robert the box.

Robert carefully lifted the lid of the box to reveal its contents. 'You've found the Mattleton Seal!'

Chapter 17

4th June 1982

Charlie, our farm hand, is undeniably a remarkable man who, despite my frequent mistakes, always manages to remain patient with me. Sometimes, I wonder if he secretly sees me as a hopeless case, though. Take yesterday. I had no way of knowing that the gates had to be kept closed at all times to stop the cows escaping down the lane did I? I didn't even think about it for a split second after I had been into the field to fill their water trough. They were busy eating grass when I left them. Oh, dear, I've never seen Charlie so angry when he and Tom had to chase after them to get them back in. In hindsight, the incident was both hilarious and a bit scary, and I learned a few words that weren't in any dictionary I'd ever read! I enjoy spending time with him and his son Tom, and I'm eager to learn all I can, whatever the task at hand is. During the busiest time of lambing season, I devoted practically every waking hour to help care for the orphan lambs, fully committing myself to feeding them every four hours, including during the night. I wonder if this experience has honed my caregiving skills and prepared me for motherhood. That's way down on my wish list, so I doubt it. One thing I do remember is how proud I felt when, despite all odds, one lamb survived with my help. But the euphoria of joy was somewhat marred yesterday as I watched them happily playing in the fields alongside all the other sheep, knowing that they were about to be auctioned off today. Given my medical background, one might assume I would be emotionally disconnected from this natural progression. But the truth is, I have developed a strong emotional bond with these lambs, making their eventual fate all the more bittersweet. Still, despite my constant struggles and mistakes, Charlie never gives up on me and includes me in everything, such as taking me to the auction today so I can understand how that works.

I have made the renovation of the dilapidated servants' quarters my number one personal project. I have set a goal for myself to transform the living area into a comfortable space not only for Charlie, but also for Tom. The state of the quarters, which were only supposed to be temporary after the fire, was truly appalling when I moved to North Hall. I'm determined to provide Charlie and Tom with a proper home, one that they deserve. They work tirelessly day and night for the estate, especially during lambing season. They are always on tap to help with the birth of calves when needed. In an unexpected twist of fate, I even found myself playing the role of a midwife recently, assisting a cow through a difficult delivery. It was an unbelievable sight to see its head emerge from the birth canal, its mother bellowing as the contractions got stronger. I've seen and delivered many a baby, but this calf's birth is one I will never forget. Although I had to rely on Charlie's strength for the final stages, I must mention, in my defence, it was a massive calf!

Mrs Scarr has recently started to stay over in the servants' quarters with Charlie and Tom, presumably to distance herself from Jack, who, I've learned firsthand, is prone to violent outbursts. Mrs S treats Charlie and Tom as if they were her surrogate family, offering her unwavering support since the passing of Charlie's wife, Isobel, last year. They, unlike her son Jack, appreciate anything Mrs Scarr does for them, especially her cooking. Could it be that she's smitten with Charlie?

'Charlie is here to collect you to take you to the auction, lass,' Mrs Scarr called up from the bottom of the stairs.

'Thank you, Mrs Scarr. I'm on my way,' Mary answered, laying down her pen and

She'd had no prior experience with auctions and was looking forward to this one-of-a-kind experience. Albeit, some lambs in the auction would be the ones she'd hand-reared.

'I wonder what it'll be like seeing my lambs sold today, not knowing where and what they're destined for,' she'd said to herself as she made her way down the stairs.

Charlie was leaning against the doorway, waiting for her.

Mary was momentarily taken back on seeing his weathered face freshly shaved and his mop of unruly grey hair slicked down and wearing a crisp white shirt with a striped navy tie.

'Good morning, Charlie! You're looking very dapper this morning.'

'Why thankee, miss,' Charlie mumbled, looking down at his feet.

'Are we all set to head out?' Mary asked.

'Aye, miss. Tom has loaded the lambs in the trailer, so best be goin'.'

'What about your breakfast, lass?' Mrs Scarr called out to Mary just as she was leaving the house. 'Can't be running on an empty stomach!'

'You're right, I should have made time for breakfast.

But there's no time now, Mrs Scarr,' Mary called out as she turned, closing the behind her.

'You should make time for it,' Mrs Scarr admonished, wagging her finger.

But her advice fell on deaf ears. Mary was already gone and hurrying after Charlie, who was gallantly standing with the door of his green battered jeep open. Despite his rough exterior, Mary had found Charlie to be a gentle soul with unwavering loyalty.

'There you are, miss.' He smiled, holding open the door with his calloused hands. 'I give it a clean for you inside,' he said and chuckled.

Mary had driven many times with Charlie in his old battered jeep. She'd even got used to the strange smell coming from somewhere and having to make room for her feet amongst the clutter on the floor. While Mary accepted that he most probably knew the roads like the back of his hand. It didn't, however, make her any less nervous when he veered dangerously close to the edge of the road when taking a bend wide. She frequently found herself clutching her seat in terror, her knuckles going white while looking down out of the window beside her at the steep precipice just inches away. Or found herself bouncing up and down on the car seat as he drove rough-shod along the unmade tracks, bringing back memories of the fairground rides she'd experienced at the Sydney Easter Show.

Today's outing would be no exception, she reflected as she made sure her seat belt was firmly across her body and safely fastened. Today, however, Mary had something else to distract her – the little animals in the trailer being towed behind them. They would be subjected to the full brunt of Charlie's driving.

Mary felt uneasy as they drove, dreading the thought of selling the lambs in the trailer behind them. After hand-rearing and watching them develop, they had become almost like her children. Still, she reminded herself she was a farmer now. Therefore, as Charlie had already pointed out, there was no room for sentiment.

'We're here, miss,' Charlie announced, pointing to the Hawes Auction Mart sign.

Mary looked around, astounded by the number of people already queued up with cars and trailers, waiting to be directed to their drop-off holding pen locations. Charlie had warned her it would be busy with farmers travelling from all over. Still, she never imagined there would be so many in attendance.

'So, tell me again, Charlie. What do we do once we've unloaded the lambs into the holding pen?' Her brow furrowed in confusion.

'You don't have to do nowt, miss. I'll do paperwork and take lambs into the ring when it's time to show them,' he explained. 'You can watch from the gallery and take all the credit,' he added, his amusement evident in the sound of his laughter.

Charlie directed her to the main auction rooms. She found the auction room was hectic. The chaotic atmosphere engulfed her like a whirlwind. Mary stood for a moment, excitement building inside her, before moving up to the wooden gallery seating to take a seat. She sat down next to a friendly-looking man. He doffed his cap.

'Morning, missus!' he said with a wide grin, revealing his missing front teeth. 'It's a fine day for the bidding.'

She guessed he was a farmer by the clothes he wore. His three-piece tweed suit had seen better days, with its leather-patched elbows and leather-edged cuffs. She suspected he was a heavy smoker based on his ginger-tinged, grey-haired, walrus-style moustache and his nicotine-stained fingers.

'Good morning,' Mary replied, clasping her hands tightly in her lap, a little uncomfortable at his over-friendly greeting.

'Ah ain't sin you around these parts afore. You be new

here, aren't you?' the farmer inquired, giving Mary a curious look.

How, she wondered, had he guessed it was her first time? She'd hoped to blend into the background. 'Yes! Yes, it is. How did you know?'

'I heard you was coming,' he said and laughed aloud. 'Ol' Charlie did tell me. You be the one taking over from that no good, Jack Mattleton, at the big house.'

Mary paused briefly. Had her arrival already become the talk of Yorkshire? Back home, it would've taken years for the news to circulate.

'Yes. I'm Mary Mattleton, the new owner of North Hall Manor,' Mary introduced herself, extending her hand. 'How do you do?'

The farmer doffed his hat once more and, grinning, took hold of Mary's hand, shaking it vigorously.

''ow do!' he replied in his thick Yorkshire accent, his voice resonating through the bustling auction room. 'It's reet good to have you here,' he added, a warm smile spreading across his face, firmly clasping her hand in both of his.

Mary smiled. 'Thank you,' she said, trying to release her hand from his grip.

As the auction began, Mary soon became captivated by the auctioneer's fast-paced and melodic speech, blending into an incomprehensible jumble.

'Two fifty, two fifty. I've got two fifty. Do I hear two seventy-five?'

'I have seventy-five whatiwannagive eighty?'

'Eighty, I'm bid, anyone else?'

'All done at eighty?'

'Sold!' the auctioneer announced triumphantly, banging his gavel down hard on the lectern, the sound reverberating throughout the sale room and making Mary jump.

Mary continued to watch as if she were under a spell, intrigued by the entire procedure as the auctioneer's voice rose above the crowd's babble. Electric energy filled the room, sending a shiver down her spine. She was mesmerised by the way the auctioneer skilfully responded to each bid, his experienced eyes interpreting and acknowledging the bidders' gestures with a nod of understanding.

Mary eagerly waited for the bidding to start on her beloved lambs, her heart pounding with anticipation as each new batch entered the ring. The excitement was growing inside her. It was as if someone was gradually winding up a spring tighter and tighter in her stomach as she waited for her lambs to appear.

Finally, she saw Charlie, his crook in hand, confidently leading the lambs into the ring. A surge of pride and hope swelled within her. Mary sat upright in her seat and grinned, her hands clasped tightly in her lap.

'Next lot here we have North Hall Manor Swaledales,' the auctioneer announced.

'See those lambs over there?' she whispered to her neighbour, pointing towards the ring. 'They're mine,' she said proudly.

The farmer gave out a loud, hearty laugh. 'Aye. I knows they are.'

'Who'll start me off? One fifty.' The auctioneer pointed into the audience. 'I've got one fifty,' he said, pointing to someone over in the corner.

'One seventy-five, bidder now, two bidders now. Do I hear two fifty?'

Mary couldn't take her eyes off the auctioneer.

'Two fifty, thank you.' He nodded to the man in the front row.

'Two seventy-five, two seventy-five. Thank you.' The auctioneer nodded.

'Oh, I see two eighty, thank you.'

'Two eighty I'm bid. Anyone else?'

Mary found herself sitting on the edge of her seat,

listening to the quick bidding, creating an atmosphere charged with anticipation.

'I'm at two eighty.'

'All done at two eighty?'

'I'm selling at two eighty...'

With a forceful strike of his gavel, the Auctioneer proclaimed. 'Sold!' Prompting Mary to jump and bring herself back to reality.

A bittersweet smile tugged at the corners of her lips upon seeing Charlie herd the lambs out of the ring and out of her sight for the last time.

'Thank you for bringing me along, Charlie,' Mary said as they drove back to North Hill. 'It was an experience I'll never forget. You've really opened my eyes to a whole new world, not that I could understand half of what the auctioneer was saying!'

'Next time, thou'll naw what to expect, lass.' Charlie laughed, his Yorkshire accent adding a touch of warmth and kindness to his words.

Next time ... Was this going to be her life from now on? Mary pondered. Had those days of sterile environments and pristine white coats vanished and been replaced by this? She wondered, looking down at her jeans tucked into her muddy leather boots and her casual, un-ironed check shirt.

'It would seem that way.' Mary chuckled to herself. 'And I wouldn't trade this life for anything,' she murmured softly.

Chapter 18

18th June 1982

It's been a while since I last saw Molly and her family, and I'm starting to miss them. Could it be because I've been too preoccupied with other things? I'm keen to learn if Molly was able to persuade her mother to follow my suggestions for Thomas' treatment. I'm not sure how much faith I have in the remedy I've suggested. It's not like prescribing the usual modern-day treatment for rheumatic fever, so I'm a bit out of my comfort zone. I sincerely hope that it was successful, as I'm filled with dread at the possibility of a different outcome. I must find a way to contact Molly to find out. It's strange how I can only be seen by Molly and not by anyone else.

'Duty calls!' Mary exclaimed, grabbing the stack of paperwork from her desk that Robert had given her to read. She flipped through the various documents until she came across the yellowed document of Leonard Mattleton's foundling adoption papers. Upon further inspection, because of the fading ink, she discovered that the name of Leonard's mother was indecipherable. 'I wonder who Leonard's mother was?' Mary said aloud. The only information Robert had uncovered was that she was a local girl who died while giving birth.

'Lunch is ready, lass!' Mrs Scarr called up from downstairs.
'Thank you, Mrs Scarr. I will be right down,' Mary

shouted. This could be my opportunity to find some answers about Leonard's mother from Mrs Scarr. Mary pondered, still trying to decipher the writing on the document in her hand.

'Help yourself, lass,' said Mrs Scarr as Mary walked into the kitchen.

'This looks wonderful!' Mary exclaimed, her eyes widening in wonder as she gazed at the array of vibrant salads and accompaniments. 'You always put on such a feast, Mrs Scarr. No wonder I'm putting on weight.' Mary added with delight, her mouth watering at the sight of Mrs Scarr's pork pies and cold meats. 'I hope you are joining me today, though. There's enough here to feed an army!' Mary added, chuckling.

'Yes, lass. I need to sit down. I have been on the go since daylight,' Mrs Scarr replied, brushing the loose strands of her silver hair away from her face and clearly looking as though she needed a break.

'Charlie doesn't need my help today. Is there something I can help you with?'

'Nay, lass, I wouldn't want to be troubling you. You have enough on your plate running this place, which, if the truth be told, is men's work!'

Mary smiled to herself at Mrs Scarr's traditional ideas on gender roles. She was clearly one of the old school. The kitchen and child-rearing were a woman's domain, whereas managing a farm and making decisions was men's work.

'Tell me, Mrs Scarr, do you think it's right that women should confine themselves to running a household and not have a say in running a farm, for instance?'

'Nay, lass, it's not for me to say.' Mrs Scarr's voice carried a mix of resignation and fondness. 'Leonard always believed a woman's place was in the house.'

Mary laid down her knife and fork. 'But is this that your belief as well?' she asked curiously.

'Whether or not I believe it. I knows no different. It was

the same when I was growin' up, which I would guess don't sit reet with the likes of you young uns now,' Mrs Scarr grinned. 'Pa treated me ma the same and us wee bairns, though the boys were treated differently compared to us girls.'

Mary concealed a hidden sadness behind her smile while considering Mrs. Scarr's inherited beliefs. 'I understand that was often the situation. Fortunately, there has been progress in recent years, leading to greater educational and professional opportunities for women.'

'Oh Lordy! I can't picture meself as one of them woman.' Mrs Scarr replied with a soft chuckle. 'Besides, Leonard used to call me gormless,' she added quietly.

'That wasn't a very kind thing to call you.' Mary said, frowning.

'Nay matter, lass. He called me many things. I got used to it.' She chuckled. 'It seems the sibling thing messed with his head.'

'The sibling thing?' she asked. 'I don't understand. Can you explain that?'

'Leonard says his pa would always favour his brother over him. Leonard and his brother didn't get on, you see.'

'Ah, yes. That's quite often the case, and occasionally, it still is. Personality clashes arise when siblings become jealous of one another.' Mary nodded with understanding.

'Aye, I suppose that was the case with them,' she agreed. 'When Leonard was drunk once,' she said in a low voice, glancing anxiously around her as if afraid of being overheard. 'He says to me he felt like an outsider since learning he was abandoned and then adopted.'

'And did his father treat him as such?'

'Well, he reckoned he did, 'specially when he found out that his brother was getting the house and the farm when their parents died, leaving him with only a small inheritance. That was when Leonard decided to handle things himself.'

'Are you telling lies about my pa again?' Jack bellowed as

he burst through the kitchen door. 'You have always hated Pa, and now I catch you spreading lies about him!'

'Your pa was no good!' Mrs Scarr retorted.

'That's not true! You are just trying to ruin Pa's reputation like you always do!'

Mrs Scarr's eyes narrowed, her lips pressed into a thin line, and she crossed her arms. 'What are you doing here any-road?' Mrs Scarr asked.

Jack noisily dragged a chair out from under the kitchen table and sat down. 'What gives you the idea I'm here for anything?' he scoffed, grabbing a large piece of pork pie from the plate and sinking his teeth into it. 'Lucky I am here to help you with all this food, eh?' he smirked.

'Not lucky at all! You are like a bad penny, showing up when you want summat.' Mrs Scarr sighed. 'So, I ask you again. What brings you here?'

'I've stumbled upon something that has the potential to set the cat amongst the pigeons,' Jack said excitedly, nearly choking on the pork pie. 'I sent it to that fancy solicitor of yours. If I am reet, your days are numbered!'

Mrs Scarr rolled her eyes. 'Some things never change. You have always been a troublemaker, just like your Pa.'

Jack wiped his mouth on his sleeve. 'You don't believe me? Well, listen to this …'

The telephone rang, interrupting Jack's revelation, breaking the tense atmosphere in an instant. Mary rushed to answer it, grateful for the temporary reprieve from the escalating conversation.

'Hello, the North Hall Estate…'

'Mary, this is Robert. Something extraordinary has come to light. I'm in London at the moment, trying to get to the bottom of it. I'll be back in touch at the earliest opportunity.' He paused. 'Brace yourself.'

Chapter 19

19th June 1982

I'm eagerly waiting for Robert to call me back today to give me an update on yesterday's phone call. I've been racking my brains since his call as to what he can mean by 'something extraordinary has come to light'? Ordinarily, I enjoy solving puzzles, but this. Where do I start? The suspense has bugged me all day, and I won't rest until I find out what he's talking about. Also, what could Jack have meant by 'your days are numbered'? Was that meant as a threat or a warning? I should mention that to Robert when he calls and see what he thinks.

Mary closed her journal and breathed out a weary sigh, her chest heavy with mental exhaustion and her shoulders tight with tension. Her gaze drifted towards the window as she reflected on Robert's phone call and Jack's cryptic comments while absentmindedly twirling a strand of her hair between her fingers. What was the true meaning behind Jack's statement? She wondered as the sense that something was wrong settled in her stomach.

Desperately trying to escape the thoughts of Jack's unexpected appearance, Mary reached for her crossword book, which sat on the table alongside her.

'I need a distraction!' she whispered to herself as

she opened the book to the page she had bookmarked. 'Something to take my mind off Jack's words,' she added, her eyes frantically scanning the clues as if searching for answers to a much bigger mystery.

Try as she might, Mary couldn't disregard the ominous impression that his words might be a veiled threat. 'But what if Jack's words were intended as a threat to my life?' she muttered, staring into space. 'No, that's not possible,' she answered her own question, dismissively shaking her head and trying to dismiss her own fears, desperately seeking a rational explanation. Her mind raced with possibilities.

Mary laid aside her book. 'Perhaps I'm overthinking this,' she said, closing her eyes to block out her fanciful notions. 'It's possible that Jack was intentionally being obscure just for the fun of it.'

Mary yawned, stretched out in her armchair, and closed her eyes.

***

'Mary, wake up! Wake up,' a voice urged in a loud whisper, jolting Mary from her sleep.

Mary's eyes snapped open, and her gaze darted around her room in a desperate search for the source of the voice.

'Over here!' the voice called out.

Mary rubbed her eyes, trying to focus. It was as if she were staring through a hazy curtain as she strained her eyes to see who was calling her. Suddenly, materialising before her, she saw the petite figure of Molly, dressed in her usual brown overalls with her wild, curly blonde hair cascading down onto her shoulders. Perhaps I'm dreaming? Mary questioned, pinching herself. 'Ouch!' she cried out, wincing. No, she wasn't dreaming!

'Molly?' Mary asked, her voice filled with both confusion and relief.

'Aye, of course it's me. Who else were you expecting?' Molly giggled.

Mary looked around her. The last thing she could remember was sitting in her chair in her bedroom doing a crossword. Yet here she was in Thomas's bedroom. Mary recognised his tousled, fair hair peeking out from beneath the blanket, lying asleep in his bed.

'Wait, how in the world did I get here?' Mary asked, surprised.

'Ah dunno?' Molly shrugged. 'Ah was thinking about you, and then … poof! There you were!' She giggled, her eyes sparkling with mischief.

Mary took a moment to reflect. She had read that some people believed in the power of telepathy. The power to communicate solely through their minds, bypassing the traditional use of speech. But, to her logical mind, that sort of thing was reserved for stage magic shows. However, I should keep an open mind. Mary thought. After all, maybe telepathy can transport people to other places. Suppose telepathy is a type of extrasensory perception, or The Sight, as Molly refers to it, and she uses it to transport me back to her time. But … If that's not the case, how else did I end up here?

'So many possibilities,' Mary said in a hushed tone.

'What are you saying?' Molly asked.

'Nothing.' Mary pulled herself together. 'So, let's get this straight. You thought of me, and I suddenly appeared here in Thomas's bedroom?' Mary asked.

Molly giggled, her unruly blonde curls bouncing as she nodded. 'Aye, I reckon so.'

'In that case, you've definitely caught me off guard then. Why were you thinking about me in the first place?' Mary asked.

'I got to thinking about our Thomas and wishing you was

here to make him well again when suddenly … there you were!' Molly said, her words rushing out excitedly.

'How is Thomas?' Mary asked, leaning in towards him, studying his pale complexion and intently listening to his shallow, laboured breathing. 'I expected him to be up and about by now.'

'Give him a chance; it's only been a day, you knows!'

'Days? But surely you mean a week? It's been more than a week since he fell ill …'

Molly cut in. 'That'll be in your world … here, only a day have passed.'

'And there's me been wondering how Thomas was for days,' Mary said quietly under her breath.

Mary stopped in mid-sentence, interrupted by a female voice calling up the stairs.

'Molly, Molly! Where are you, girl?'

'Who's that calling you?' Mary asked in a loud whisper.

Molly plunged her hands into her dungaree pockets. 'It's me, Ma!' she replied. 'I have me jobs to do,' she added sulkily, going down the stairs with her head bent. Mary followed her down the stairs.

Molly's mother greeted her upon entering the kitchen. 'Where have you been?' she asked crossly. 'I've been calling you!'

'To see our Thomas with …' Molly stopped in mid-sentence and looked over towards Mary, who was pressed against the wall.

'Our Thomas don't need you bothering him,' she declared, shaking her finger. 'After your breakfast, I want you to feed the chickens, fetch the coal and the kindling, then help wash the milk bottles so as Bertha can fill them.'

'Yes, Ma!' Molly grumbled as she picked up her spoon and started to eat her porridge. 'When is our Thomas going to get out of his bed and take his turn with the jobs?' she asked sullenly.

'I can't say, lass, he's badly, that's for sure,' she said, exhaling. 'He had a high fever during the night. I have been up all night sponging him down,' she added wearily.

Noticing her mother's anxious expression, Molly volunteered, 'Should I fetch the doctor?'

'Nay, lass, the Doctor can't do no good. He says we have to wait on for the fever to break.'

Molly had learned from the past not to talk to her mother about her gift of The Sight and the premonitions she often had, but as it was Thomas. 'Ma! I knows what's wrong with our Thomas?' Molly blurted out.

'Don't be daft, our Molly. Get on with your breakfast, then go out and bring me back some eggs.'

'But, Ma, I knows what ails him. I spoke with this lady.' Molly indicated with her head at Mary.

'What lady are you talking about?'

'I see her. She's a doctor and …'

'Enough of you seeing folk.'

'I do see her.' Molly paused, wondering whether to go on. 'She's here now!' Molly glanced over towards Mary. 'I saw her the night our Thomas took sick. She was in the bedroom. She says she is a doctor, and she takes a look at him and tells me what ails him and what would make him better …'

'Enough of your nonsense!' Mary's mother shouted, grabbing Molly's half-eaten bowl of porridge. 'Get yourself outside and fetch me some eggs like I told you to. And take that basket of scraps with you.'

Molly gave Mary a quizzical look. Mary smiled back at her.

'We have to do summat, Ma. The lady told me what would cure him. I wrote it down here,' Molly said, pulling out a small piece of paper from her apron pocket.

'Stop!' her mother cried, raising her hand. 'I don't have time for your stories.'

'But Ma, please listen to me. This piece of paper says

what would make our Thomas better,' Molly pleaded, her voice laced with desperation.

'Ah won't tell you again! Stop mithering me and go get the eggs as I asked. Now be off with you!' she replied, pushing Molly out of the door.

Molly trudged across the yard, dragging her feet and stirring up a cloud of dust that covered her worn-out shoes and left a trail behind her. Mary followed.

'It's not fair!' Molly angrily stomped her foot to the ground when they reached the henhouse before giving the henhouse door an angry kick, startling the chickens and sending them into a frenzy of feathers and squawking.

A stooped, white-haired older man with weathered skin peered around from behind the henhouse, startling them both.

'Nah then, what's to do?' he shouted.

'Oh! You startled me, Grandpa!' Molly exclaimed, almost dropping the basket she was carrying.

Mary stepped back, unsure if the older man had spotted her. He looked familiar – she'd had seen him at the family gathering in the kitchen last time she was there.

'You're a reet mardy little bugger this morning! What ails you?' he asked gruffly, making no acknowledgement of Mary.

'Why do I always have to do everything while Thomas gets to lie in bed? It's not fair!' Molly's voice cracked with pent-up resentment.

'Cos he be sick, that be why. Think on this; you should be helping your ma, not throwing a strop!'

Molly lowered her head into her chest. 'I've tried helping her, but she won't listen,' she mumbled sullenly. 'Ah knows what ails Thomas. This lady standing here with me is a doctor, and she do tell me how to cure him.' Molly turned and pointed to Mary. 'But Ma won't listen to me. She don't believe I see this lady,' Molly added, sulkily scuffing her foot in the dirt.

'Aye, your ma told me you've a notion to talking to folks who ain't there. Just like the old woman indoors.'

'You mean Grandma?'

'Aye, she reckons she sees things too. Daft bat!' He said, letting out a loud belly laugh. 'Now, set about the work your Ma gave you. Don't you forget I need help with washing the milk bottles too. And Bertha is waiting on you to help fill the bottles with milk, thou knows!'

Molly scattered the kitchen scraps from her basket out onto the ground while keeping an eye on her grandfather strolling back across the yard to the milking parlour. She opened the henhouse door, quickly jumping aside. Mary followed suit as the chickens surged through the doorway in a flurry of feathers towards the scattered scraps of food, like a swarm of hungry locusts.

'I hate this job!' Molly grumbled to Mary while she searched around in the corners and crevices of the henhouse. 'Move over, Bellina!' Molly shouted at a plump chicken with black and white feathers sitting firmly on a nest, refusing to move off when Molly attempted to retrieve the eggs she was sitting on. 'Ouch! That hurt!' Molly yelled when Bellina promptly pecked her hard on her hand for her trouble!

Mary stifled a giggle.

'Stay there, see if I care!' Molly yelled to the bird, rubbing her hand where Bellina had pecked it before picking up the basket of eggs and closing the henhouse door behind her.

Mary walked alongside Molly as they returned to the house across the yard. 'Molly, what about Thomas's potion?' Mary asked. 'You need to get it made up without delay.'

'Don't fret thee sen,' Molly said in her broad Yorkshire accent.

'But it's serious. Without proper treatment, Thomas may have lasting damage to his heart, or worse still, he may die!'

'I've got an idea!' Molly tapped the side of her nose. 'Summat Grandpa said. I will talk to Grandma. She knows the local wise woman. I will tell Grandma about you and give her the list for your potion. She'll see him reet.'

'Your grandma? The local wise woman?'

Molly nodded. 'Aye. Some folks say the wise woman be a witch …'

'And is she?'

'Nay, course not!' Molly laughed. 'She's what you call a healer, I'd say. She makes folks better.'

'Does she have any medical training?' Mary asked, then realised what a silly question that was. 'I mean, what treatments does she use?' she asked, her voice laced with scepticism, wondering what unconventional treatments they used.

'Why, herbs and stuff, a bit like you tell me to use for our Thomas? Cumin and carom seeds. Garlic, ginger. As well as wild plants that grow in the hedgerows, berries and seeds from the trees and bushes.'

'That's all very fine, but he needs this medicine urgently if he's to pull through. Do you understand?'

'Don't fret thee sen; they can mix up the potion today, and I will see that Grandma gives it to our Thomas. He'll be reet don't worry.'

'I do worry. I can't help but wonder if we're running out of time.'

***

Mary woke up suddenly, her heart racing.

'What's happening?' she gasped, her voice full of fear as her eyes scanned the dimly lit room to find herself seated in her chair, the crossword book on her lap. 'How did I get back here?' she asked herself as she attempted to reconstruct the bits she remembered.

The very last memory she had was of talking to Molly.

Mary rose from her chair. The coldness from the wooden floorboards on her bare feet caused her to shudder as she cautiously walked towards the window to look outside. It was pitch black!

'I wonder what time it is,' she said, glancing over at the clock next to her bed. Its old-fashioned hands, illuminated by a soft, eerie glow, showed it was just past midnight.

'Did any of what I remember really happen? Or did I dream it all?' she said aloud, her mind searching for explanations.

Mary went back to her chair. 'Yes. Perhaps the whole thing was a dream, broken by the annoying clock chiming at midnight.' she uttered, tapping her fingers on the table beside her, cluttered with scattered papers, the half-empty coffee mug and, her crossword book. The puzzle was still unfinished.

She stood up from her seat. 'Oh! I don't know … I can't think straight anymore,' Mary admitted wearily as she slumped onto the bed, fully clothed. 'I'm so tired,' she whispered, her words barely audible. The weight of confusion and uncertainty engulfed her, pulling her into a deep sleep.

Chapter 20

20th June 1982

After last night, I'm now convinced that Molly and I exist in parallel worlds and, based on what happened last night, it appears that Molly is the force that draws me into this time-travelling vortex. While I find this truly remarkable, I am unsure of the reasoning behind it. Nor do I clearly know how I travel to Molly's realm. Is it possible for a time portal to exist in the mirror on my dressing table? I say this because, even though I distinctly recall covering the mirror with the curtain each night, I often find it uncovered in the mornings. Despite my doubts, I'm beginning to enjoy my time with Molly. She's such an engaging child, and she reminds me a lot of me at that age. I hope that, in time, the remaining family members will know and recognise my existence. But more importantly, I hope that next time I go, I'll find that my patent herb remedy was effective, and that Thomas is thriving. If that proves to be the case, maybe I should write a paper on it for the medical journal. On the other hand, maybe not. I could find myself being burned at the stake as a witch!

'Burned at the stake as a witch?' Mary said aloud, unable to contain her laughter. 'My mind is getting as fanciful as young Molly's, it seems!' Mary closed her journal and stood up. 'Enough of this frivolity, time to tackle those invoices!'

Sitting at the desk in the library, surrounded by the pile of farm invoices, Mary couldn't avoid being overwhelmed by the rows of numbers and business jargon on them. She could be reading a foreign language for all she knew. This only served to intensify her desire to escape from the mundane reality they represented. Admin was, without a doubt, the most unpleasant aspect of farm life, she concluded as she shuffled the invoices into date order.

'Pay… File … Ask Charlie ….' Mary mumbled to herself as she sorted the invoices. When she'd finished, she looked listlessly out of the rain-streaked window while absentmindedly flicking the pen in her hand. The *Ask Charlie* pile had grown. Mary groaned and sighed, patting the pile of invoices on the desk.

Her yearning for human connection had become palpable at times amidst the solitude of the Manor. Deep down, while she loved her new life, she was lonely. Mary's heart ached for the laughter and conversation she used to share with her friends. She missed the familiar hum of activity that filled the hospital corridors, the sound of urgent footsteps. Mary's pen froze mid-flick when she noticed the postman's van coming up the drive. She jumped up and rushed to open the door, eager to escape the monotony of the farm invoices, almost colliding with Mrs Scarr in the hall in her eagerness to see what the postman had brought.

'It's all right, Mrs Scarr, I'll get the door.' Mary sang out, her voice infused with affection for the older woman who had become a surrogate mother figure.

'Morning miss. I've got a big pile of post for you today!' the postman said, thrusting a pile of assorted-sized envelopes into Mary's waiting hands.

'Thank you, Mr Duncan. It's an awful day to be out and about outside today. Why not come in out of the rain and have a cup of coffee? I believe Mrs Scarr has some on the go?' Mary offered with a friendly smile, sensing Mrs Scarr was hovering in the background, ready to pounce and ask the same question.

'Aye. I don't mind if I do. Thank you kindly,' Mr Duncan replied, stepping inside, taking off his cap and shaking off the raindrops, leaving a small pool of water on the floor.

'Good. Come on in; Mrs Scarr will look after you,' Mary said, pointing to Mrs Scarr, who was hanging back in the corner of the hall, beaming at the postman. 'I'll take my coffee in the library, if that's alright with you, Mrs Scarr?'

'Aye, miss, I will fetch it directly,' she said.

As Mary made her way back to the library, she flicked through the pile of envelopes, eagerly scanning each one for the sight of something more interesting than invoices, groaning inwardly each time she came across a brown envelope that could only mean one thing – yet another bill!

Mary sat back down at the desk. Sorting through the mail, methodically removing the brown envelopes and known farm correspondence and putting them into a 'deal with later' pile. The rest she left in a mound on the desk.

'Well, no one could accuse me of not trying to be efficient!' Mary chuckled, masking her internal frustration with a forced laugh. However, she knew full well that the 'deal with later' pile might well still be there in a week or, indeed, be a permanent fixture – paperwork was not her favourite pastime!

Mary picked up the ornate silver letter opener and carefully slit open the first envelope. It was an invitation to the local Harvest Festival Supper and asking for donations. Setting it aside, Mary mentally reminded herself to add the invitation to her calendar and to seek Mrs Scarr's guidance on an appropriate donation.

Mary picked up each envelope as if on autopilot, opened it, and read through its contents before placing it on the relevant pile until she came across a white handwritten envelope. Mary paused and studied the unfamiliar handwriting.

'I wonder who this is from,' she muttered under her breath, a puzzled frown on her face.

She slit open the envelope with the letter opener. She took out the letter, carefully unfolded it, and smoothed out the crisp white paper before her.

2 Mews Cottages
Sowerby
North Yorkshire

17th June 1982

Dear Mary,

Please excuse the intrusion. I have been working overseas and have only recently returned to my hometown. On my return, there was a letter waiting for me from my cousin asking me to contact him. I understand from him that a solicitor by the name of Mr Robert Hart had been in contact with him, informing him of the death of our relative Leonard Mattleton. Mr Mattleton was related by marriage to my mother's sister, Sybil Mattleton, who I believe was your great-grandmother?

Mary's heart quickened as her eyes landed on the name *Sybil Mattleton*. 'But … That was my great-grandmother's name!' she exclaimed.

Eager to see what else the letter revealed, Mary continued reading….

I spoke to my cousin today, and he told me that upon the death of Leonard Mattleton, you inherited and recently moved into North Hall Manor. I imagine you must be busy finding your way around the old place at the moment, but if you have time, it would be wonderful to meet up with you at some point. I don't live very far away from the Manor, and I'm available to meet with you anytime you say. My phone number is 623 596 if you'd prefer to call me instead of writing back.

Best wishes
Eleanor Featherstone (Miss)

Mary slumped back in the chair, overcome with emotion after reading the letter. Her mind was filled with joy and curiosity upon the realisation that she may have discovered a long-lost cousin. Robert mentioned to her that she had numerous relatives, but she hadn't come across any until now. But, as she re-read Eleanor Featherstone's letter, doubts began to creep in. Should she believe what was in this letter? Or was it just a prank? The continuous ticking of the grandfather clock exacerbated Mary's concerns. She stared out of the window, watching the rain pelting against the windowpane as she doodled on the blotter, lost in her thoughts. It was too wet to venture out for a pre-lunch walk and contemplate the contents of the letter. She would instead talk to Mrs Scarr about her long-lost cousin during lunch and gauge her reaction.

'What do you know of this family, Mrs Scarr?' Mary asked after she'd shown her the letter.

'Well...' Mrs Scarr stared into space and scratched her head. 'I do rightly remember Molly's ma had a sister.'

'What was her name? Do you remember?'

'Nay! It was too long ago. Any road, she might be dead now.' Mrs Scarr remarked.

'Hmmm,' Mary said, drumming the table with her fingers. 'Yes, yes, maybe you're right. But in this letter from her daughter, she didn't mention her mother, dead or alive though, did she? Do you find that a bit strange?'

'Well, lass. There's only one way to find out.' Mrs Scarr replied, leaning closer and patting Mary's hand.

'Oh? What's that?' Mary frowned.

Mrs Scarr gave a loud chuckle. 'Ring her!'

Mary returned to the library after lunch and took a seat at the desk. Doubts and questions continued to fill her mind. She stared at the mountain of mail that still needed to be sorted, but her heart wasn't in. Mary pushed it to one side with an enormous sigh before reaching for Eleanor's letter.

She dialled the number. Her stomach filled with butterflies as she braced herself while she waited for the phone to be answered. *Could this call be the breakthrough she's been waiting for in finding her family?* she wondered.

'Hello,' a voice answered.

'Is that Eleanor Featherstone?' Mary asked.

'Yes. May I ask who is calling?'

Mary hesitated. Unsure if she should refer to herself as Eleanor's cousin – that was yet to be established – Mary debated with herself. Perhaps she should wait to use that term and see how their conversation unfolded.

'This is Doctor Mary Mattleton,' Mary heard herself answer in a formal voice.

'Doctor … Doctor Mattleton?' Eleanor stammered. 'Oh! Are you the Mary Mattleton who lives at North Hall Manor?' she asked tentatively.

What possessed her to use such a formal approach? Mary chastised herself.

'I'm sorry. Yes, yes, I am. Forgive me; I didn't mean to come across so formally.' Mary responded with a nervous laugh. 'It's just that receiving your letter out of the blue has come as a surprise.' Mary paused. 'A pleasant surprise, I might add, though!' she added quickly.

'Oh, I'm pleased to hear it was a pleasant surprise,'

Eleanor said with relief in her voice. 'I wasn't sure whether you'd want to know me. After all, our families have been estranged for many years, so I was unsure how my letter would be received.'

'Not at all,' Mary said, eager to reassure her. 'I meant it. I was delighted to hear from you, and I'd love for us to meet up. When are you free?'

'Tomorrow for lunch? … Or is that too soon?' Eleanor asked.

'No! That would suit me just fine! Are you familiar with The Red Lion Inn just outside of Reeth?'

'Am I familiar with it? I'll say I am! It used to be my local haunt before I ventured overseas. I used to practically live in there.' Eleanor giggled.

'Great. Say twelve o'clock?'

'Perfect… until then.'

'Wait!' Mary said urgently. 'How will I know you?'

Eleanor chuckled. 'Don't worry, I'll find you. I'll know everyone else in the pub. Bye for now.'

Chapter 21

Mary draped her cardigan over her shoulders and picked up her bag. Her upcoming lunch date with Eleanor Featherstone filled her with both excitement and nervousness. After taking some time to decide what to wear, Mary finally settled on her mint green tailored pants and matched them with a cream-coloured top. As it was such a warm day, she'd done her hair in a low, messy bun and kept her makeup to a bare minimum. She assessed her appearance in the mirror.

'After all,' she said aloud to her reflection. 'I want to make a good impression, and another woman notices what you're wearing and how you look, right?' Mary laughed and nodded.

On reaching the bottom of the stairs, she was surprised to find Mrs Scarr diligently dusting in the great hall.

'I'm going out now!' She greeted her cheerfully.

'Goin'? Goin' where?' Mrs Scarr asked.

'You know? I'm going to The Red Lion to meet Eleanor. Remember I told you I'm not in for lunch today?'

'Won't you be a tad early, lass?' she asked, glancing over towards the grandfather clock.

'No! I plan to stop off at the post office to post these cheques off on the way,' Mary explained, grabbing the pile of neatly stacked envelopes from the hall table that she'd placed there earlier. Smiling to herself, she looked down at the envelopes in her hand, which served as a reminder of her dedication to her responsibilities over the past few days.

'You go careful, lass!' Mrs Scarr warned, waving her duster at her.

'I will,' Mary shouted over her shoulder as the clock chimed eleven, signalling that she was running late if she didn't leave now to post the letters before her meeting with Eleanor.

Mary felt a cool breeze as she made her way to her car. She congratulated herself on not forgetting to bring a cardigan. Her wardrobe was beginning to reflect her growing understanding of the British weather. Dressing for summer over here meant being ready for any weather, whether it's sunny, rainy, or snowy, she'd learnt. She was about to get into her car when she noticed Jack's jeep coming thundering down the driveway, music blaring loudly from its open windows. Mary's heart skipped a beat as Jack's jeep screeched to a halt, its tyres leaving skid marks on the gravel driveway as it came to a halt, stopping inches away from the rear end of her parked car.

Jack jumped out of his car, slamming the door closed behind him.

'Ah want a word with you!' he shouted as he approached Mary, his jaw clenched and his footsteps heavy on the gravel.

This was all she needed! Mary paused, taking a deep breath to calm herself.

'Good morning, Jack. How are you this morning?' she asked politely, silently reminding herself to stay calm and collected, despite Jack's aggression and focus on keeping her composure. As he got closer, she could smell alcohol on his breath. Mary wondered where he'd spent the night before, noticing his hair was messy and his clothes were crumpled.

'That solicitor of yours still hasn't give me the papers for things in the settlement of this here place.'

'I see. I'm not sure how I can be of help,' Mary said.

'That gormless secretary of his says you have the papers.'

'I'm sorry, but I am not aware of any papers belonging to you. Have you asked Mr Hart for them?'

'Course I 'ave! Thou are as gormless as that secretary!'

Mary could feel a surge of anger building up inside her. 'There is no need for rudeness, Jack,' Mary responded curtly, determined not to let Jack's insults get to her. 'I believe Mr Hart is away at the moment. I suggest you ask him when he returns from his trip,' Mary said, her voice trailing off as she glanced at her watch, realising she was running late. 'Now, if you wouldn't mind, please move your car. I have an appointment.'

The tension between them was palpable as Jack stood momentarily, staring at Mary. Then, dragging his feet and cursing under his breath, he returned to his car, slamming the car door behind him with such force it made Mary jump. After starting the engine with a roar, Jack slammed the gears into reverse. He shot backwards up the drive, disappearing as quickly as he had appeared.

Mary heaved a sigh of relief as she watched him disappear out of sight before getting into her car and driving up the driveway. When she reached the main road, there was no sign of Jack. He'd long gone.

The Red Lion Inn, with its cosy fireplace and rustic wooden beams, radiated a welcoming ambience, making Mary feel instantly at ease upon entering the pub. She quickly scanned the faces of the people standing around the bar. On her drive to the pub, Mary tried to imagine what Eleanor looked like. Was she fair hair like herself? Or maybe she took after her father's side?

'Mary! Mary, over here!' a voice called out, cutting through the noisy chatter of the pub.

Mary felt a sudden surge of nerves. Someone had recognised her – but who? She looked about at the faces of the crowd, hoping to see who it was calling her name. She suddenly experienced a tug on her arm.

'Mary. At long last we meet!'

Mary spun around to see a girl of a similar age to herself

with dark skin and a shock of untamed black corkscrew-coiled hair framing her face.

Mary stared; her mouth dropped. 'Eleanor?' Mary gasped.

'I'm not quite what you expected, eh?' Eleanor said, joking. She placed her hands on her hips and grinned, revealing a perfect set of gleaming white teeth.

'Oh … No! … Yes…' Mary stammered. 'It's nothing like that! Sorry, it's just that with all these people and …' Mary stumbled over her words, her cheeks flushing with embarrassment.

Eleanor put her arm through Mary's. 'I know. I'm quite a shock to everyone's system, as you've just found out! So, no apologies needed,' she said, letting out a loud, infectious laugh. 'Come with me. I've grabbed us a table over there in the snug. It's quieter there, and the locals won't disturb us.' Eleanor's voice trailed off as she guided Mary to their table.

Mary gathered herself together. Why had she been so shocked at seeing Eleanor? She wondered. After all, Eleanor was no different from the various ethnic backgrounds she encountered at work, was she? Mary wrestled with her own thoughts.

'Here we are – the snug,' Eleanor announced.

Mary entered a cosy area separated from the other parts of the pub by frosted glass partitions. It had a low ceiling and exposed brickwork walls, with a black wrought iron fireplace surround and comfortable chairs and tables scattered around. Eleanor was right, Mary reflected. The space was far more private, providing a quiet place for them to chat away from the noisy bar. 'I know it's possibly a little bit naughty given the time of day and all that, but I've arranged a nice bottle of wine to go with our lunch, see?' She was pointing to the silver ice bucket in a stand next to a table marked 'reserved.'

'Now, what would you like to order?' Eleanor asked,

handing Mary a menu before quickly adding, 'Oh, and they have a special on the fish and chips today!'

'Lovely! However, the last time I was here, I had a ploughman's lunch; it was delicious. I'll try that again, please,' Mary said, handing the menu back to Eleanor.

'I'm with you there! Okay, they are short-staffed today, so I'll go up to the bar and order, and then we can talk. Won't be two ticks!'

Mary gazed out of the large casement window beside her. She noticed everything looked so green and lush after the previous day's rain. The rolling green hills beyond were bathed in the soft glow of the late morning sun. Its picturesque view serving as a reminder of the beauty of the countryside of her newly adopted country.

'All ordered!' Eleanor announced, flopping down on the chair. 'Now, I'm dying to know all about you. No topic is off-limits. Just a heads up, I tend to talk a mile a minute, so feel free to interrupt me or tell me to shut up, as most people do! Want some wine?' Eleanor said, hardly taking a breath.

Mary was captivated by the striking-looking slim girl on the other side of the table, with her large, round, wide-set brown eyes, full lips, and smile that lit up the room. Could she possibly be related to Eleanor? Mary pondered. Her skin, in contrast, was fair, whereas Eleanor's was black.

'Yes, please, I'd love a glass of wine.' Mary smiled, holding out an empty glass.

'Good! I'd hate to have to drink it all myself,' Eleanor said, pouring two large glasses of wine and handing one to Mary. 'I've done it before, and believe me, it's not a pretty sight! I remember the time …. oops, there I go again, off on a tangent — sorry. Tell me about yourself. I understand you were born and raised in Australia.'

'Yes, that's right. In fact, the first time I travelled out of Oz was just a few months ago, when Uncle Leonard died. Did you know Uncle Leonard?'

Eleanor took a large sip of her wine before moving her head from side to side. 'No. Not really. My family was estranged from the rest of the family.'

'Oh? Why was that? Was there a falling out or something?' Mary asked, curious to understand how family members who live so close to each other could be estranged.

'Yes! I suppose you could call it a falling out. The family disapproved of my mother's choice of husband.'

'Disapproved of your father?' Mary quizzed. 'Why didn't they approve?'

'Because Daddy is Black… black as the ace of spades, as the saying goes. That's why I'm brown, in case you've been wondering.' Eleanor laughed aloud.

Mary was initially taken aback by Eleanor's openness but quickly regained her composure.

'These days, does anyone really notice things like that?' Mary asked, gesturing with her head.

'Perhaps not so much these days.' Eleanor paused, taking a sip of her wine. 'But back in the fifties, when Mummy married Daddy, it was a different story.'

'Oh? I'm a bit too young to know what went on in the fifties,' Mary remarked with a sarcastic grin. 'Why was it a different story back then?' Mary asked.

'It turned out that it wasn't just Mummy's family who disapproved of their marriage. Back in those days, it was highly frowned upon by society for a white Caucasian girl to be involved with a Black African, let alone enter into marriage. Mummy's father told her that if she married Daddy, she would never set foot in the house again!'

'Did he mean it?'

'Oh yes! There's no doubt he meant it! They also found that other people held a similar view on mixed-race relationships. Their early years of marriage were tough. People shunned them. They found it difficult to find anywhere to live because no one would rent rooms to a Black man. They had very little money as Daddy was a medical student and Mummy was training to be a nurse.'

'Your father is a doctor?' Mary asked, raising an eyebrow.

'Well, yes, sort of. Daddy is a top surgeon in London now,' Eleanor boasted proudly.

Mary's eyes widened in surprise. During her recent research on tropical diseases, she remembered reading an article about a well-known surgeon named Featherstone.

'Is your father, Samuel Featherstone, by any chance? The renowned surgeon?' she asked.

'Yes! Do you know Daddy then?'

'Well … not exactly. I've read some of your father's papers on tropical diseases, but I can't say we've had a personal introduction. Goodness me, what a small world.'

Eleanor took a big sip of her drink. 'Not small enough sometimes.' She grinned, replenishing her glass, which was now empty. 'A top-up?' she asked, holding the bottle out to Mary.

'No, I'm fine, thank you. What about you then? What do you do? You said in your letter that you have just returned from overseas?'

'Yes, I'm just back from Guana. I got my medical degree a couple of years ago. But I couldn't see myself tied down to the routine of doing the rounds in a hospital or in a practice as a GP sitting behind a desk all day. That's all a bit too rigid for me. So, Daddy suggested I try out tropical medicine so I get a chance to travel, and I absolutely love it!'

'What a coincidence we're both involved in the world of medicine in our own ways,' Mary exclaimed.

'I know! What are the chances, eh? Must be something in the genes.' Eleanor chuckled. 'Now … enough of me. I want to know all about you. No holds barred,' she added, leaning forward eagerly. 'Spill the beans, girl!'

Chapter 22

8th July 1982

Eleanor's presence in my life has boosted my spirits immensely. We have so many things in common and share so many interests and experiences; it feels like we're soul sisters instead of cousins. I've noticed that I'm starting to open up and confide my deepest thoughts and fears with her in the same way that I used to with Aunt Molly. A wave of emotions hit me when I woke up this morning, anticipating the long-awaited meeting with Aunt Ruth, Eleanor's mother, later today. Although I was heartbroken to learn that she has Alzheimer's disease, she's only seventy-two. I admit, when I heard this initially, selfishly, I felt robbed, knowing that Aunt Ruth's illness may have taken away the one chance I had to uncover untold stories about my mother. Aunt Ruth, being four years older than my mother, could have provided me with valuable insights about her.

However, Eleanor has filled in a few gaps for me. The other day, she brought over her family photograph album for me to look at. It was like stepping into a time machine as we went through the photographs of our mothers growing up. I was especially enthralled when Eleanor relayed the stories behind each picture, like the one of our mothers covered in flour when they were making an apple pie together. I could almost hear my mother's voice and laughter looking at that photograph because it reminded me of the pies Aunt Molly and I used to make together and the mess I often got into. Sadly, we both have to face up to the fact that Aunt Ruth's fight against Alzheimer's could steal more of the priceless memories already lost to Eleanor.

I did, however, find the sheer number of family connections in Eleanor's photos overwhelming, and it appears these connections are escalating. I'll be meeting her brother, David, and his family soon as well. So, it seems Robert was right all along. I do have an extensive family, and I'm trying to come to grips with its vastness as I look at the family tree that branches out into a labyrinth of unknown faces and untold stories.

But am I ready to embrace all these connections?

Mary sat in the kitchen, staring into space, lost in contemplation, while sipping her coffee. She was anxiously awaiting Eleanor's arrival to drive her to the care home. While Mary was familiar with her aunt's medical condition and knew a little of what to expect, it didn't make the impending visit any less daunting. This was her own flesh and blood, her mother's sister, whom she was about to meet. Although Eleanor had shown her a photograph of her aunt, it didn't prepare her for the kind of woman Aunt Ruth might be.

'Did you know my Aunt Ruth, Mrs Scarr?' Mary suddenly asked.

Mrs Scarr stopped stirring the big pot of stew on the stove and turned to face Mary, stroking her chin as she tried to remember. 'Hmmm…' She paused. 'Now you come to mention I remember she came here once to visit with Molly's ma. She didn't stay long, though.'

Mary frowned. 'Oh? Why was that?' Mary leaned forward, eager to hear more about her aunt's visit.

'It was a reet rum do I remember.' Mrs Scarr recalled sitting down next to Mary at the table.

Mary folded her arms and sat back in her seat. 'Oh? What was strange about it?' she asked.

'I was only a youngun at the time. But I seem to remember she came with a tall, handsome, dark-skinned man, and old Mr Mattleton saw them off. There was lots of shouting, and that poor woman was crying. I have no idea what it was about, but it fair upset poor Molly's ma.'

'Who's upset who now?' Eleanor asked, breezing through the opened back door with a playful smile.

'Oh! No one, really,' Mary answered quickly. 'I'm ready. Shall we go?'

'Hey! Is that freshly brewed coffee I can smell by any chance?' Eleanor asked, sniffing the air.

'Yes, lass, sit yourself down. I'll pour you a cup,' Mrs Scarr said, getting up from the table and fetching a cup and saucer from the dresser. 'Have one of them to go with it,' she added, pushing a plate of flapjacks towards her.

'Oh! Flapjacks, my absolutely all-time favourites,' Eleanor replied excitedly, grabbing one and taking a big bite out of it. 'Mmmm. Yummy,' she murmured with a mouthful of cake and rolled her eyes upwards.

Mary inwardly groaned. Not that she begrudged Eleanor a cup of coffee or a flapjack. In fact, she'd not finished her own coffee and cake. It was just that she was eager to get going and get the initial meeting with her aunt over with. Eleanor, on the other hand, didn't appear to be in any hurry and proceeded, in between mouthfuls of flapjack, to give a blow-by-blow account of what her mother used to bake before Alzheimer's struck her.

'Ought we to be making a move?' Mary asked eventually, checking her watch. 'We're going to miss visiting time if we don't go now?'

'Oh, lummy! Check out the time. You really do need to

stop me from rambling on, Mary. You know how I can talk! Thanks for the coffee and flapjacks, Mrs S. Next time I come, remind me to tell you about—'

'Do come on, Eleanor!' Mary said, her voice filled with amusement, as she held the door open wide for her.

'Sorry,' Eleanor said with a sheepish smile as she climbed into her car. 'Oh, wait! Before we go, did you remember to bring those photographs of your family in Australia, as I suggested?'

Mary patted the bag that was in her lap. 'Yes. I have them in here.'

'That's great. Some days, Mummy is quite lucid and remembers stuff,' Eleanor explained. 'Although she doesn't always recognise me,' she confessed, her voice heavy with sadness. 'But maybe today will be different,' she added optimistically.

Eleanor, as usual, kept Mary entertained with the stories of her work and the family throughout the trip to the care home. Mary listened attentively, occasionally asking questions or laughing aloud at the amusing circumstances Eleanor found herself in.

'Here we are,' Eleanor said, the gravel crunching beneath the car tyres as they turned into the drive of an imposing Yorkshire stone building.

'Will your father be there today? I'd love to meet him.'

'No. Daddy is at the hospital in London today. Possibly he'll be around next time.'

They parked the car. 'This way, follow me,' Eleanor said, pointing towards the building ahead of them.

Mary stood briefly, taken in by the natural stone building that stood before her, nestled amidst towering trees and, surrounded by immaculately manicured lawns and gardens that seamlessly blended with the natural surroundings. The building appeared to give off an aura of warmth and tranquillity, shattering her preconceived expectation of seeing a sterile, impersonal institution like the ones she'd been involved with in Australia.

After announcing themselves through the front door security grill, the door opened, and they stepped inside. The welcoming atmosphere enveloped Mary like a comforting embrace, dispelling any lingering expectations about what she might find and replacing them with an air of peace and belonging.

'Good morning, Matron,' Eleanor greeted a tall, pleasant-looking woman wearing a dark blue cotton dress. 'I'm here to see Mummy. This is my cousin Mary Mattleton,' Eleanor said with a smile, gesturing towards Mary.

My cousin – the words echoed in Mary's head. This was the first time she'd been acknowledged as a family member to an outsider.

'Good morning, ladies. If you'd both just like to sign the register, I'll show you to Mrs Featherstone's room.'

They both signed the brown leather visitors' book. They followed the Matron down the long, carpeted corridor to Eleanor's mother's room.

The Matron pushed open the door. 'Visitors, Mrs Feathersone,' she called out brightly.

'Hello Mummy. Look who I've brought to see you!' Eleanor exclaimed, her voice filled with excitement, as she rushed over to her mother, who was sitting in the chair by the French windows that led out to the garden. Draped over her knees was a soft-knitted multicoloured blanket and a book sat open next to her. Eleanor gently kissed her cheek while her mother continued to stare ahead.

Mary lingered in the doorway and glanced around the large high ceiling room. An assortment of paintings hung on the walls. A variety of ornaments and souvenirs adorned the shelves encompassing the room. Some she suspected were from Eleanor's trips, each item holding its own memory.

Eleanor's mother suddenly looked at Mary and half-smiled. Mary smiled back while focusing her gaze on her aunt's snowy white hair, which was illuminated by the sunlight streaming through the windows. Her skin was pale and almost translucent, resembling a wax dummy. Aunt Ruth's once vibrant eyes, full of life, now held a distant look. Her head constantly nodding as if agreeing with a conversation no one else could hear.

'Come closer so she can see you,' Eleanor beckoned to Mary.

Mary entered the room and walked over to her aunt. She passed by the dresser just inside the room, which displayed faded photographs and testimonies of her aunt's vibrant past. She noticed a monochrome wedding portrait of her aunt standing smiling beside a dark-skinned man, a head taller than her. Her aunt was holding a bouquet of flowers and wisps of feathery fern cascading down to a point. Amidst the photographs, there was a vase of half-dead yellow roses.

As Mary got closer, her aunt's eyes locked onto hers, radiating a sign of familiarity. Time appeared to stand still. Then, unexpectantly, her aunt's lips curved into a broad smile that seemed to light up the room.

With tears forming in her eyes and her arms outstretched towards Mary, she whispered, 'Catherine, my dear sister, you've come at last. It's been so long. I've missed you.'

Eleanor knelt down facing her mother and took hold of her hands.

'No! Mummy. This is Mary. Aunt Catherine's daughter. Remember I told you about her?' she said softly.

'Catherine…'

'No! Mummy.' Eleanor corrected emphatically. 'This is Mary.'

'You're lying! It's Catherine! Get out of my room!' Ruth screamed angrily, pushing Eleanor away with such force she toppled over backwards.

Mary approached her aunt slowly and knelt down where Ruth could see her.

'Hello, Ruth. How are you today? That's a pretty top you're wearing,' Mary said softly, her eyes lingering on the delicate embroidery of her blouse.

Ruth stared back at Mary, her brow furrowing, eyes searching for answers. Mary held out the posy of flowers she was holding towards Ruth. 'I picked these roses this morning for you from the garden in the Manor. Aren't they a pretty shade of pink? They almost match your top. Would you like to smell them?' Mary asked, holding the flowers towards her aunt.

Ruth took the flowers and placed them in her lap without smelling them. A long, heavy silence hung in the air as she stared at Mary. 'Who are you?' Ruth asked, frowning, peering into Mary's face for answers.

Mary hesitated for a second, thinking about her experiences working with Alzheimer's disease patients back home. She reminded herself to stay composed and patient if she was to find a way to connect with her aunt, even if it meant starting from scratch. After all, she could always come back and see her another day when she may be more lucid.

'I'm Mary. I've come to visit you,' she said brightly. 'Shall we go for a walk around the grounds? It's such a beautiful day today,' Mary suggested as she stood up and looked out onto the sun-drenched gardens.

Chapter 23

Mary felt a sudden surge of uneasiness as her eyes searched her surroundings, trying to determine where she was. The last thing she remembered was collapsing on her bed, mentally drained from her visit with Aunt Ruth.

'Where am I?' Mary said aloud, frantically scanning the room. 'This looks like the great hall. But wait! Something is missing. Where is the portrait of the lady with her children? And where have the treasures gone from the cabinet?' she uttered, the empty display cabinet staring back at her.

'There you be,' Molly said, appearing as if by magic as she descended the stairs.

'You startled me, appearing out of nowhere like that, Molly!' Mary cried out, her hand flying to her chest as she took a quick step back.

As the initial shock subsided, Mary quickly realised she had once again entered Molly's parallel world. The question of how she'd got there still baffled her.

'You took your time!' Molly said with urgency.

Mary frowned. 'Took my time? What do you mean, took my time?'

'Ah called you an age ago. I bin waiting to show you summat important. Follow me quick!'

'Oh! Is it Thomas? Is he still unwell?' Mary asked anxiously.

'Nah! that potion worked. He's up 'n about and being annoying as ever!'

'I'm pleased to hear it!' Mary answered as she hurriedly followed Molly down the dimly lit passage to the servants' rooms.

'In here …' Molly said as she opened the door at the end of the corridor. 'This here be Bertha, the milkmaid. She helps Pa with the milk and making the cheese. She's right poorly.'

Molly came across Bertha in bed, gasping heavily and battling to catch her breath.

'Pull back her bedclothes, please, Molly,' Mary said.

Mary stared down at Bertha's slight frame, which was covered in a bright crimson rash, standing out starkly against her pale skin.

'Has she seen a doctor?' Mary asked.

'Nay. Grandma went to see the wise woman who sez to give her boiled-down saffron and milk and a poultice for her chest for her breathing.'

'Molly, this poor girl has measles, and I would guess she also has bronchial pneumonia.'

'Mezzles? What be Mezzles?'

'It's a highly contagious infection that can lead to complications if not treated,' Mary warned.

'That's why I brought you here. Can you give Bertha summat to make her well again, like you did with our Thomas?' Molly asked, her voice laced with concern and desperation.

Mary hesitated for a second. She'd had little exposure to severe cases of measles because of the successful vaccination campaign. She was also concerned about undermining Molly's household trust in the wise woman's treatments, even though it conflicted with her own treatments.

'There's very little more I can suggest other than what you are already doing,' Mary said, her voice filled with sympathy. 'Except, see how Bertha is squinting against the sun coming through the window?' Mary gestured towards the window.

Molly nodded.

'Well, her condition is making her eyes very sensitive, so you might get someone to darken the room by putting a blanket up at the window. Also, fill a bowl with boiling water, add a few drops of oil of camphor, and place it near her bed and keep topping it up. The steam from that will help her breathe,' Mary suggested.

'Ah will see to it straightaway. Bertha is my friend 'n ah want to help. I don't want her to die!' Molly solemnly replied as she walked over to the bedroom door.

'One more thing … Bertha must not mix with the others in the household. Anyone who attends to her must wash their hands thoroughly afterwards. That includes you, Molly. Do you understand?' Mary said.

'I understand.' Molly nodded her head vigorously.

***

9th July 1982

As I sit here in the early morning, jotting down these thoughts in my personal journal, I find myself overwhelmed by all that has been happening since arriving at the Manor. I am caught between reality and Molly's realm, and I'm losing my grip on what is real.

Once again, when I woke up this morning, I found myself in my day clothes with no memory of falling asleep and questioned whether I had indeed travelled to another time or if it was all a figment of my imagination. Even so, my visits with Molly always feel natural, so it's hard to believe that it could just be a dream. Upon reflection, I am beginning to think Molly possesses the remarkable ability to serve as a conduit, enabling her to transport me to her time by traversing the intricate realms of mental transference. I need to find someone who understands this phenomenon and confirm whether what I'm experiencing is possible and that a profound reality exists beyond my comprehension. I wonder if this is something I could share with Eleanor and get her opinion. I need answers.

Unfortunately, I couldn't gather much information about my mother from Aunt Ruth during yesterday's visit. During our walk in the garden, we mostly remained silent to avoid any confusion between me and her sister Catherine, my mother, and to prevent another outburst if I mentioned I wasn't her sister. Poor Aunt Ruth could be forgiven for mistaking me for my mother in her regressive state. While examining my mother's photographs, I couldn't ignore the uncanny resemblance between us. It makes me curious about other similarities between my mother and I. Oh! I so wish I knew!

Mary sat for a minute, fiddling with her pen and looking off into space. In some respects, both she and Eleanor were alike. They had both lost their mothers. Eleanor's through Alzheimer's, and hers through death. She laid her pen down on the desk and closed her journal.

'Enough of these maudlin thoughts — coffee time!' she announced out loud.

As she was about to sit down with her coffee and toast, Eleanor barged into the kitchen without knocking as usual, catching her off guard.

'Am I in time?' she asked breathlessly, her eyes scanning the kitchen.

'In time for what?' Mary asked, raising an eyebrow. She was surprised to see Eleanor, and a little taken aback since she had just been thinking how nice it would be to have her company today.

'Why, for a Mrs S breakfast special, of course!' she answered, laughing, pulling out a chair, sitting down on it, and looking around the kitchen. 'I *am* invited, aren't I?' she asked hopefully.

'Well, ordinarily, you would be invited for breakfast, of course, but you'll have a long wait today. It's Mrs Scarr's day off!' Mary replied.

Eleanor leaned backwards in her chair. 'Drat! I was looking forward to one of Mrs S's big breakfasts. It was to have been the only decent food I would get today! Daddy has disappeared for the week to his London clinic. Our maid is gallivanting off somewhere for the day, so I am all alone and no one to feed me at home,' Eleanor explained, rolling her eyes. 'Where's Mrs S disappeared to when I need her?' she added, thrusting out her lower lip in a playful pout.

'She's gone to the farm to sort out, Jack, no doubt. I'm pretty sure she'd rather be here to feed you, though.' Mary laughed. 'I can offer coffee and toast.'

'I suppose that will have to do then.' Eleanor sighed dramatically. 'By the way, I'm sorry your visit to Mummy was a washout yesterday. Are you game to try again sometime next week?'

'I'd love to, yes. I want to learn more about your mother and your father, how they met et cetera. And, of course, my mother. She must have heaps of stories of her to tell locked away in her memory!'

'Oh! Yes, Mummy and Daddy have lived a high old life, I can tell you. Well, I can only tell you about the bits they've shared with me, of course.' Eleanor giggled. 'Enough of that. What are your plans today, then – fancy some company?'

'Actually, yes, I'd love your company, and I'd like to run something by you. Here's your coffee and toast. Help yourself with the butter and marmalade,' Mary said, placing the tray in front of Eleanor.

'Thanks! I am eternally grateful. But can I say it doesn't look half as appealing as Mrs S's grub?' Eleanor said, looking down at the plain toast on the plate. 'Oh, well, beggars and all that!' She shrugged her shoulders. 'So, what's on your mind?'

'When I woke up in my bed this morning, I found myself fully dressed, and I don't remember even going to bed!' Mary blurted out.

'What!' Eleanor exclaimed. 'How come? Did you have a skinful last night?' she asked, laughing aloud, her eyes sparkling with amusement.

'No!' Mary replied indignantly. 'I'm serious!' Mary insisted. 'This has happened to me a few times during my time here. It started with the reflection in my dressing table mirror…'

'Reflection in your dressing table mirror? You've lost me now. What's that got to do with anything?' Eleanor said, tossing her head.

Mary could see Eleanor could be another non-believer like Robert, and she was beginning to regret bringing the subject up. Still, as she'd started, she'd have to continue. 'It's like this … I appear to wake up to use a simple expression, in a parallel universe, in this house, only it's in a different year … sixty years ago, to be exact, when my ancestors lived here.'

'You seriously believe in all that stuff?' Eleanor chimed in, her tone laced with scepticism. 'I've got a friend who believes in all that mumbo jumbo!'

Mary sighed. 'To be honest, I'm really torn right now. I'm uncertain what to believe. All I know is that somehow, I am finding myself in another time with my Aunt Molly, who brought me up after my parents died. She is a child of around eleven and is the only one who can see me.'

'Oh! Come on, Mary. Are you asking me to believe that your Aunt Molly, who is now a child, has a hotline from a parallel universe and is calling you back to her time?' Eleanor said, with a smirk on her face.

Mary's heart sank. Why should she expect Eleanor to believe her when she had doubts herself?

'I understand that, from a logical standpoint, this whole situation appears far-fetched. However, despite any of my misgivings, talking to Molly feels undeniably real.' Mary paused, noticing Eleanor pulling a face. 'I know, I know – Robert poo-pooed the situation when I talked to him about it, too.'

'So, I'm not the only one who thinks you've gone ga-ga then?' Eleanor burst into laughter.

'Humph! I might have expected you to say something like that!' Mary replied, voicing her indignation at Eleanor's response. 'You mentioned having a friend who might relate to my experiences. Can you put me in touch with them, please?'

'I apologise if I appeared sceptical. That's because I am.' Eleanor grinned and pulled a face. 'However, yeah, I do know someone who is in touch with their soul, as they call it. I will give you his phone number, and you can call him to find out what he thinks.'

'Thanks, I appreciate that,' Mary replied, finding odd comfort in the hope of discovering answers.

Eleanor pushed her plate away and got up from the table. 'Look, let's get out of here. Perhaps a change of scenery and some distractions will clear your mind. I know, how about a spot of shopping and a bite to eat at the pub? That should do the trick. There's no point in hanging around here, anyway. There's no one to feed us!'

'Good idea, even though shopping isn't my favourite pastime.' Mary laughed. 'Help me stack the dirty dishes in the sink, would you? Just in case Mrs Scarr comes back. I'll get a telling-off if I leave the place in a mess!' Mary said.

'Oh! I adore shopping,' Eleanor gushed, a glimmer of excitement in her eyes. 'Shops are like a second home to me.'

'Sorry, I can't share your enthusiasm for it, Eleanor.

However, I'm willing to tag along with you today. All I ask for is a nice lunch afterwards as a reward.' Mary chuckled.

'Glady,' Eleanor replied, vigorously nodding and grinning.

'Come on, then,' Mary said, linking arms with Eleanor and stepping outside.

Eleanor's love for shopping quickly became apparent to Mary as she was dragged along from shop to shop while Eleanor tried on clothes and shoes. How many pairs of shoes can a girl need? Mary couldn't help but wonder as Eleanor tried on her sixth. Or was it her seventh pair of shoes that day?

'What are your thoughts on these? Don't you agree they're nicer than those? They've got more of a ….'

Mary interrupted Eleanor's excited chatter about the shoes she was trying on, saying. 'I don't know about you, Eleanor. I could do with a sit-down and a drink. Let's go grab lunch at the pub, shall we?'

'Okay. But I'd like to pop in next door first. I saw some of the prettiest earrings when I looked in their window the other day. They would look good with my red top, you know, the one with the scooped neckline?'

'Another day, perhaps?' Mary replied, her patience wearing thin.

'Okay, you win. I get the message! Let's go eat!' Eleanor replied, linking arms with Mary.

'You and your shopping obsession, Eleanor.' Mary teased, lightly nudging Eleanor's arm as they walked back to the car laden with bags. 'It's beyond me how you manage to spend so much time and money on clothes and shoes.'

'Oh! That's easy… but it's made me work up an appetite. Let's eat!' Eleanor giggled.

Upon arriving at The Red Lion Inn, Eleanor parked the car and, they walked into the pub together arm in arm. They found the bar was empty.

'It's like the grave in here today!' Eleanor remarked. 'I'll see if I can raise someone and order the drinks. You go see if our table in the snug is free,' she added, waving her hand dismissively.

'Yes, all right.' Mary nodded before heading towards the snug.

Eleanor was right. This place is like a grave today, Mary thought as she walked past the empty tables and over towards the snug, which was tucked away in the far corner.

As she drew near the snug, she stopped dead in her tracks. Her eyes grew wide in shock, and she drew in a quick breath. She saw Robert, sitting in the corner, with his arm around a man of a similar age, their murmured words lost to her ears.

She was just about to turn and leave before she was seen when Robert looked up and saw her. He quickly released his arms around the young man.

'Mary…Mary… it's not what it seems…' Robert called after her as she fled from the pub.

Chapter 24

10th July 1982

The isolation of North Hall, ever since Mrs. S went to help at the farm, has been something of an adjustment for me to make. I am eagerly awaiting her return today, not only for her company but also for the tantalising smell of her cooking. Just imagining it makes my stomach growl with hunger. A girl can only exist on tea and toast for so long! Last night, I slept soundly, free from any dreams or encounters with Molly. Perhaps that was down to sheer exhaustion from yesterday's shopping expedition with Eleanor after carrying her heavy shopping bags that dug into my fingers and the throbbing pain I had in my feet. The experience was enough to knock me out like a tranquilised elephant! I might have to be conveniently busy next time she invites me! While lying in bed this morning, my mind wandered aimlessly to Robert and the mysterious man I saw him with in the snug. A part of me desperately would love to uncover the truth behind Robert's rendezvous. Still, another part of me reminds me it's not my place to pry into his affairs! However, my imagination truly knows no bounds these days, and I found myself getting carried away into a realm of endless possibilities with my thoughts spiralling like a tornado sweeping me away! I'm getting as bad as Eleanor. I really must rein it in.

The sudden ringing of the telephone jolted Mary out of her thoughts, causing her to pause in her writing. She got up from her desk to answer it.

'Hello … what have you misplaced this time?' Mary chuckled, fully expecting it was likely to be Eleanor calling, asking about something she might have left behind during her visit yesterday. Last week, it was her house keys, and she'd had to drive all the way back to the Manor for them.

'I'm pretty sure I've not lost anything to my knowledge?' Robert replied hesitantly.

'Oh! Sorry, Robert.' Mary chuckled. 'I was expecting you would be Eleanor. How can I help you?'

'I'd like to come and see you and explain about yesterday…' Robert sounded hesitant.

'Explain about yesterday?' Mary repeated casually, trying not to sound too curious.

'Yes. I want to talk to you about who you saw me with in the snug at The Red Lion,' Robert said.

Although Mary had been burning with curiosity about who the man she'd seen Robert with, she had convinced herself that it was none of her concern. 'There's no need. It's none of my business …'

Robert interrupted her quickly. 'I think that there is a necessity. I'll be over in about thirty minutes, and I'll bring a bottle of wine because there is also something I'd like to share with you. Okay?'

Mary hesitated. Robert wanted to share something with her – could this be more than just a professional meeting?

Intrigued, she replied. 'Yes. Yes, that's fine…'

After replacing the receiver, Mary ran her fingers through her hair, contemplating whether she should tie it back before Robert's arrival. She hurriedly went upstairs and looked in the full-length mirror. Should she also change and put on some makeup? Mary wondered.

'What am I even thinking about?' Mary scolded herself

as she looked in the mirror. 'It's getting on for mid-day, and it's not like Robert is asking me out on a date. Anyway, it's possible the man I saw him with yesterday was a new client. Robert wants me to help him celebrate securing his account – or something as simple as that,' she muttered to herself.

To avoid dwelling on Robert's visit, Mary occupied herself by organising laundry in her bedroom, which Mrs Scarr had left before her trip to the farm. The doorbell rang, making her jump. She hurried across the hall and opened the door.

'Come in, Robert. Let's go through to the library; it's nice there at this time of day. We have a beautiful view from the window of the sun over the hills in the distance …'

She paused mid-sentence and chuckled to herself, realising how absurd she must sound, rambling on about the view of the hills. As if Robert would care. She was definitely beginning to sound like Eleanor.

'Thanks for the wine,' she said, placing the bottle along with two glasses on the small round table. 'But what's the occasion?'

'There's no occasion as such. I just … I just thought we could enjoy a drink together,' Robert stammered. 'Would you like me to uncork and pour?' Robert asked.

'Yes, please.' Mary smiled, masking her disappointment that she'd been under the impression they were about to celebrate something.

Robert carefully poured the rich, ruby-red wine into two delicate crystal glasses. He handed Mary a glass before they took their seats in the oversized chairs on opposite sides of the fireplace.

Robert took a large gulp from his glass. 'I can only imagine how surprised you were when you caught sight of me with Christopher yesterday,' he blurted out.

Mary interrupted. 'Look, Robert. Like I said on the phone, it's your concern, not mine!'

Robert took another large sip of his wine. An agonising silence stretched between them. 'Dutch courage!' he exclaimed, half-smiling and setting his almost empty glass noisily down on the table. 'There's no easy way to say this – Mary, I am a homosexual.'

Mary sat motionless, her hands clenched tightly in her lap, attempting to appear composed. In reality, a whirlwind of thoughts tore through her mind. His news had hit her like a thunderbolt, leaving her momentarily stunned. Not that she had anything against homosexuals per se. Even though, unlike in England, homosexuality was yet to be decriminalised in NSW, Australia. However, Robert? *How did I miss the fact that he was gay?* she wondered. How could she have been so blind? Why hadn't he mentioned it before? Her thoughts raced as she searched for the right words to say, sensing Robert was bracing himself for her reaction.

'Are you shocked?' Robert asked, breaking the silence.

'No! Not at all,' Mary said. 'But I'm wondering why you think you should tell me. After all, it's your business, not mine.'

Robert filled up his glass of wine. 'I've been wanting to tell you for a few weeks now.' He paused, taking a deep breath and toying with the stem of his wineglass. 'It's not always easy to find the right words when coming out to people you care about. There's always a chance of being judged when others discover the truth about you.'

'I would never have a lower opinion of you, Robert, no matter who you say you are,' Mary affirmed. 'You are among the kindest people I have ever known. And I value our friendship too much to let something like this change that.'

'Thank you, Mary! That means a great deal to me,' Robert said, his voice filled with gratitude and relief. 'Telling you the truth about who I am will allow me to be myself with you now.'

'No worries!' Mary responded in an exaggerated Australian accent and laughed. 'But seriously, Robert, you've meant a lot to me these past months. Leaving behind my life in Australia and relocating halfway across the world has been an emotional rollercoaster. I have sincerely appreciated your support and guidance throughout this transition.'

'I've been pleased to help, and to be honest, it has taken my mind off other things.'

'Oh? What other things, if you don't mind me asking?'

Robert slowly placed his glass down on the table and sank back into his chair, inhaling deeply. 'It's my partner, Christopher. The recent situation with his health has been tearing me apart,' he admitted, his words tinged with a combination of desperation and anguish. 'I can't even begin to describe the fear and worry that's been consuming me of late. I've been wanting to share this with you, but I was reluctant because ….'

Mary leaned forward toward him, placing a comforting hand on Robert's knee.

'What's wrong with him?' she asked with genuine concern.

'I've been worried sick about him for weeks. He can't eat. He's lost so much weight. I had to push him hard, but he finally went to see the doctor. The blood test results came in yesterday and …' Robert paused, his eyes brimming with tears as he mustered the strength to share his devastating news with Mary. 'His HIV test came back positive!'

'But how?' Mary exclaimed. 'As far as I know, there are very few instances of HIV in this country. Isn't it predominantly prevalent in African countries and, more recently, in America? How did Christopher contract it?'

Robert nodded slowly. 'It's true. HIV cases are rare in our country, but because of Christopher's work with the Red Cross, he often finds himself in high-risk areas,' Robert explained. 'Sierra Leone is one such place from which he's recently returned.'

'He takes the necessary precautions, though?'

Robert nodded. 'Yes, of course! But sadly, it seems he still managed to contract the virus while over there.'

'I see.' Mary paused while observing Robert's trembling hand pour another glass of wine for himself. 'What is Christopher's prognosis?' she asked softly.

'We were in the middle of discussing his prognosis when you walked into the snug. Even though the doctors haven't played down the severity of Christoper's condition, they have said by starting treatment early, there's hope of preventing it from progressing to AIDS.'

With a defeated expression, Robert slumped into his chair. Mary stood and knelt before him.

'I'm truly sorry, Robert. I can't even begin to imagine what you must both be going through right now. I'm sure that Christopher has his own medical team, but if there's anything I can do for either of you, please don't hesitate to ask.'

Robert sat in silence. Mary's words hung in the air.

'Thank you, Mary. Your support means the world to me,' Robert replied, placing his hand over hers.

'Not at all. After all, you've been my sounding board over the past few months, even though you've ridiculed me at times,' Mary remarked with a wry smile. 'But you have made it easy to share my problems, and I hope I can do the same for you.'

Mary's hand reached for her glass. 'Here's to Christopher's full recovery and to many more years of our friendship!'

Chapter 25

'Oi! Shift thee sen Marigold!' Charlie shouted, prodding the rump of the black and white cow with his hazel stick. The cow had halted to feast on the vegetation in the hedgerow. Marigold turned around and gave out a loud bellow in protest.

'Why are you bringing the cows inside tomorrow, Charlie?' Mary asked, walking alongside him as they followed the cows back to the field after the afternoon milking.

'Because of the rains,' he replied. 'It be like a quagmire in them there fields reet naw. They always cum in for the winter anyhow.'

'They do? Why?' Mary asked, surprised.

'Cos otherwise they get mardy!' he added with a hearty laugh.

Mary frowned. 'Seriously? Cows get miserable. How in the world do you know that?'

'Charlie knows! That's how.' Charlie tapped the side of his nose. 'They hate the cold, just like ol' Charlie. It gets right down into my bones; 'tis the same with the cattle. They have to huddle together to keep warm when that old north wind do blow, and they lose ground.'

'But I'm still not sure how you can tell they're miserable,' Mary remarked, her uncertainty growing as she wondered if Charlie was stringing her along.

'Simple, the milk yield goes off, and they lose weight. I usually waits till November cos there's still a bit of grass around. But this year, with all this rain and the snow to come, we need them off the pastures.'

'What will they eat then if there's no grass around?' Mary asked.

'Why, they eat the hay we gathered in the summer instead, of course.' Charlie explained.

Mary's ears had pricked up at the sound of a potential snowfall, instantly transporting her back to a snowy day at Thredbo on her ski trip back home.

'We're quite high up here. Are you expecting much snow?' she asked hopefully.

'Oh aye!' Charlie chuckled, nodding vigorously. 'We always get snowed in up here! The snow ploughs can't reach us, you see.'

'How wonderful! So, will that mean I could get in some skiing then?' She asked, her eyes lighting up with excitement.

'Skiing?' Charlie burst out laughing. 'You won't be doing much skiing, lass,' he exclaimed, looking amused.

'And why not?' Mary asked indignantly. 'I'm an excellent skier!' she added, her voice laced with determination. She was always ready to face any challenge that came her way, including conquering a small amount of snow.

Charlie chuckled. 'Cos one step outside and you'll sink into the snow up to your waist and beyond, that's why, and I'll have to dig thee out like I have to do them sheep that are daft enough to get themselves buried in the snow.'

Mary's face reddened. 'Oh! I see,' she mumbled. Once again, she'd shown how little she knew of life in the Yorkshire Dales.

So as not to lose face, Mary asked, 'Would you and Tom like some help with the cows tomorrow?'

'Aye! If you feel you're up to it!' Charlie replied, looking her up and down.

'Of course, I am – see!' Mary replied mockingly, flexing her arm. She'd surprised herself in the shower the other day by discovering she'd developed muscles in her upper arms. It's incredible how much she's changed since arriving at the farm six months ago. Mary had thought.

The following morning, Mrs Scarr knocked on Mary's door. 'Charlie's here and waiting for you,' she called through the door.

Mary prised open her eyes and peered at the alarm clock on her bedside table. 'It's only five o'clock. What does Charlie want?' she replied sleepily.

The bedroom door opened. 'He's ready to move the cows?'

Mary inwardly groaned. Yes, she'd agree to help, but at five o'clock in the morning! Reluctantly, she sat up and swung her legs over the edge of the bed.

'Tell him I'll be down in a minute, please, Mrs Scarr,' she replied, letting out an enormous yawn.

Mary shivered as an icy blast of air hit her on stepping through the doorway to the yard outside. She quickly pulled her jacket tighter around herself before walking across the yard to where Charlie and Tom were waiting for her. The air had a crisp, slightly sharp autumnal smell. A heavy dew still lay on the ground, and the early morning sun's rays peaked through the mist that hung low over the trees. The colour of the leaves on the trees were changing. Soon, the landscape would paint itself in vibrant reds, oranges and, gold, just like she'd seen in books. Mary was filled with anticipation as she realised that this autumn would be her first in her adopted country, marking the beginning of another new chapter in her life.

'Which ones are we bringing in first?' Mary asked.

'Why the milkers, of course!' Charlie shouted over his shoulders as he set off at a pace down the lane. 'Gotta get milking done first, thee knows.'

Charlie was fond of his *lady friends,* as he called his twenty or so milking cows. He'd given them all names. They displayed a gentle nature and came to Charlie when he called them in from the fields at milking time. Mary had grown fond of them as well and was no stranger to help bring them for the afternoon milking. But it was her first time getting up early to help with the morning milking routine.

As they reached the field, Mary could see the cows had gathered by the gate. Their two-tone black and white coats and gentle eyes expressed calmness and contentment that mirrored the peacefulness of the morning, patiently waiting to be herded to the parlour for milking.

Once the milking was done, Charlie and Tom settled the cows into their new home in the next barn before going into the Manor for breakfast.

'Right then, let's be having you!' Charlie announced, pulling on his boots after breakfast.

'Where are we going?' Mary asked, getting to her feet.

'To get the heifers from the fells,' Charlie replied. 'Just got to fetch the tractor.'

Why on earth would they need a tractor? Mary thought. Should she ask, or could this be another one of Charlie's and Tom's mischievous pranks? She braced herself for the unexpected.

Mary walked for what felt like miles to find the heifers with Tom, Meg, the collie dog, with Charlie leading in the tractor.

'There they be!' Charlie suddenly called out.

Mary's face dropped upon spotting the heifers high up on the fells and spread out.

'How are we going to round them up?' Mary asked nervously.

'Tom. You take the right, and I will go t'other side. Mary, you take the middle with Meg,' Charlie shouted.

The initial roundup went far smoother than Mary expected. Tom vigorously rattled a bucket of nuts, encouraging the heifers to follow him down the slopes and across the field to the lane. Mary, unsure of her role, followed the cows with Meg, coaxing them along with Charlie's hazel stick as they headed down the lane back to the farm. Charlie, on the tractor, brought up the rear.

As they approached the farm, the carefully orchestrated plan of herding the heifers crumbled. In a sudden and unexpected turn of events, one of the heifers broke free from the herd and sprinted along the lane at great speed, leaving the remaining cattle in a state of confusion. Mary, her heart in her mouth, watched as the other cows then panicked and chased after the heifer as it bolted down the lane.

'Move yourself!' Charlie shouted to Tom. 'Catch them buggers!' he roared.

Tom ran after them, with Mary and Meg following. Just around the corner, they found the heifers in an unfenced field of winter turnips, contentedly grazing on their lush green tops.

'At least they were on the farm,' Tom reminded his father, who was none too pleased Tom had let them run off.

Charlie interrupted, 'But if you'd done as I said, we'd still have a crop of turnips to harvest. As it is …'

Mary removed herself from Charlie and Tom's argument to the sanctuary of the library. She collapsed onto the chair by the blazing fire. Her body felt battered and bruised.

'Thank you!' Mary said as Mrs Scarr placed a cup of tea beside her. 'I've never walked so far in my life. My feet are killing me,' Mary moaned.

'Aye, lass. It's a tough old job, that's for sure,' Mrs Scarr sympathised. 'Wait there, I have something for them feet of yours.'

Mrs Scarr returned and placed a white enamel bowl of steaming hot water on the floor at Mary's feet. 'Put your feet in here.'

'What's in it?' Mary asked.

'Why! It's the best remedy in the world – Epson salts!'

Mary slipped off her shoes and peeled off her thick woollen socks. 'Ahh,' she sighed as her feet slowly submerged in the hot water. 'Thank you, Mrs Scarr,' she said, letting out a loud yawn. 'I cannot believe how tired I am tonight. I'll go to bed after this.'

***

'Mary! Mary! Wake up!'

'What … What is it?' Mary mumbled, her words slurred with sleepiness as she half opened her eyes.

'Come with me,' Molly called from the opened bedroom door. 'I've got summat to show you.'

Mary reluctantly sat up in bed, swung her legs around and placed her bare feet on the icy cold floor.

'Where are you taking me?' she asked sleepily.

'You'll see, come on,' Molly urged with a grin.

Mary put on her slippers and reluctantly followed Molly down the dimly lit back stairs used by the servants. They finally appeared at the end of the passage, close to the great hall.

'This way,' Molly called over her shoulder, beckoning Mary to follow with a wave of her hand when they had reached the bottom of the staircase.

Molly stopped at the library door and went inside. Mary followed.

Crossing over to the large inglenook fireplace, Molly ran her fingers along the stones at the side of it. 'Ah! Here tis!' she shouted, pressing a stone that was poking out.

Mary gasped, and her eyes widened in astonishment upon seeing one of the wall panels slide open, revealing a narrow passage.

Is this the hidden passage Mrs Scarr told her about? She wondered.

'Follow me,' Molly beckoned, tilting her head towards the hidden passage.

Mary cautiously stepped inside the passage, wrinkling her nose at the musty, stale air that hung heavy in her nostrils. She suspected it hadn't been disturbed in years. 'Where does this lead to?' Mary asked in a half-whisper, her voice barely audible in the narrow and cramped space.

'It leads to outside,' Molly answered, giving a quick nod towards the hidden passage.

Mary frowned. 'Do people use this as a shortcut, then?'

'Nay. It's only used by us children to play now, but I'm sure I saw Uncle Leonard the other day hiding summat behind a stone in the wall just inside the entrance on the other end.'

'What did he hide? Did you get a look at what it was?' Mary asked, her curiosity piqued.

'Nay! I got called to do me jobs. Come on, let's see if we can find it. We don't have much time afore I need to help in the kitchen, and afore Uncle Leonard comes back,' she added, racing on ahead.

Mary was reluctant to follow. She found the narrow passage and its low ceilings cramped and claustrophobic. 'Come on!' Molly urged. 'Hurry up will you!'

'Molly, Molly, where are you, girl?' Mary heard a woman calling, her voice echoing through the passage.

'Who's that calling you?' Mary asked.

Molly swung round to Mary and placed her finger on her lips. 'Shhh,' she hissed quietly. 'That's Ma. She's outside looking for me. I got to go. You stay here and look for what my Uncle Leonard hid. I will get back to you as soon as I can,' she said as she rushed towards the exit.

'I'm coming, Ma!' Molly shouted, racing down the passage to the outside.

Mary ventured deeper into the secret passageway, her vision adjusting to the dim light, allowing her to navigate with increased certainty. She was suddenly aware of a faint smell of pipe tobacco. She heard approaching footsteps and muffled voices growing louder coming up the narrow passageway towards her. Mary began to panic. She pressed her body tight up against the stone wall.

'Nah then, we'll wait till back end o'night. I will leave you the paraffin and matches in the fireplace in the library. I reckon them books in there will go up a treat. Then I will set a little fire in the hall. Them wall panels in there will make a good bit of kindling, eh?' The man chuckled. His laughter resounded around the passage as he and his companion made their way towards the library. 'Till tonight then …'

As the approaching footsteps behind her grew louder, Mary's sense of urgency increased, fuelling her determination to reach Molly before it was too late.

Filled with panic and her heart pounding, Mary turned on her heels. 'I have to warn Molly!' she whispered to herself, her voice barely a murmur as she raced down the passageway and back to the library.

Chapter 26

Mary was abruptly awakened from a deep sleep by the loud chimes of the clock, resonating through the room like a sharp knife as it struck twelve.

'Where am I?' she whispered, her voice tinged with alarm as her eyes flitted around the dimly lit room. 'How did I wind up here?'

She sat for a moment, desperately trying to piece together the fleeting memories of her lost hours.

'The last thing I remembered …' Mary rested her hand under her chin as she pondered. 'I was overhearing those men planning to burn down the Manor and running to tell Molly.' She paused and looked around her room, searching for clues. 'And now I find myself back in my bedroom. It makes little sense,' she muttered, shaking her head in frustration. 'Has reality shifted, and I'm trapped in some sort of twisted nightmare?'

Mary drew in a quick breath as she stepped onto the icy wooden floorboards with her bare feet before walking towards the window to gaze outside. It was pitch black. A chilling sensation of isolation swept over her as she returned to her chair.

'Could I have dreamt it …?' she quietly whispered to herself, tapping her fingers on the cluttered table next to her. ' But if it wasn't just a dream,' Mary reasoned, 'and there was a fire, then it would not only destroy the Manor but also my family and, in turn, also threaten my very existence.' She stopped for a moment, contemplating. 'No! It wasn't just a dream. Deep down, I know there is something terrible about to happen. I need to find a way to warn Molly about the fire before it's too late!' she said aloud.

***

'Good morning, lass!' Mrs Scarr greeted Mary as she walked into the kitchen.

'Morning, Mrs Scarr. I am sorry, but I seem to have slept in this morning. Have I missed breakfast?' Mary asked apologetically.

'Nay, lass, come sit yourself down. I'll rustle you up some scrambled eggs. Will that do you?' Mrs Scarr asked warmly.

'Yes. Thank you. I am famished!' Mary said with a grateful smile, her stomach growling in agreement.

'I'm not surprised, lass, you've had nowt since yesterday lunch,' Mrs Scarr declared, her words laced with concern and a hint of scolding.

'Yesterday lunchtime? But I remember having dinner last night … didn't I?' Mary asked, her brow furrowing in deep thought.

'Nay lass. You went to your room soon after returning from herding the cows, and when you hadn't come down for supper, I looked in your room, and you were nowhere to be seen.'

She was nowhere to be seen. Mrs Scarr's words played on her mind as she earnestly attempted to reconstruct her jumbled recollections of her meeting with Molly and the mysterious men she'd overheard in the secret passage the night before. Did she really hear those men planning to set fire to North Hall? Or could it have been just a figment of her imagination?

'There, get that down yourself,' Mrs Scarr said, placing a

large plate of scrambled eggs with two chunks of thickly buttered toast balancing on the side of the plate onto the table.

'Thank you!' A wave of hunger swept over Mary as she smiled at the towering plate of golden eggs, realising she had missed dinner last night, just as Mrs Scarr had pointed out after Molly had called her to check out what Leonard had hidden in the passageway.

'Mrs Scarr … what do you believe Leonard intended by stating he would personally address the situation after discovering he was adopted and that his brother James was in line to inherit the North Hall Manor estate?'

Mrs Scarr took a seat beside Mary. 'Ah don't rightly know what Leonard meant by it. He was mighty drunk at the time and made no sense.' Mrs Scarr sighed.

'I see,' Mary responded, absentmindedly moving her scrambled egg around the plate, finding her appetite had suddenly disappeared.

'But … I heard talk after the fire that Leonard knew summat about it,' Mrs Scarr blurted out.

Mary laid down her knife and fork and sat bolt upright. Was it, she wondered, Leonard she'd heard plotting the fire with someone else? Her curiosity piqued. If so, she hadn't dreamed it after all, then!

'The fire? Yes, Robert told me there had been a fire at North Hall. Where was it exactly?' Mary asked.

'It was here in the west wing. I don't like to think about it, even now. It was reet bad!'

'It was a big fire then. How did it start?'

As Mrs Scarr sank further into her chair, she let out a heavy sigh, her fingers nervously twisting her handkerchief.

'I don't rightly know how it started. It was a long time ago, thou knows. I remember I was about eleven back then and getting ready to start me new school. Not the same school as Molly, though. She was starting at the grammar school. I weren't as clever as her. I was goin' to t'local school.'

'So, that night when the fire broke out?' Mary prompted. 'Please, tell me what you remember, Mrs Scarr?'

Mrs Scarr's eyes shifted away from Mary, lost in contemplation, before turning back to her. 'On t'night of fire,' she began. 'I was staying here in the servants' rooms with ma. She had a lot of sewing to do for the mistress. As I says I was just a youngun, so they had me staying to play with Molly,' Mrs Scarr explained.

'Go on,' Mary urged.

'It were pitch black, and Molly came banging on the door, shouting and telling me and ma the place was on fire and to run for our lives. It frightened the life outta us.'

Mary's eyes widened. 'Molly alerted you about the fire?'

'Aye, she did.' Mrs Scarr nodded vigorously. 'It was just as well, as we would have gone up in flames along with everything else.'

Mary frowned. 'But how did she know of the fire?'

'After the fire, she says to me she had a premonition … or something like that, she called it. She was always a bit queer like that, telling me things that was going to happen.'

Mary took a moment to process the significance of Mrs Scarr's words. Had Molly's premonition come from her? Had Molly overheard Mary's desperate plea warning her about the conspiracy to set fire to the Manor?

'How severe was the fire?' Mary asked.

'As I says, it was bad, lass,' Mrs Scarr replied in a low voice, with a mournful gesture. 'Ma and me was in the rooms at the back. By the time we ran out and around to the front of the house, the flames was coming out the windows and folks was rushing in and out of the west wing with their belongings and running all over the place.'

'Were the fire brigade called?'

'Aye, the fire brigade came, but they were beaten by the heat and the smoke, you see, so there was nowt they could do to save it except it from spreading to the east wing. Most of the west wing were lost.'

'This wing of the house was lost in the fire?' she repeated. 'But it's all here now,' she remarked, frowning. 'So, how could that be?' she asked, a note of disbelief in her voice.

Mrs Scarr sighed. 'Aye, all the inside of this wing was gone in the fire. Only the stone walls, stone staircase and fireplaces was left. It's been built up again since.'

'I can't even begin to picture the scene from that night. You were fortunate to have escaped the fire unharmed.'

'Aye. If it weren't for Molly …' Mrs Scarr's eyes glazed over for a moment, lost in a painful memory. 'It looked even worse the next day,' she murmured. 'Blackened books, the wall panelling, debris everywhere and a strong smell of smoke hanging heavily in the air. It was then I suspected Leonard had summat to do with it!'

'What makes you say that?'

'Well … I saw summat that caught my attention,' Mrs Scarr added quietly.

Mary leaned in closer, her own voice barely above a whisper. 'You saw something? What did you see?'

'Aye. I saw Leonard and the farmhand,' Mrs Scarr muttered, as if afraid to speak the words aloud. 'They was running away from the fire with lit torches.'

'He was running from the fire, are you sure?' Mary asked in astonishment.

Mrs Scarr nodded. 'Aye. And Leonard had summat tucked under his arm.'

Mary recalled what Robert had told her at their first meeting, that Leonard had been spotted escaping the fire with a box under his arm. *Could this be the same box found hidden in the fireplace with Leonard's adoption papers?*

'Was it you who told Mr Hart about seeing Leonard with a box running away from the fire?' Mary asked.

'Aye. I kept quiet till after Leonard died.' Mrs Scarr's shoulders slumped as she breathed a heavy sigh. 'But when the solicitor came alookin' for Leonard's papers, I says to him about t'night of the fire and that I sees Leonard running away t'fire wiv a box under his arm, just like I'm telling thee now. I'm not sure Leonard was the same after that night,' Mrs Scarr explained, her broad Yorkshire accent thickening, leaving Mary having to strain her ears to understand.

'What do you mean Leonard wasn't the same after the fire?'

'Long after I came to live here, I caught him looking at some papers afore sticking them in an old metal box.'

A jolt of realisation shot through Mary. That could be the very same box that had been found in the hall fireplace. So, it could have been Leonard who hid it there!

'I asked what the papers were,' Mrs Scarr continued. 'Leonard got all riled up and wouldn't tell me no more. I never asked again.'

'I understand Leonard's mother died in childbirth. Have you any idea who she was?'

'Nay, not rightly. But some says she was a young servant girl working for old Mr Mattleton. Some even say old Mr Mattleton was Leonard's pa!'

Mary stopped playing with the handle of her coffee cup and shook her head. 'That's just gossip, Mrs Scarr! Mr Hart said—'

'What did Mr Hart say?' Robert jovially interjected as he walked into the kitchen. 'I'm sorry about the intrusion. I've been trying to call you, but I couldn't get through. Your phone must be out of order.'

'Oh? I'd better try to get someone out to look at it …. not sure how, though?'

'No need, I've already reported it.' Robert replied briskly. 'Now, is there somewhere where we can go? I've got some important papers for you to go over that need your urgent attention.'

'More papers?' Mary groaned and rolled her eyes. 'How about some coffee first?'

'No, thank you. Some unprecedented facts have come to light that will have a big impact on the incumbents of North Hall Manor, so business first!'

Chapter 27

To whom it may concern

I, Thomas William Mattleton of North Hall Manor, Bainbridge, in the county of Yorkshire, declare and swear that Leonard Mattleton of North Hall Manor, Bainbridge, Yorkshire, is my illegitimate son. I give and appoint him to be the lawful joint heir to my fortune alongside my legitimate son, James Mattleton of Third Avenue, Macquarie Fields, New South Wales, Australia. I lay my hand to this as a codicil to my Last Will and Testament, signed and dated the 28th day of August 1901.

In all other respects, let my Last Will and Testament stand.

AS WITNESS my hand this 11th January 1922.

SIGNED by: Thomas William Mattleton

In the presence of:

Albert Makepeace	*Margaret Dent*
Butler	*Maid*
North Hall	*North Hall*
Bainbridge	*Bainbridge*
Yorkshire	*Yorkshire*

Wearing a puzzled expression, Mary frowned as she carefully examined the document before giving it back to Robert.

'Could you explain to me again what this means, please?' she asked, doubt gnawing away in her mind.

'Of course.' Robert nodded, spreading the codicil out in front of him. 'As you know. I've just come back from your great-grandfather's solicitor's office in London. Some weeks ago, they discovered a box containing journals and letters of your great-grandfather, including this document.'

Mary shook her head and frowned. 'So, where does this leave me?' she asked, still struggling to grasp the implications of the document and the very foundation of her family history.

'This document acknowledges Leonard Mattleton as your great-grandfather's heir apparent. Which means Jack, as Leonard Mattleton's heir, becomes the co-owner of North Hall alongside you.'

'I'm starting to believe that everything I thought about my family has just been turned upside down,' she added, tears welling up in her eyes. 'I have no sense of who I am anymore.'

'I'm sorry, Mary. I never wanted to be the bearer of such news. I can only imagine the impact this has on you,' Robert replied, reaching out and lightly touching her hand.

'So be it!' Mary said firmly, pulling herself together. 'We needed to uncover the truth, Robert. We can't waste any more time worrying about it. But answer me one thing that is puzzling me. The adoption papers clearly stated that Leonard was a foundling and that his mother died in childbirth. There was no mention of the father. Is that correct?'

'Yes, that is correct.' Robert nodded, his eyes fixed on Mary. 'The adoption papers did read that way. However, while I was searching through the other papers and journals in the box, buried deep within the pages of your great-grandfather's journals and letters were secrets that have re-written your family's legacy. So, while I initially thought this codicil might not be legally valid,' he paused, unfolding a letter he'd retrieved from his briefcase. 'I found this letter from your great-grandfather to his solicitor dated 28th December 1921, along with journal entries written around that date. They appear to provide the answer as to why your great-grandfather adopted Leonard, yet didn't acknowledge him as his son at the time. Here, I'll read you an extract from the letter.'

> *In my youth, I engaged in a foolish dalliance with a young maid of fourteen years who died giving birth to my illegitimate son. I was not in a position to recognise and name this child as my flesh and blood at that time, lest it be made known to my young wife, Elizabeth. Subsequently, I adopted him as a foundling at a year old and named him Leonard Mattleton. I hereby now recognise Leonard Mattleton, my beloved son, as a rightful joint heir to my estate alongside my son James. Their equal inheritance shall reflect the bond I hold with each of them. I kindly ask you to draft an addendum to my Last Will and Testament, specifically acknowledging Leonard Mattleton's rightful claim as a legal heir, in equal standing with my son James.*

Robert carefully refolded the letter and then placed it down before him.

'Has Jack seen this?' Mary asked.

'Yes. Yes, Jack has seen it. The solicitor tracked Jack down and sent him a copy of the codicil to your great-grandfather's Will and this letter, which Jack passed on to me.'

Mary glanced out of the window, desperate to understand her place in the larger scheme of things in light of what had been uncovered. So that was what Jack must have meant when he said, your days are numbered, Mary realised. The sudden realisation that she was about to share the estate with Jack unsettled her. Even though Mary experienced periods of loneliness in the quiet corridors and empty rooms of North Hall, it had, on the other hand, become her sanctuary. Was she ready to change all that and open her home to Jack, or would she be inclined to consider a return to Australia? Mary released a deep sigh.

'Why the big sigh, Mary?' Robert inquired.

Mary clasped her hands tightly in her lap. 'Oh! Robert, what do I do now?' she asked.

Before he could answer, Eleanor burst into the room. 'Hi! Cuz! Guess who?' she said, her laughter filling the air and bringing joy to the atmosphere. 'Is this a private party, or can anyone join in?' she asked cheerfully, embracing Mary and kissing her on the cheek.

There's one thing about Eleanor struck Mary. She can always be relied on to lighten anyone's mood.

'Private party or no, you know you're always welcome here, Eleanor,' Mary replied, placing her arms around Eleanor's shoulders. Then, turning to Robert. 'We're about finished here, I believe, Robert?'

Robert nodded and smiled. 'Yes! I think so. I need to do a little more investigating on this matter, and I'll get back to you. Meanwhile, don't worry about a thing.'

'Now, what dull business stuff are you boring my darling cuz, with now? Shame on you!' Eleanor said, wagging her finger and grinning at Robert. 'You'd be better off employed planning another evening out with you and your gorgeous partner Christopher for us to enjoy instead.'

Robert laughed. 'Yes, your ladyship, I'll do just that. Let me check our calendar when I get home.'

'It's a pity Christopher bats for the other side!' Eleanor giggled. 'Otherwise, I'd …'

'Eleanor!' Mary chastised. 'How is Christopher, by the way?' she asked. 'We've not seen him for a few weeks.'

'He's doing well. His doctor is happy with his progress.' Robert smiled.

'Give him my love.' Mary smiled as she opened the front door for Robert.

'And mine!' Eleanor added playfully, poking Robert's arm.

'I will.' He grinned.

Robert turned to Mary. 'Don't worry about that other matter,' he whispered. 'I'll sort something out.' He squeezed her arm.

'Bye Robert. And thank you,' said Mary, waving goodbye to him as he walked down the path.

'Where's Mrs S today? I had hoped to grab some lunch from her,' Eleanor asked eagerly as they returned to the kitchen together.

'She must have gone down to the village. If you're hungry, we could check the fridge to see what culinary delights she's got hiding in there,' Mary suggested with a grin. 'Or we could indulge in a pub lunch. Your choice.'

'Now you're talking! Let's treat ourselves to a pub for lunch. By the way, what did Robert want? When I barged in, you both looked deadly serious about something. Did he bring you some bad news or something?'

'I'll tell you later. In fact, I'm glad you popped in…'

'Oh? Before I forget,' Eleanor butted in. 'The other reason I'm here is I'm going to visit Mummy after lunch. I wondered if you would like to join me. She was positively radiant yesterday. But if, after Robert's visit, you're not up to it …'

'Yes, I'd love to do both,' Mary cut in quickly, laughing. There was no doubt about it, Mary thought; she could always count on Eleanor to lighten her mood. 'Wait while I quickly leave a note for Mrs Scarr, and then we can head out,' she added, her hand moving swiftly across the writing pad as she wrote the note.

True to form, Eleanor chattered incessantly throughout

the drive to The Kings Arms in the next village. It had become their new favourite place, being so close to the Manor. Mary was only partially paying attention, her mind occupied by Robert's news.

'Let's sit here,' Eleanor said, entering the pub and gesturing towards the table next to the large window that overlooked the hills. 'We will be out of the way, and you can tell me what Robert wanted.'

Eleanor handed Mary the menu. 'What do you fancy?' she asked. 'It's your turn by the way. I paid last time, remember?' Eleanor remarked, playfully nudging Mary's arm.

Mary studied the menu. 'Oh, that's easy. I'm going to have the Lamb's Fry!' she announced.

Eleanor frowned as she scrutinised the menu. 'Lamb's Fry? Is that some fancy Aussie dish, or are you making it up? Either way, you're out of luck. It's not on the menu.'

'Yes. There it is … see!' Mary exclaimed, pointing at the menu.

'Put your glasses on that says, Lamb's Liver and Bacon with onion gravy, and you wouldn't want that now, would you?' She grimaced.

Mary frequently slipped back into Aussie mode without realising it. 'I would! I love lamb's liver. I forget where I am sometimes. Back home, we call it Lamb's Fry.'

'Well, you can order it. I'm not!' Eleanor said, pulling a face. 'But you'd better order it in English! And while you're there, I'll have good old British scampi and chips in a basket, please,' she added.

'Now, let's have it!' Eleanor demanded of Mary on her return from ordering their food. 'What were you and Robert talking about when I rudely interrupted? You had a serious look on your face and looked upset,' Eleanor said, probing.

Mary took an envelope out of her bag and slid it across the table to Eleanor. 'Take a look at this.'

Eleanor took out the copy of the codicil from the

envelope. Her brow furrowed in concentration as she sat quietly, reading. After a moment, Eleanor settled back in her chair, raised her eyebrows, puffed out her cheeks and let the air out slowly.

'You lost me, I'm afraid,' she declared with a shake of her head. 'What's all this mumbo jumbo supposed to mean?'

'If Robert confirms this document is legal, then the estate is no longer exclusively mine; it also belongs to Jack. That's what it means!' Mary's voice, laced with concern and frustration, explained.

'You get to share it with Jack?'

Mary nodded slowly, her eyes downcast. 'I'm afraid so …' She was suddenly overcome with uncertainty. Would she really be able to open up her sanctuary to Jack?

'Well … that's not so bad, is it?' Eleanor asked, placing the codicil back in the envelope and passing it to Mary. 'After all. North Hall is a big house with masses of grounds to rattle around in. You needn't come across each other,' Eleanor added, her voice laced with a trace of optimism.

'Yes, I've told myself that. But the truth is, I'm hesitant to open up what I think of as *my* home to Jack. Am I being selfish?'

'Well, ask yourself, what other choice do you have?'

Mary sighed. 'I'd have no other choice but to return to Australia,' she said with a heavy heart. 'And I need to make a decision soon.'

'Oh! Come on, girl, that's a bit drastic! Granted, it's a difficult situation, but running away isn't the answer, is it?'

'I know, and I don't really want to.' Mary's gaze drifted to the view outside the pub window. 'I feel a deep connection to this place,' she admitted, her voice tinged with nostalgia. 'It's hard to imagine leaving all this behind,' she added softly.

'You're seriously contemplating going back to Oz?' Eleanor exclaimed.

Mary nodded. 'Yes, I'm afraid so…'

Eleanor sprung up from her chair. 'Crikey! So, if Robert says this is legit, you're planning to go back to Oz. Which means I won't have you around anymore? No! I take it all back. You've gotta fight this!' Eleanor exclaimed.

Chapter 28

A surge of emotion washed over Mary as she drove with Eleanor to visit Aunt Ruth at the Care Home. The mere existence of Eleanor's parents was, at times, a reminder to Mary of the tragic loss of her own parents. Her concern for Aunt Ruth was sometimes overshadowed by a wave of envy. She longed for the parental love Eleanor took for granted.

Mary forced a smile onto her face as she turned to Eleanor.

'I hope Aunt Ruth is in fine form today, as you say she was yesterday.'

Eleanor sighed. 'Me too! It makes life easier when she's in a good place.' With a sudden motion, Eleanor's hand slammed on the steering wheel. 'Damn!'

'You made me jump!' Mary exclaimed, jolted back from her thoughts. 'What's wrong?'

'I've completely forgotten to bring a fresh box of tissues,' she exclaimed.

Mary frowned. 'What did you need those for?'

Eleanor sighed, her shoulders slumped over the wheel, her gaze fixed on the road ahead. 'Because some days, when she's not in a good place, she cries constantly. Nothing will placate her. Poor Mummy, it's so hard watching her like that.'

Mary lightly touched Eleanor's arm. 'Although, as a doctor, I've seen similar struggles with patients, I can't imagine what it must be like for you and your father. It must be very difficult seeing someone you hold dear suffering like that.' She paused. 'Still, let's hope today is a good day, even if it's simply for my own selfish reasons,' Mary said with a hopeful smile.

'And what is your selfish reason for hoping today goes well?' Eleanor asked.

'Because I'd really like to get to know Aunt Ruth,' Mary replied. 'To be able to have conversations with her about her childhood growing up with my mother. I was thinking the other day she might be the only person left who truly knew her well.'

'Hmm. I'm not sure you'll get much out of Mummy on that score, even on a good day,' Eleanor said. 'So don't set your expectations too high.'

'I understand.' Mary nodded. 'I think I'll start by getting her to speak about the black and white wedding portrait on her dresser. She looked so elegant in her wedding dress, holding her bridal bouquet and standing beside your father. He looked tall and upright, proudly holding the arm of his new bride. They were the epitome of youth and promise ...'

'Yeah. That's as, maybe. But that was before ...'

'Before? Before what?' Mary asked, wondering what significant event she was referring to.

'That was before reality struck ...' Eleanor replied, her voice trailing off.

Mary was hesitant to ask what Eleanor meant and remained silent.

'The reality is ...' Eleanor blurted out, breaking the silence. 'It's tough being a different colour to everyone else sometimes. I should know!'

'But ... surely these days ...'

'Yes. Our colour is more widely accepted these days than it was when Mummy and Daddy were newly married, as I've told you before,' Eleanor stated, with thick emotion in her voice as memories resurfaced. 'Back then, being Black, Daddy had a tough time providing a roof over their heads and food on the table and, Mummy never got over how mean people were to her.'

'Why did they act unkindly to her?' Mary asked.

'Because she'd married a black man. No! I doubt Mummy would want to remember those days. It would trigger too many painful memories for her.'

'I'm sorry. I didn't realise,' Mary replied thoughtfully.

'And why would you?' Eleanor paused for a moment, collecting her thoughts. 'Fortunately, we have come a long way since then,' she remarked with a note of optimism.

Eleanor's words lingered as Mary took a moment to process them. 'Thank you for sharing this with me,' she said, lightly touching Eleanor's arm.

'Right! Here we are – hang on to your hat!' Eleanor exclaimed while deftly turning the car into the driveway of the familiar imposing Yorkshire stone building ahead of them.

It was a bright early November day, and with the sun shining on her, Mary had felt quite warm in the car. However, on getting out of the vehicle, a bone-chilling gust of wind sliced right through her. She clutched her coat, pulling it tightly across her. She sought its warmth as she shivered from the icy wind. Would she ever get used to these cold winter days? Mary pondered as she hurried after Eleanor up the steps to the front door to get into the warmth of the care home. Eleanor pressed the bell.

'How can I help you?' a female voice said over a speaker.

'It's Eleanor Featherstone. I've come to see my mother, Ruth Featherstone and, I've brought her niece along with me, Mary Mattleton,' Eleanor replied, with her mouth pressed up against the speaker.

'Good morning, ladies.' The Matron greeted them politely as the door swung open. 'Do come in. I'll take you to Mrs Featherstone's room after you both sign the register.'

'Thank you, Matron,' Eleanor replied as she signed the

register. 'Here, your turn, Mary,' she said, handing Mary the pen.

'You'll find Mrs Featherstone is quite lucid this morning,' Matron called over her shoulder as she marched down the corridor.

The Matron opened the door. 'Your daughter and niece have come to see you, Mrs Feathersone,' Matron announced brightly.

'Hello, Mummy,' Eleanor said, rushing towards her mother, flinging her arms around her and kissing her cheek. 'Look who has come to pay you a visit!' Eleanor said, pointing to Mary, who stood in the doorway.

Ruth Featherstone looked over towards Mary. 'Hello dear. How lovely it was for you to come and visit me! Do, please, sit down here so I can see you,' she replied, patting the seat of the chair next to her. Looking intently at Mary. 'Oh dear, I appear to have lost my glasses.'

'They're on your head Mummy!' Eleanor piped up.

Ruth frowned. 'What would my glasses be doing on my head, you silly child?' she asked, clearly agitated. 'Now, where did I put them?'

'Your glasses are on your head, Mummy!' Eleanor replied, indicating to the top of her mother's head. 'You put them there, remember?'

'I had my glasses a few moments ago. I'm sure I did,' Ruth said. Her trembling hands fumbled in frustration among the books and magazines scattered on the table next to her. 'What a blessed nuisance. I can't see a thing without them. Where could they have got to?' she grumbled.

'I told you,' Eleanor replied loudly. 'They're on your head, Mummy!' she pointed to her mother's head once more.

Mary stood up. Quietly and carefully, she removed the glasses from her aunt's head. 'Are these what you are looking for?' she asked, smiling, handing the glasses to Aunt Ruth.

'How clever of you to find them. Thank you, dear,' Ruth

said, putting on her glasses with a relieved smile. 'Ah! That's better. Now, let me get a better look at you,' she said, peering closely at Mary, who had sat down alongside her.

'I told you they were on your head,' Eleanor mumbled sulkily.

'Don't be so tiresome, child. What would they be doing on my head?' Ruth replied, dismissing the idea.

'Because …' Eleanor began before catching Mary slowly, moving her head from side to side.

Ruth turned to Mary. 'Now, where was I?' she asked, adjusting her glasses. 'My goodness, you bear a striking resemblance to my sister Catherine when she was younger. Do you know her, by any chance?'

Mary paused for a second, realising this might be her opportunity to inquire about her mother. Charged with anticipation, she leaned forward in her seat. 'No, I'm afraid I'm not acquainted with her. However, I would love to learn more about her though.'

Ruth sat gazing out of the French windows briefly, as if gathering her thoughts, before turning her attention back to Mary. 'I've not seen her for a few days since … since we both sailed off in a big boat to somewhere. I've forgotten the name of the place. There were lots of people with us. I do remember that. Where was that place?' Ruth muttered, tapping her fingers on the arm of her chair, getting visibly frustrated as she struggled to remember what it was called.

'It was Australia, Mummy,' Eleanor whispered.

'It was Australia,' she said in a quiet voice. 'Yes. I remember now,' she said, nodding. 'When the guns stopped, Catherine and I went to Australia to work as nurses…' Tears welled up in Ruth's eyes. 'But it was such a big place …' Her voice broke. 'I don't remember seeing Catherine again,' she added, tears rolling down her cheeks.

Eleanor tenderly wiped away her mother's tears with a tissue. 'That's where you met Daddy, right?' Eleanor exclaimed. 'And he swept you off your feet, and then you both returned here and got married. And then came David, and later, me. We all lived happily ever after … didn't we?' Her words came tumbling out rapidly.

'But … but where did Catherine go? Did she find happiness like me?' Ruth asked.

'Catherine? Oh, she got married too!' Eleanor answered brightly, passing a tissue to Ruth. 'And they lived happily ever after too … well, until …' Her words trailed off as her hand flew to her mouth, her eyes pleading with Mary to continue.

'What Eleanor is trying to say is … well, it's quite a story,' Mary said quickly. 'Catherine met my father, Thomas. They fell in love, they got married and had me!'

'And did they find their happily ever after?' Ruth asked.

Mary and Eleanor looked at each other as they stood before the dresser full of Aunt Ruth's old photographs. Where do we begin? Mary considered. How do you relay the stories of love and loss to someone like Aunt Ruth?

'You handled Mummy very well,' Eleanor remarked as she drove them back to the Manor. 'You have a way of comforting Mummy that no one else does. I seem to annoy her more than anything,' Eleanor confessed. 'You know, I used to be her favourite, but now it feels like I barely know her. Perhaps it's because I forget she has Alzheimer's and I expect her to remember things.'

'It's not easy for anyone,' Mary responded. 'Remember, I've had some training and, as I mentioned earlier, I'm sure it's more difficult when you're dealing with a close family member. Remember this,' Mary continued, her tone softening, 'she may not recall specific days and people. But, on good days, she will remember moments.'

'I still envy your patience,' Eleanor conceded. 'I'm afraid I'm more likely to drive her crazy than help her remember anything.'

'Oh, don't worry.' Mary chuckled. 'You'll have your own experiences with Aunt Ruth. It's a bit like riding a rollercoaster, unpredictable and filled with ups and downs. But remember, what matters most is how she feels in those moments.'

Chapter 29

The biting wind penetrated Mary's bones as she stood alongside Molly amidst the skeletal stone remains of the west wing of North Hall Manor. It carried with it the acrid smell from the fire, catching her throat and making it difficult for her to breathe.

The scene before her was just as Mrs Scarr had described it to her a few weeks earlier. Lost amidst the fallen beams and debris, Mary observed the destruction. The flames had devoured nearly everything in its wake, sparing only the odd single porcelain ornament Mary spotted that had miraculously remained in one piece and was partly hidden under the debris. A delicate survivor within the ruins. The once vibrant paintings now lay in tatters, their colours muted and lifeless. Her heart ached as she looked upon the cherished memories that were lost forever in the fire. The chard and blackened wall panelling in the great hall clung to the walls like ominous shadows, serving as a grim testament to the fire's destructive power. The only things left standing in the west wing were the beautifully carved stone fireplaces in the hall and library, along with the majestic stone spiral staircase, now all covered in soot and ash.

'How could something so beautiful turn into something so ugly?' Mary whispered, staring at the charred remains.

She turned to Molly. 'Why have you brought me back here?'

'So's you knows why I must go from here,' she murmured,

her gaze fixed straight ahead on the charred remains as she poked the ground with a burned piece of wood.

Mary frowned. 'I don't understand. Why must you go away from here? With the west side gone, there's still plenty of space for you and your family in the east wing, isn't there?'

'Aye, there is … but …' Molly's voice trailed off.

'But what?' Mary pressed.

Molly threw down the charred piece of wood and turned to face Mary. 'Uncle Leonard told Grandpa it was Pa who lit the fire, and he says we got to go,' Molly said as her voice quivered.

Mary sensed Molly was on the verge of tears.

'But Molly! It wasn't your father that started the fire – it was your uncle. I overheard him plotting. I tried to warn you, but ….' Mary stopped mid-sentence.

'Ah knows you did. I heard you.'

'You … you heard me?' Mary asked, surprised.

Molly nodded and smiled.

'But … but…' Mary's mind raced as she endeavoured to piece together what Molly had said. 'But, of course! Now I understand …' she muttered to herself with a mix of excitement and apprehension churning inside her as the truth began to dawn on her: 'Molly has been using her gift to communicate, and I appear to have the gift, too?'

As Mary's mind embraced a newfound gratitude for the shared gift with Molly, everything started to fall into place. She remembered the cherished childhood moments she'd shared in the company of her aunt. The laughter, the shared secrets, and the deep bond she had with her aunt, although precious, went undervalued.

The times when Aunt Molly approvingly smiled while she watched her complete tasks without being asked. When the memories of her parents' car accident haunted her in her nightmares, unleashing deep-seated grief and pain. Her aunt was always there to help her come to terms with her grief by transporting her to a different place in her mind to help her come to terms with her grief. They proved to serve Mary as a lifeline, connecting her to the here and now.

In those moments, while experiencing detachment from her own body, her senses became heightened, enabling her to see, feel and, smell. Whether it be standing in a beautiful garden, breathing in the delightful fragrance of flowers, or experiencing the silky petals brushing over her fingertips. Or standing on top of a mountain, breathing in the invigorating air with the valley below stretching out beneath her feet, mirroring the vastness of her heart, open and vulnerable to the beauty and pain of life. Or the times she'd hear and watch the water cascading from a waterfall and stand on the edge of a pool below, the mist spraying her face as each droplet of water delicately touched her skin, bringing a sensation of liberation, completely washing away the weight of her grief.

Yes! Mary pondered, looking back. Aunt Molly always seemed to understand her needs, and she was always there to guide her towards moments when the world seemed boundless and brimming with opportunities.

Mary turned to Molly. 'So, why didn't you warn anyone about the fire if you heard me?' she asked pointedly.

'Ah did. I told my friend Elsie Scarr, who were staying that night.' Molly hung her head on her chest and muttered, 'Ah also tried to tell Grandpa, but he says he'd give me a whipping for telling him lies.'

Mary studied Molly's crestfallen face. 'I'm sorry. You clearly did everything you could,' she replied.

'Oh! Mary! We are leaving on a gurt big boat in two days!' Molly wailed. 'Ah won't ever see you here again!'

Standing in Molly's parallel universe and looking into her face, Mary felt a mixture of sadness and helplessness. Her arms ached to wrap themselves around her, to hold her tight and provide the comfort that only a loved one's embrace could bring. But she'd learned her role in Molly's realm was merely that of an observer and advisor. The parallel universe functioned as an impenetrable physical barrier between them, crushing her hopes of delivering a warm embrace to reassure Molly that she and her family would be alright and that they would meet again in another world.

As she inhaled deeply, she could sense Molly's apprehension about her future intensifying, compelling Mary to seek clarity about her own current situation as the image of Molly faded away.

'Molly …. Molly….'

She would miss these visits with Molly.

Mary sensed a sudden lightness in her head and a heaviness in her feet. She succumbed to the growing darkness as she shut her eyes. Her heartbeat settled into a steady rhythm as she drifted off to sleep.

***

Mary awoke the following day to the sound of tapping on her bedroom window. She rose from the bed and pulled back the curtains. An overhanging limb from the tree silhouetted against the grey skies was rhythmically tapping on the glass of her bedroom window. It was just getting light, and a new day had just begun. Shivering, Mary returned to her bed and snuggled under the blankets. As she was settling down, she was startled by the creaking sound of her bedroom door opening. Her gaze widened with anticipation as she watched it slowly reveal who was on the other side of it.

Mrs Scarr peered around the door with a cup of tea in her hand. 'Good morning, lass!' she greeted Mary. 'I've brought you a cuppa. Sup it up while it's hot!' she said, placing the steaming cup of hot tea on her bedside table.

Mary sat up in bed and pulled the bedclothes up under her chin. 'It's a bit early?' Mary remarked, looking at the faint light of dawn coming through the window and down to her clock on the bedside table. 'How did you know I was awake?'

'I heard you move around a bit in the night.'

'I'm sorry, did I wake you?'

'Nay, lass.' Mrs Scarr chuckled. 'I roam these here corridors half the night if the truth be told. But lass, what ails you?' she asked, looking concerned.

'I had the strangest of dreams, I dreamed …' Mary's voice trailed off as the memories of her visit to Molly came flooding back. Was it a dream? Or was it real?

'I heard you calling out for Molly. What was that all about?' she asked, sitting down on the chair over by the window.

Mary drew in a deep breath, pulling the soft, warm blanket even tighter around herself as she hesitated for a moment. Dare she share her secret visits with Molly since coming to live here with Mrs Scarr?

'Mrs Scarr,' she began tentatively, 'since coming to the Manor, I've been observing the lives of the family who used to live here many years ago.'

Mrs Scarr raised an eyebrow. 'You been seeing ghosts, you mean?' she asked.

Mary noticed the bewilderment on Mrs Scarr's face and realised her explanation wasn't coming across clearly. 'Let me rephrase,' she said, gathering her thoughts. 'I've been witnessing the presence of actual people, living their day-to-day lives as they did years ago.' Mary explained.

As Mary took a sip of the hot sweet tea, she began to question the wisdom of telling Mrs Scarr of her visits to Molly's parallel world, especially since Robert and Eleanor had dismissed her claims. Mary silently wished she'd kept quiet as she watched a look of scepticism cross Mrs Scarr's face. She knew she had to provide more convincing evidence if she wanted Mrs Scarr to believe her.

'That picture in the hall downstairs, the one with the lady

and the children. That's my grandmother with my father Thomas and my aunt Molly as children, right?'

'Aye, but how did you know who those people in the portrait were?'

'Molly told me! You told me you didn't know who they were when I asked you.'

'I didn't tell you for fear of upsetting you when you heard about the fire and the family being sent away. That picture was hung by ol' Mr Mattleton after the west wing was rebuilt. It was his favourite; he bought that blue dress your grandmother was wearing. The one that got left in your wardrobe.'

So, I was right about the dress then! Mary thought.

'My great-grandfather sent my family away?' Mary questioned.

'Aye, he did. He regretted it till the day he died and rued the day he handed this place over to Leonard. But, as for you seein' young Molly, she's long gone, so that's not possible. You must have dreamed it!'

'Since coming to the Manor, I've been watching Molly and her family, my family,' Mary said, correcting herself and continuing, 'going about their day-to-day lives before the fire and before they emigrated to Australia.' Mary paused, gathering her thoughts.

'Nay lass, as I said afore, you must have dreamed it …'

'Not true!' Mary interrupted. 'I've spoken with Molly multiple times. She called upon me when Thomas had a high fever, and I treated him for rheumatic fever. He could have died, and if he had, that would mean I wouldn't have been here now!'

'I still think …' Mrs Scarr interjected.

Mary's mind raced, attempting to find something else she could say to convince Mrs Scarr she was telling the truth.

'And I warned Molly about the fire,' Mary added, 'after I overheard Uncle Leonard planning to burn down the

Manor. So, if Molly hadn't warned you, you may have died in the fire, so you wouldn't be here today either.' Mary paused; she could see the confusion on Mrs Scarr's face. 'Maybe I'm not explaining this very clearly, but I do think it highlights how intertwined our lives are?'

Chapter 30

Mary sat stone-faced, her hands clasped in her lap, listening to the grandfather clock's steady ticking in the great hall. Each second amplified the sense of expectation, causing Mary's shoulders to tighten and her body to become a tightly coiled spring that could snap at any given moment. Rather than look at Jack sitting opposite her, she turned her attention to the portrait of her grandmother, with Molly and Thomas, on the wall behind him.

'First, let me apologise for the delay in getting back to both of you regarding the recent revelations of the codicil that has come to light regarding your great-grandfather's Will,' Robert announced solemnly. 'I can now reveal the full extent of your great-grandfather's wishes.'

'Finally! It's about bloody time we heard summat! It's taken thee long enough,' Jack bellowed angrily, pounding his fist on the dining room table, and making Mary jump.

Robert gave Jack a stern look and cleared his throat. After gathering the bundle of papers on the table, he continued. 'I have had a top lawyer in London check the legality of these documents …'

'Why?' Jack asked impatiently.

'A codicil is an addendum to a Last Will and Testament for the purpose of making minor changes, such as adding, removing, or changing provisions in a Will, without having to rewrite the Will. However, the codicil that your great-grandfather had drawn up recognising Leonard Mattleton, your father Jack, as his biological son and the heir apparent to his estate, could be considered a significant change to his Will.'

'So, what's to do then?' Jack asked gruffly, crossing his arms tightly across his chest.

Filled with eager anticipation, Mary fixed her eyes on Robert as he meticulously laid the bundle of papers onto the polished oak dining table. 'Your great-grandfather's letter, which you both have copies of, appears to provide solid evidence that Leonard Mattleton was his biological son. Along with the entries I uncovered in his journals, confirming his wishes regarding who were to be the benefactors of his estate. This all contributes to the legitimacy of this codicil and your great-grandfathers' directions.'

'Which means, which means?' Jack asked impatiently, his fingers drumming on the table. 'Spit it out!' he exclaimed impatiently.

Robert paused, glancing at Jack before continuing. 'Your great-grandfather's Will provides that upon his death, his son, Leonard Mattleton – your father Jack – and his son, James Mattleton, your grandfather, Mary, are to inherit a life interest in North Hall estate. Each to have an equal share. Upon their death, Mary, as the sole living descendant of his son James, and you, Jack, being Leonard Mattleton's son, inherit their life interest share of the estate. Which means, upon your deaths, your descendants will inherit the estate and subsequently pass it onto their descendants.'

A triumphant grin spread across Jack's face. 'Yes!' Jack shouted, unable to contain his jubilation, his fist punching the air with a mix of joy and determination.

A feeling of despair washed over Mary as she observed Jack's exuberance filling the room, fully aware that the burden of their shared inheritance would soon be upon her. She silently contemplated the uncertainties that lay ahead of her to preserve her inheritance. Not only would she have to share the Manor with Jack, but she would also have to divide the income. And with no children, who would inherit the estate from her?

Jack scowled, his brows furrowing in confusion. 'Wait a moment! What's this life interest bit?'

'As I explained to Mary a few weeks ago,' Robert replied. 'Life interest means you can access the property and estate for the duration of your life.'

'I'm not daft, tha' knows. It means I've been left this here place to do what I want with. So, I asks again, what is this lifetime bit?'

'As I was saying …' Robert sighed, trying to maintain his patience. 'In terms of this Will, it means during your lifetime, you are prohibited from selling or mortgaging any portion of the property, and when you die, the estate automatically passes to your next of kin, who bear the name Mattleton or who is a direct descendant.'

Jack stood up, drew in a deep breath and, drawing himself to full height, his eyes blazed with a fiery mix of frustration and impatience. 'It's my inheritance. I be damn if anyone tells me what I can or can't do with it!' Jack exclaimed, his voice a thunderous roar that reverberated through the room.

'As I've already pointed out. Your great-grandfather's last wishes and the codicil prevent you from selling any parcels of the estate,' Robert replied calmly.

The room fell into an uncomfortable silence. Robert sat staring at Jack, who was leaning in towards him, his hands firmly planted on the table, his face contorted in a fiery rage.

'So, you say I'm not allowed to sell any bits of this here property? Bugger off. I'll not stand for this nonsense. You'll be sayin' I can't breathe next,' Jack exclaimed. 'It's my bloody property. Never mind with the I can't sell bit!' he roared, his voice charged with anger and disbelief.

Robert drew back and composed himself. 'Well, Jack, it seems your great-grandfather was quite adamant about keeping the estate intact.' Robert paused, letting the weight of his words sink in before continuing. 'I understand your position, but we must respect your great-grandfather's wishes.'

Jack's frustration grew. 'This don't make naw sense! I can't sell, and I have to share me inheritance with her.' Jack's eyes narrowed in resentment as he gestured towards Mary. 'As the head of the household, it should have all come to me anyroad. So, why would me great-grandfather do this to me?'

'It appears when your great-grandfather drafted this codicil to his Will, he also wrote a letter to his solicitor. This would have been around the time the fire broke out in January 1922. I came across a journal entry that might explain why he felt compelled to make this change to his Will. I have taken a facsimile, which I will read to you both,' Robert announced, holding a piece of paper facing him.

A significant transformation has taken place in my life over the last few days, leaving me with a profound sense of loss. Not only did the fire destroy the west wing of my beloved North Hall, but the flames also consumed everything else I held dear, the breakdown of my relationship with my beloved son, James. In a fit of rage, I banished him from the Manor upon receiving information from Leonard that James, along with one of the hired hands, had been seen holding lit torches, suggesting it was them who were responsible for the fire. James, who took me at my word, has made the decision to emigrate to Australia along with his wife Sybil and their two children, Molly and Thomas. When I look back on my life, I am filled with deep regret and sorrow. I'm burdened by the awareness that time is running out and I might never reconcile with my estranged son.

Besides this emotional burden, I am also faced with the daunting task of managing the estate on my own. To this end, I felt compelled to update my Last Will and Testament to acknowledge Leonard as my biological son and include him as a joint beneficiary of my estate alongside James. I hope James will forgive me one day before I die and will return to the Manor along with his family to take up his rightful place at North Hall.

Jack got up from his seat and pushed his chair back noisily. 'Well … the ol' bugger! Pa was right when he say his Pa only used him!'

'Wait, there's more …' Robert said.

'Nay. I have heard enough!' Jack roared. 'I will fetch me stuff and move back into me ol' room next week.'

Mary frowned. 'Your old room?' she asked, confused.

'Aye. The big room in the east wing what me pa had.'

Witnessing the sudden shift in her family's dynamics, Mary's feelings of uneasiness deepened. 'But … but that suite of rooms is mine,' Mary stammered, realising that the redecorated suite of rooms she called her own might now be in jeopardy. 'I had them redecorated when I moved in,' she added.

Jack strode over to where Mary was sitting and towered over her. 'Let's get one thing straight!' he barked, his eyes narrowing. 'There's goin' to be some changes round here!' Jack's voice thundered through the room, filled with anger, as he declared his intent to reclaim what he believed was rightfully his.

'Changes? What changes, may I ask?' Mary said, looking Jack straight in the eyes.

Robert raised his hand. 'Wait a minute,' he interrupted in a stern voice. 'May I remind you both this property is now under joint ownership? Any changes should be at the discretion of both parties.'

'We will see about that! As I say. I will move back into me old room. You can have the west wing. Ma will move to t'farm.'

'Oh! Yes? And who's going to be in charge of the house if Mrs Scarr isn't here, then?' Mary asked sarcastically.

'That will be you!' Jack's voice boomed. 'You'll be where you belong — in the scullery,' he added, storming out of the room.

Chapter 31

The chill in Mary's bedroom mirrored her sense of loneliness and isolation following her recent confrontation with Jack. As she looked around the room, her colourful patterned duvet, the cosy knitted blanket draped over her armchair, the stack of books on the small table next to the chair, the little ornaments she'd brought over from Oz, her friends had given her as parting gifts. She had grown accustomed to these things and to her room. She wondered how much longer she could still call this room her own.

'This room holds so many memories,' she murmured, gazing at the once-covered mirror that had sat ominously on her dressing table. The mirror was now left uncovered, symbolising her newfound understanding and acceptance of its purpose. Mary sighed. 'I do miss seeing Molly,' she whispered.

'It's freezing in here!' Mary said out loud as she swung her legs off the bed and instinctively reached for her warm dressing gown from the bottom of the bed. The fire had died hours ago. Mary walked barefoot on the creaking floorboards across to the window.

With a firm grip, she yanked back the heavy velvet curtains to reveal ice crystals that had formed themselves into intricate lacey patterns clinging to the windowpanes like delicate frosty webs on the inside of the glass. She took in a deep breath. As she exhaled, her breath transformed into a visible cloud of vapour, creating a foggy mist as she breathed out onto the glass. Using the sleeve of her dressing gown, she carefully rubbed away a portion of the intricate snowflake pattern, revealing a clear patch for her to see through the window.

Mary peered through the cleared pane of glass and gasped in surprise. 'It's snowing,' she exclaimed with delight. 'It's snowing!'

Soft, white snowflakes were gracefully descending from the cloudy grey skies, creating a tranquil atmosphere and covering the entire world in a serene, snowy stillness. As Mary looked out of her bedroom window, she noticed that the familiar view had undergone a complete transformation. In its place were snow-covered hills and fields adorning the landscape, extending as far as her eyes could see.

It was approaching Christmas. The anticipation of her first real cold Christmas brought a spark of excitement and anticipation to her heart like a glowing ember reigniting a dying fire. 'It looks just like a winter wonderland,' Mary whispered to herself. 'A Christmas wonderland.'

Filled with a strong sense of urgency and eagerness to share her excitement with Mrs Scarr, Mary wasted no time in getting dressed and descended the stairs with great speed.

'Mrs Scarr, Mrs Scarr, it's snowing,' Mary exclaimed, bursting into the kitchen, her eyes sparkling with excitement. 'Come and take a look!' she added, grabbing hold of Mrs Scarr's hands.

'I knows, lass!' Mrs Scarr chuckled warmly. 'And if the snow keeps goin' we're here for the duration!'

Mary stopped in her tracks. 'Here for the duration?' she asked, trying to comprehend the implications.

'Aye, lass, unless the snow ploughs can reach us. We'll be snowed in.'

'Snowed in?' her reply laced with surprise as she repeated what Mrs Scarr had said.

'Aye,' Mrs Scarr replied. 'Just like them folks at Tan Hill Inn, I'll be bound.' Mrs Scarr chuckled.

'I've been up there. Robert took me up there soon after I arrived here.' she furrowed her brow, struggling to understand the connection. 'I don't recall him saying anything about the likelihood of being snowed in, though. Although…' Mary paused. 'He did say the pub was sitting on the highest point in the country. I, for one, believe him, having travelled up that steep and winding road leading to it. Do you know the place, Mrs Scarr?'

'Aye, I do. Here, get this down, you and I'll tell you about the Inn,' Mrs Scarr said, pouring a mug of freshly made coffee into a mug.

Mary pulled out a chair from beneath the table and sat down. 'Thank you.' Mary smiled, picking up the mug and cradling it with both hands. 'Just what I need to warm me up!' She took a sip, relishing the rich warmth that spread through her body. 'Ah, that tastes *so* good! Now then, tell me about Tan Hill Inn.'

'Aye. Mr Hart is right. It is the highest pub in England. When we have a bit of snow, and the snow ploughs can't get through, the Inn is cut off from everybody and everything till the snow melts.'

'Cut off? From everything?' Mary asked, wide-eyed. 'So, what happens if people get stranded there?' Mary's curiosity grew.

'Why, they have to just sit it out till snow melts. That's what they do,' Mrs Scarr replied casually, with a dismissive wave of her hand.

'How do they keep warm? What do they eat? How long does it take to melt?'

'Oh! My! So many questions!' Mrs Scarr raised her hands up in the air. 'It takes as long as it takes,' she replied, chuckling.

'Yes! But meantime … how do they survive up there?'

'The landlord keeps a well-stocked larder and freezer and always has a good stock of fuel for the fires. They do just fine; some even enjoy it.' Mrs Scarr added.

Mary paused for a moment, remembering how deep the snow was when she went skiing at Thredbo. It was over her boots in places on the snowfields. Yet, there was no talk of being cut off there. She stayed in a nice, cosy cabin and enjoyed delicious hot food. The snow ploughs kept the roads clear. So, what's so different about Tan Hill Inn? she wondered.

'But how much snow are we talking about? What about the snow ploughs? Surely, they can keep the road clear?' Mary asked.

'Aye. We have got big snowploughs. But when the wind whips off the moors, the snow be over three feet or more in places. Nowt can get through to places like Tan Hill Inn or here for that matter!' Mrs Scarr leaned in, her voice dropped to a whisper, her words barely audible, 'Legend has it that the ghost of a lost traveller still haunts the Inn.'

'And I suppose you can hear eerie whispers and mysterious footsteps echoing over the moors and along the corridors of the Inn late at night?' Mary laughed out loud, her scepticism evident. 'Seriously, you don't believe in all that, do you, Mrs Scarr?'

Mrs Scarr leaned in toward Mary with a deadpan face. 'The locals claim the Inn was built on sacred grounds. Some believe that ancient spirits still roam the place …'

The back door suddenly swung open, and Mary felt a sudden blast of icy air on the back of her neck, giving her goosebumps.

'There's no such thing as ghosts …' a voice boomed out from behind her, interrupting the conversation, and making Mary jump.

Mary turned towards the door, and her eyes widened in surprise.

Standing in the doorway was the silhouette of a person dressed in a bright yellow snowsuit, an orange knitted bobble hat pulled down over their ears and forehead, a matching scarf covering their nose and mouth, and wearing oversized sunglasses.

'Eleanor?' Mary asked. 'Is that you?' she pointed to the figure in the doorway.

In a slow and deliberate movement, the mysterious figure shed its gloves and scarf. Then, after struggling with their numb and cold fingers, they finally removed their hat to reveal a head of wild, black, corkscrew-coiled hair.

'Ta Dah! Surprise!' Eleanor grinned, revealing a row of perfect white teeth and throwing her head back, roaring with laughter as she shook the frozen snow from her hat onto the floor.

Mary gasped. 'It is you ...' Mary said in a stunned state. 'What in heaven's name are you doing here?'

'Is that all the thanks I get for risking life and limb to come and see if you and Mrs S are all right?' she asked, affronted.

'Sorry, I mean ... here, sit yourself down.' Mary pulled out a chair, offering it to her. 'What's wrong with the telephone? You should have just telephoned rather than come out in this weather,' Mary said, helping her off with her boots.

'Your phone is out of order. Most of the phones are around here. I pictured you all alone here, with Charlie and Tom away, and I was worried about you. So ... here I am!'

'We're very grateful, of course, aren't we, Mrs Scarr?'

Mrs Scarr nodded.

'So, as I've made it in one piece, how about one of your legendary breakfasts for a weary traveller, Mrs S? I see there's still some left in the frying pan?' Eleanor grinned mischievously, looking at Mrs Scarr with her head cocked to one side.

'Right away, lass. Sit yourself down.' Mrs Scarr chuckled, pouring Eleanor a large mug of steaming coffee.

Mary walked briskly over to the telephone and picked up the receiver. She rattled the cradle while pressing the receiver close to her ear, straining to catch a dialling tone amidst the static.

'You're right! It's dead,' she said, exhaling deeply as she slowly replaced the receiver. 'How will we reach out for help?'

'You can't,' Eleanor replied, holding a forkful of food poised midway to her mouth, ready to dig into the plate of food Mrs Scarr had just served. 'That's the beauty of snow days – you're uncontactable, isn't that wonderful?' She grinned before opening her mouth wide and taking in the forkful of food.

'Uncontactable on snow days.' Mary repeated Eleanor's remark to herself. Jack was unlikely to move in while there was snow on the ground, was he? She convinced herself. 'That gives me a bit more time to plan,' she added.

'I guess the snow is pretty widespread in this area, then?' Mary asked nonchalantly.

'Err – yeah, of course. It isn't just going to drop the stuff over North Hall, is it?' Eleanor laughed out loud.

Aggrieved by Eleanor's condescending attitude, Mary replied quietly, 'I'm sorry … but this sort of weather is new to me, you know…' Mary dropped her head into her chest.

Eleanor leapt from her chair and flung her arms around Mary. 'Hey cuz, I'm sorry too. You've integrated so well that I forget you're not a native. Forgive me,' Eleanor said dramatically, clasping her hands together and pouting.

Mary looked up. 'Of course,' she replied, laughing aloud at Eleanor's antics.

'Thanks!' Eleanor kissed Mary's cheek. 'But why the question?'

Mary had yet to fill Eleanor in on Robert's recent visit and the bombshell he'd dropped, confirming she was officially joint owner of North Hall with Jack. 'Robert called in the other day confirming that the codicil to my great-grandfather's Last Will and Testament is legitimate.'

'Oh! Crikey! What does that mean?' Eleanor asked, frowning.

Mary sighed as she felt the weight of the news she was about to share with Eleanor. 'In short, it means Jack is moving in, and Mrs Scarr is moving out.'

Eleanor's hands flew to her face in shock. 'What do you mean, Mrs Scarr is moving out? Moving out where?' she exclaimed loudly, unable to contain her surprise.

'Shh,' Mary said, putting a finger to her lips. 'She will hear you. I saw her disappear with her feather duster and stuff, so I'm guessing she's only next door in the library.'

'Sorry,' Eleanor replied in a loud whisper. 'When is this move taking place?'

'That's the problem. I have no idea. Mrs Scarr is pretending it's not happening. Charlie is walking around with a long face …'

'Why the long face? Have those two got something going on between them?' Eleanor asked, giggling.

Mary chuckled. 'Yes, I believe they have,' she replied with a knowing look. Then, hesitating and with her expression shifting, she said, 'But seriously, don't you see, with Mrs Scarr living at the farm looking after the animals, Jack is free to move back in here, and he's threatening to take over everything, even my room! What am I going to do, Eleanor?'

The sudden noise of someone pounding on the front door caused them both to jump.

Mary looked at Eleanor. 'Who could that be?' she said, her face etched with concern.

'You won't know till you go and see, will you?' Eleanor grinned.

Mary sat rigid in the chair, staring at Eleanor. She was consumed by a feeling of impending doom.

'Want me to go?' Eleanor asked brightly.

Mary stayed close to Eleanor, following her into the great hall, stopping short as Eleanor approached the front door and opened it.

It creaked as she opened it wide.

'Yes. What can I do for you?' Eleanor asked.

Mary squinted, straining to make out the figure standing hunched over in the porch. His face was hidden beneath his snow-covered hat, pulled down low over his eyes, and the collar of his long coat was turned up to protect the rest of his face.

'It's me, Robert. Can I come in?' he sputtered, his voice strained as he stood shivering, clutching his black briefcase in his gloved hand.

Mary rushed forward. 'Oh! My goodness! What are you doing here? Come on in out of the weather,' she exclaimed, taking him by the arm and guiding him to the worn leather armchair by the fire. 'What can be so important that brings you here in this weather?'

'Your phone isn't working,' he replied, peeling off his gloves, removing his hat and, unbuttoning his coat. He went over to the fire, crouched down, and held his hands out near the fire.

'I know it's out of order. Eleanor says everyone's phone is out of order … but what could be so urgent to bring you all the way out here on a day like this that couldn't wait?' Mary asked.

'I bring some tragic news, I'm afraid …'

'Tragic news?' Mary asked, almost afraid to know what it was. 'What … what tragic news, Robert?'

'There's no easy way to put this – Jack is dead.'

Mary's eyes widened. 'Dead? Jack is dead?' she repeated. 'But when? How?'

Feeling her legs about to buckle under her, Mary sat down heavily on the chair by the blazing fire.

'Tell us what happened, Robert?' Mary asked quietly.

Robert sat down next to her. 'The snow ploughs noticed a white van overturned down a gully on the Buttertubs Pass this morning. In fact, they could only see the wheels. The rest was almost buried under the snow. They are under the impression Jack's van has been there since yesterday. The men managed to climb down to see if there was anything they could do for the driver. They found Jack, still in the driving seat, dead.'

'But how could they be sure it was, Jack?'

'They identified him from his driving licence in his jacket pocket.' Robert reached out and touched Mary's arm. 'I'm sorry,' he added.

Mary's head swam with disbelief. 'Whatever was he doing up on the Pass? It's dangerous enough at the best of times, let alone in the snow!'

'It seemed to me he was planning to move into North Hall last night. His van was full of his belongings, they say.'

Mary, overwhelmed by the news, sat silently, her gaze fixed on the dancing flames, her mind filled with a mixture of emotions. 'Jack was about to move in, and now he is dead,' she said to herself. She wasn't sure how she felt. Sad? Relieved?

Robert got up and knelt before her. 'You've gone very pale, Mary. Are you alright?'

'Yes, yes, I'm alright,' she said quickly, composing herself. 'I must go and break the news to Mrs Scarr. Please excuse me,' she added, getting up from her seat. 'Eleanor will look after you.'

Chapter 32

'Ninth of April nineteen eighty-three!' Mary read aloud, gazing at the date ringed in red on the calendar hanging on the wall ahead of her. 'It seems impossible that an entire year has passed since I moved in here,' Mary said aloud to herself, her voice tinged with disbelief. 'It certainly has been a year of ups and downs, that's for sure.' She sighed.

Mary spun the pen in her hand as she reflected on the past year while enjoying the warmth of the fire and the dancing shadows it created. She closed her eyes, momentarily overwhelmed by her memories.

On hearing her bedroom door creak open, her eyes sprung open. Mary turned to see who was there. She momentarily imagined she saw Molly wearing khaki dungarees and grinning at her. Quickly realising those days were in the past. There was no one there. 'It must have just been the wind blowing it open.' Mary sighed in disappointment. She missed Molly's visits just as much as she missed her Aunt Molly's presence.

The last few months had been challenging ones, she reflected. She'd found herself forced to stay indoors for days on end because of the fierce winter weather and snow. This all served as a reminder of the harsh cold that had crept into her bones despite what appeared to be endless shopping trips with Eleanor to acquire appropriate winter clothing to keep her warm.

The Christmas season, which she had been looking forward

to the most, had been overshadowed by Jack's untimely death. Instead of a festive occasion, it appeared as if all the joy had been sucked out of it. It passed by in a blur. Initially, upon learning of Jack's death, Mary secretly felt relieved, as she knew he would no longer pose a challenge to her inheritance. Yet she couldn't escape the sensation of guilt for harbouring those sentiments. Burdened by guilt and fearing judgment, she kept her thoughts hidden, even from Eleanor.

Mrs Scarr, too, appeared to go about her days as if nothing had happened. Could it be that she also was hiding her own secrets beneath the façade of normalcy? Or was it the impending marriage to Charlie that had put colour in her cheeks and a spring in her step? Indeed, things had moved fast in that direction over the winter months, Mary mused, recalling the conversation she'd had when Mrs Scarr announced her and Charlie's plans. Was that only two months ago?

'I'm not getting any younger, you know!' Mrs Scarr had announced over breakfast one dark February morning.

'None of us are,' Mary had replied, absentmindedly stirring her cup of tea after heaping in two large spoons full of sugar and about to add a third. Unsweetened coffee she could drink, but Mrs Scarr's rich, dark beige strong tea she could not. Once, when she'd dared Mary to add more milk, telling her in no uncertain terms that the correct way to serve tea, according to Mrs Scarr's pa, was to be strong enough to trot a mouse across without it sinking.

'Aye, true enough, we're not getting any younger, that is for sure,' Mrs Scarr replied. 'So, I have decided to accept Charlie's offer,' she said, pouring tea from the large earthenware teapot into her cup.

Mary stopped stirring her tea and looked up. 'Offer? What offer is that?' she asked, her curiosity aroused.

'Why, to get wed and move on, of course! I was threescore years and ten last birthday, and Charlie isn't far behind me. We've decided it's time we retired.'

Mary's eyes widened as if a thunderbolt had struck her. Mrs Scarr was planning to get married to Charlie and move out. She'd had an inkling that they might be an item, as the saying goes, especially now that Charlie's son Tom was walking out with the next-door farmer's daughter, Margaret, and would soon be off his hands. She knew Tom and Margaret had been discussing marriage for a while now, once they could find a place to live. But Mrs Scarr and Charlie moving on as well? Where would that leave her? Who would run the farm? Was she ever going to be free from this endless cycle of heartache and uncertainty? As Mary grappled with her own emotions at Mrs Scarr's news, a wave of nausea washed over her, fuelled by unanswered questions and the need to support Mrs Scarr's happiness.

'I … uh …' Mary's hands fidgeted with the hem of her jumper, and her gaze shifted between Mrs Scarr and the floor as she tried formulating her words. 'I mean, congratulations,' Mary stammered. 'So, when is the wedding to be?' she asked, her attempt at a smile faltering for a moment.

Mrs Scarr paused. 'Spring, aye spring, I think … the month of May,' she replied, looking out of the window with the rain pelting hard against the windowpane. 'I have always dreamed I'd like to be a spring bride if I ever got wed,' Mrs Scarr paused before continuing in a dreamy, faraway voice. 'I dream of me standing under a cherry blossom tree with flowers in my hair—' She stopped in mid-sentence; her cheeks flushed a rosy pink. 'Never mind this silly talk. We have lambing season to tackle first up,' she said, laughing aloud and getting up from the table.

Mary got up from her chair and embraced Mrs Scarr. 'It's not silly talk at all. You are allowed to have your dreams, you know,' she said. Her arms tightened around Mrs Scarr as she planted a kiss on her cheek, her embrace conveying both support and a hint of longing for the love she yearned for. 'How about this: you and Charlie pick a date, and I'll make sure your wedding is everything you've ever wanted. It's no more than you deserve.'

'Get away with you!' Mrs Scarr chuckled then, frowning, she asked earnestly, 'You don't think it's too soon after …?'

'Too soon after what?'

Mrs Scarr slumped down on the chair. 'Jack's accident …. I feel guilty, like I'm betraying his memory.'

Mary drew up a chair alongside Mrs Scarr and placed a hand lightly on her arm. 'Oh! Bless you, no, of course it isn't! What happened to Jack was tragic, of course, but life goes on,' she said reassuringly. 'I don't believe Jack would want you to sacrifice your happiness and put your life on hold.'

'Pah!' Mrs Scarr exclaimed. 'You didn't know, Jack! He was as bad as his pa. Selfish and rotten to the core. His pa took me when I was but a young lass and got what he wanted. A son. He used me and continued to use me till he died. Jack was nah better.' Mrs Scarr dabbed her eyes with the handkerchief. 'He had no respect for me either,' she said, sighing heavily.

'Well, that's all in the past,' Mary replied cheerfully. 'Eleanor and I will ….'

'Oh! Yeah! What will I do, may I ask?' a voice piped up loudly.

Mary whirled around to see Eleanor standing in the kitchen doorway in a long beige trench coat with the hood up, hiding most of her face and wearing yellow Wellington boots.

'Eleanor! You made me jump!'

'God! It's absolutely disgusting out there!' Eleanor declared as she removed her rain-soaked coat, vigorously shaking it, causing the raindrops to scatter across the floor before hanging it on the peg just inside the door.

'Any food on the go, Mrs S, by any chance?' she asked, striding towards her.

'Not in them boots, my girl!' Mrs Scarr cautioned, pointing at Eleanor's Wellington boots.

Eleanor stopped in her tracks. 'Oops. Sorry,' she said, hastily backtracking and clumsily removing her boots one by one. 'Better?' she asked coyly before joining them at the table. 'So … what were you talking about when I walked in?'

'Mrs Scarr and Charlie are getting married. Isn't that just wonderful news?' Mary exclaimed, forcing a smile, trying to conceal her true feelings of disappointment.

Eleanor rushed over to Mrs Scarr, who was standing at the stove, expertly dropping another piece of bacon into the hot frying pan. Eleanor flung her arms around her.

'How utterly romantic,' she gushed. 'Your knight in shining armour has come to rescue you, and together, you'll ride off into the sunset on his majestic white charger and take you to his castle. It feels like something straight out of a fairytale.' Eleanor giggled, giving her a bear hug and kissing her cheek.

'It is the way you paint it, Eleanor!' Mary chuckled.

'Seriously, I couldn't be happier for you, Mrs S. Can I be a bridesmaid? I've only ever been a bridesmaid once, and that was for my brother ages ago, so please say I can – please?'

'Get away with your nonsense and get this down you,' Mrs Scarr replied, tossing the sizzling bacon from the frying pan on top of a thick slice of bread and putting it onto a plate.

Eleanor eagerly took the plate, lifting it to her nose to inhale the mouthwatering scent of the bacon. 'Ahhh … thanks, Mrs S,' she said, her smile growing wider as she settled into her seat and took a hearty bite. 'Now, spill the beans. When and where is this wedding to be? We'll have to go dress shopping. Oh, and a hat and a….' she rambled on, her words muffled by the mouthful of food.

'Hang on before you get too carried away!' Mary laughed. 'Let's see what Mrs Scarr wants first, eh?'

'Ah don't want any fuss. Sunday best will do me,' Mrs Scarr answered to her as she poured Eleanor a large mug of tea.

'But Mrs S …'

'Ney buts!' Mrs Scarr snapped, wagging her finger at Eleanor. Pausing, she turned to Mary. 'Except one thing do bother me. If Charlie and me leave here, who will take care of you? What will happen to you all alone here?'

Eleanor's hand shot up, her face beaming with enthusiasm. 'I know … I know,' she shouted with glee.

'You're not thinking of offering to take Mrs Scarr's place, are you Eleanor? As much as I love you, I don't see you as Mrs Scarr's replacement.'

'Oh! God no! I'm allergic to domesticity,' Eleanor replied, vigorously moving her head from side to side.

Mary laughed. 'Thank goodness for that. I thought for one awful minute …'

'No, no! Let me explain,' Eleanor continued. 'Mrs S has mentioned multiple times that Tom and Margaret are eager to marry if they can find a suitable home for themselves and Margaret's young un. Why not offer them this place? Tom can take over managing the farm, and you can hire someone to help him. Margaret can keep house for you. Problem solved! She proclaimed with a nod, settling back in her chair and crossing her arms over her chest.

Mary paused briefly, her gaze locked with Mrs Scarr's, searching her eyes for a glimmer of approval. Mrs Scarr looked back with a faint smile. Could Eleanor's suggestion be the solution? Tom, who had grown up at the Manor and had worked on the farm almost all his life, was clearly capable of running it. Margaret, who could never replace Mrs Scarr, was a nice enough girl, and Mary adored Rebecca, her little girl, who, in a lot of ways, reminded her of Molly. Mary straightened up. Yes! She agreed this place could benefit from some much-needed young blood. It was starting to feel more and more like a mausoleum.

'I believe … yes, I believe that's an excellent idea,' Mary announced. 'But first, I need to discuss it with Tom and see what he thinks, and then we can make the necessary arrangements for—' The shrill ring of the telephone interrupted Mary.

'I'll get it,' Eleanor piped up, dashing off into the great hall.

Moments later, she came back with a worried expression.

'Who was it?' Mary asked.

'It was Daddy. I'm afraid I have some unfortunate news.'

Chapter 33

Soft organ music was playing, and whispered conversations filled the space as the guests gathered in the small village stone church. The air was filled with the sweet fragrance of cut lilac and jasmine. Sunlight filtered through the stained glass window above the altar, casting vibrant hues on the polished wooden floors. Charlie, dressed in his best Sunday suit, his weatherbeaten face shaved, his thick mop of grey hair slicked back, stood nervously, running his fingers inside his collar, peering anxiously down the aisle. The only other time Mary had seen Charlie look this smart, she reflected, was at the auction last year. She caught his eye and gave him a reassuring smile; he smiled back.

I am going to miss them both dearly, Mary acknowledged to herself as she waited for Mrs Scarr to arrive to join Charlie at the altar on their wedding day. Memories of countless evenings filled with stories and laughter gathered around the kitchen table by a roaring fire on long winter nights came flooding back to her.

They have been a big part of my life for so long, and they've become almost like the family I've yearned for. Mary thought. She closed her eyes and inhaled deeply as she tried to hold back her emotions, reminding herself of the quote. 'When one door closes, another door opens.

And how true that turned out to be, Mary reflected… Just as a door was about to close on the departure of Mrs Scarr and Charlie from the Manor to Mrs Scarr's farm following their honeymoon, a new door of opportunity was about to open for her.

***

On the day of Mrs Scarr's wedding announcement, Eleanor's father delivered the unexpected news that the owner and matron of Preston Lodge, the care home where Eleanor's mother was a resident, had died in her sleep, which meant the facility would have to close unless a new owner could be found.

'If the home closes, what will happen to Mummy?' Eleanor's voice cracked, tears welling up in her eyes as she told Mary about her father's phone conversation. 'Mummy isn't in a fit state to move somewhere else. We *have* to figure something out, Mary. But what?'

A few weeks later, Mary, surrounded by paperwork on her desk, answered the telephone.

'North Hall Manor – can I help you?' she answered in a businesslike tone.

'What are you doing for lunch today?' An eager voice shouted from the other end of the phone.

Mary smiled. It is so typical of Eleanor not to bother with the pleasantries of starting a call with the usual 'Hello, so and so, or how are you so and so?'

'Er … Umm, nothing special. I have a stack of invoices to attend to, and I should …' Mary hesitated, her voice trailing off.

'Oh! Leave them,' Eleanor exclaimed. 'How about meeting Robert and me in the Red Lion at midday for lunch instead of doing that boring stuff?'

'Sounds tempting, but I really should do the invoices otherwise …' Mary began thinking about her mounting workload.

'They can wait ... we've got something we want to run past you.'

'Er ... I don't know ... I really should ...'

'Oh! Come on – my shout!'

As Mary navigated the winding lanes flanked by bright green hedgerows on her way to the pub, she sang along to the radio, tapping the steering wheel in time with the music. She didn't quite know why she was in such a good mood. Perhaps it was the arrival of spring, with the blossom bursting forth on the trees, their petals in pinks and creams, as well as fresh leaves on the previously leafless trees and hedgerows of winter. Combined with the lighter and longer days. Or was it the fun she was having with Eleanor getting caught in the flurry of Mrs Scarr's wedding plans? Either way, she was undoubtedly relieved that winter was over and spring had finally arrived, bringing not only warmer weather with it but also the anticipation of a fresh start.

'Over here!' Eleanor shouted, vigorously waving her arm at Mary as she entered The Red Lion public bar.

Mary acknowledged her with a smile and gracefully navigated the maze of tables and chairs to join Eleanor and Robert.

Robert stood up as she approached, smiling warmly. 'Lovely to see you, Mary. It's been a while. How have you been?' he asked, embracing her and lightly kissing her cheek.

'I've been well, thank you. Please accept my apologies for my absence lately. My time seems to have been swallowed up by a never-ending cycle of administrative tasks. Just as I think I've got on top of the bills; a fresh wave arrives. Then there are the wages to pay, letters to answer ...' Mary sighed in frustration. 'I'll never get used to this. I'm much more used to interacting with people rather than being buried in paperwork.'

Eleanor linked arms with Mary and giggled. 'Then this could be your lucky day and a solution to all your problems.'

Mary frowned. 'Lucky day? What are you talking about?'

Eleanor patted the empty chair next to her. 'Have a seat. I've got a drink in for you, see?' She pointed to the glass of wine on the table. Tilting her head to the side and wearing a silly grin, she added, 'Robert and I have a proposition for you. Cheers!' she said, raising her glass.

Mary raised her glass of wine. 'Cheers! But why is it I've got a feeling I might need this if it's one of your ideas, Eleanor?' Mary chuckled, taking a sip of her wine.

Robert took out a file from his briefcase and placed it down before him. Mary groaned. Her dream of escaping admin work appeared to conflict with the harsh reality of more responsibilities.

She set her glass down noisily on the table. 'Oh no! Not more paperwork – I came here to escape all that!'

'No! Not more paperwork for you to look at.' Robert grinned. 'As such, that is.' He paused. 'Let me start from the beginning.'

'I wish you would. I'm getting a bit worried as to what you two are up to.' Mary raised an eyebrow, her voice laced with caution and a hint of suspicion.

Robert settled into his chair. 'As you know, unfortunately, Mrs Selwyn from Preston Lodge Nursing Home died recently.'

Mary nodded solemnly. 'Yes, a tragic loss.'

'Yes, indeed.' Robert continued, 'While the staff can, and will, continue to run the home in the interim. In the long term, it will have to be sold and a new owner found.'

'Yes, and then poor Mummy won't have anywhere to live and …'

Robert glanced across at Eleanor, placing his finger to his lips, before shifting his attention back to Mary.

'So, as I was saying … long story short and before Eleanor interrupts again.' Robert chuckled. 'They are looking for a new owner.'

Mary, shaking her head, said quietly, 'That's not going to be easy at such short notice.' She paused before adding with a wry smile, 'Unless we stumble upon a nursing home-loving unicorn.'

'I agree ... however.' Robert paused and picked up a document from the opened file in front of him. 'It appears Eleanor's father has decided to buy the place. I have a letter of offer here,' he added, passing the document to Mary.

Eleanor's eyes gleamed with enthusiasm as she exclaimed. 'And he wants you and me to run it – can you believe that?' her words overflowed with uncontainable enthusiasm.

Mary's body stiffened. Had she heard Robert correctly? Eleanor's father was buying Preston Lodge, and he wanted her and Eleanor to run it? She felt a sudden rush of excitement. The memories of the rewarding days she used to spend tending to others gave her a sense of purpose and contentment. She could go back to doing what she loved most: looking after others. Then, a pang of bittersweet longing hit her, remembering the precious hours she'd spent rearing the lambs and the potential void that would arise if she took on this new role. It would mean leaving a part of herself behind. She felt the weight of this opportunity settle on her like a heavy cloak, both comforting and daunting.

'So, Mary, what are your thoughts on this offer from Mr Featherstone?' Robert asked.

Mary anxiously traced the table's edge, glancing back and forth between Robert and Eleanor, attempting to gather her thoughts. Finally, she announced. 'I can't deny I love the idea,' Mary replied, her voice trembling slightly.

'I knew you would.' Eleanor grinned widely.

'But I'm sorry I have to decline,' she added, her words barely above a whisper, betraying her inner conflict and the difficulty of her decision.

'No! You can't mean it!' Eleanor's eyes widened; her hands clasped together as she leaned forward. 'But why?

You were born for that role. Look how good you are with Mummy. You're a natural – you can't say no! Mary, you can't, you just can't,' Eleanor pleaded, barely giving Mary a chance to respond.

Mary looked at Eleanor's crestfallen face, her heart aching. As much as she would love to work with her cousin, who had become more like a sister to her, she knew she had to prioritise her current responsibilities and the upcoming changes at the Manor.

'Eleanor, I'm sorry to disappoint you, but with the many changes that are about to happen at the manor, Charlie and Mrs Scarr leaving, Tom and Margaret taking over, I have too much to deal with already, especially the admin side, let alone taking on Preston Lodge as well.'

'Admin? Ha! Is that all you're worried about? Tell her, Robert,' Eleanor replied, sitting down and folding her arms across her chest.

'I'll have you know, running the Manor is a very time-consuming job.' Mary exclaimed, irritated by Eleanor's lacklustre response about her workload. 'Only last week, for instance …'

'I don't think Eleanor quite meant it like that,' Robert said. 'What I've not had a chance to explain is I will work alongside Margaret on the farm's accounts, as I did with you. She is already used to maintaining her father's farm accounts and is well-versed in farm operations, so you can safely leave that side to her. The current staff at Preston's are staying on in their roles. You and Eleanor will share the role of Director of Nursing.'

Mary frowned. 'Director of Nursing?'

'Ah! That is perhaps an unfamiliar title to you,' Robert said.

Mary nodded. 'Yes! It is. What does the job involve exactly?'

'Basically, because Mr Featherstone is too busy with his

work, he is leaving the running of the home and decision-making entirely up to you and Eleanor.' Robert took out a document from the file. 'In a nutshell, he sees you, Mary, would be best suited for hiring and managing staff, as well as overseeing the care of patients on a day-to-day basis. This leaves Eleanor in charge of setting business plans and budgets, handling all new enquiries and, managing the general administration of the home. What do you think?'

Before Mary could answer Robert, Eleanor interrupted, 'I hope you approve. If you don't, it's my fault. I'm afraid I snaffled the admin job. I hope you're okay with that. I thought I'd spare you that side of things, as I know it's not your thing. In any case, you're far better with the patients than I am. I'd chew their ears off….' Her words came tumbling out without her taking a breath before pausing on the realisation Robert and Mary were laughing at her.

'Just as I'm doing now, right?'

***

Mrs Scarr walked up the aisle with regal grace and a smile on her face, carrying a bouquet of white roses and gypsophila, filling the air with their fragrance. Her silver hair was pulled back from her face, styled in a neat bun and held in place at the nape of her head with a rhinestone and black jet gemstone clasp. She wore a pale lilac suit and a matching hat. The guests leaned forward in their seats as she passed them, their eyes fixed on the radiant bride as she walked, alone, up the aisle to join her groom. As Charlie gazed at his bride, his anxious demeanour melted away, replaced by a radiant smile and tears of pure joy.

It was obvious that Mrs Scarr and Charlie were completely absorbed in each other and oblivious to the people around them, Mary thought as she approached the lectern to read from the bible.

She opened the bible to the mark page. In a nervous but clear tone, she announced. 'The chosen reading is taken from the Amplified Bible. Corinthians, chapter thirteen, verses seven and eight.'

Raising her eyes from the pulpit, she cleared her throat and surveyed the congregation. She gasped in surprise as her eyes locked with those of Molly, who was standing beside the happy couple. In that instant, Mary was overcome with a sudden sense of calm as they exchanged a knowing smile.

'Love bears all things,' she started reading in a clear voice. 'Regardless of what comes. Believes all things, looking for the best in each one. Hopes all things, remaining steadfast during difficult times. Endures all things without weakening. Love never fails nor fades or ends.'

Closing the bible, Mary looked up, searching for Molly. She had vanished. Instead, she saw Eleanor with Robert and Christopher sitting beside her. They were beaming at her and giving her a thumbs-up.

'Well done!' Eleanor mouthed to Mary as she returned to her seat.

Lost in her thoughts, Mary sat in silence, reflecting on the words she had read. There was a lot of truth in those words, she realised. Mary looked across to Eleanor, Robert and, Christopher. Faced with adversity and prejudice, they all showed remarkable courage and resilience, and their endurance paid off. Christopher was well on his way to full recovery with Robert's unfailing support. Eleanor had found her way in the world in her new role at the Care Home, where she could also be at her mother's side.

In her own case, she'd hung onto the belief and hopes of finding her family and the dream of belonging somewhere. Finally, her endurance had paid off. It turned out she wasn't alone after all. She had been reunited with the family that had been previously lost to her.

'With this ring, I thee wed.' Mary heard Charlie's voice breaking into her thoughts. 'With my body I thee worship …'

Charlie's words evoked such strong emotions in Mary that tears welled up in her eyes. Not only was she witnessing his unmovable declaration of love, but also the promise of a lifelong friendship. The world would no longer be a lonely place for them, as it would no longer be lonely for her. They would be there for each other, and she now had family and people she could trust and turn to for support. Also, through Molly's visits, Mary had been given the opportunity to rekindle memories of her immediate family. The family she'd yearned for and believed she had lost. Those precious memories would stay with her in her heart forever.

The impossible can be possible when you travel from time to time.

Printed in Great Britain
by Amazon